SWALLOW THE ANCHOR

Muriel Arnold

ISBN-13: 978-1542895750

ISBN-10: 1542895758

Cover design © Socciones

Design & formatting by Socciones Editoria Digitale
www.kindle-publishing-service.co.uk

March 1997

1

The m.v. *Welland* gains new energy, new lust for land, as she slices through the Pacific Ocean towards Guayaquil. There will be no raging storms to cope with here, flirting along the west coast of South America. Just pure seduction by smooth rolls of grey satin with soft whispers as feathery waves curl around her bows and then, when the sun decides to leave, it trails a mantle across the ocean before disappearing in an orgiastic revelry.

The Bridge is deserted except for Jeffrey Bloxham, Chief Officer. He stands near the echo sounder, staring at the panorama, sharing that energy, that lust.

He's been Chief Officer for a long time now, far too long. He knows it and at times the frustration burns him up but here he is, not half way through a three month voyage from Southampton to Chile and back, missing Linda, worrying about her. And he's anxious about Tom. Truanting again?

He glances at the calendar dangling from a hook near the echo sounder. Today is Thursday, 13th March 1997 but it could well have been Christmas Eve. Then his eyes go back to the rolls of grey satin, taunting and tantalising the *Welland*.

The Pacific is Jeff's favourite ocean. He has sailed so many of them he knows their moodiness, their sensitivities. El Niño has lurked in these waters since the beginning of time with his propensity to wipe out a civilisation here, a fishing fleet there, ruthless and unpredictable but he always feels at peace in this ocean.

The Atlantic is assertive. The South China Sea reminds him of an endless muddy pond. The Caribbean is fickle and can change mood quickly and the Tasman Sea is not to be trusted, neither is its rugged coastline which is slowly straightening itself with the help of Mother Nature.

So he's glad to be in the Pacific again. The transit of the Panama Canal had gone smoothly in spite of the problem with the pipes for the cement factory in Valparaiso. They had loosened in that unexpected storm. The *Welland* had had to reduce speed when a bitchy Force 10 whipped itself into a frenzy around The Azores. After a twenty five degree roll he and the Carpenter had gone down to the holds to check the cargo. The drums of newsprint were secure but those heavy metal pipes definitely needed to be made safe but he got no joy when at last the *Welland* steamed through the Mona Straits and came alongside in Cristóbal.

The officials had marched up the gangway and into the Chief Officer's Office as they did every voyage. The Landing Agent, the Customs, the Port Health and Immigration Officers to squeeze into his unassuming little office to check manifests, verify the stowage plans, confirm estimated time of departure before they scampered up four flights of stairs to the Bridge to go through it all again with the Captain.

The Landing Agent, a dusty little man with a thin moustache had been punctual, as always, and stood in his usual place at the side of his desk chewing on a tooth pick, as always, holding a sheaf of papers.

"Letter from Mission to Seamen. Address and phone number and good welcome. Not far from dock." He waves the letter in front of Jeff. "Put it to notice board," he points with his chin to the green baize board festooned with pieces of paper curling around drawing pins. There are other telephone numbers on scruffy cards offering equally warm welcomes.

There is not an ounce of comfort in the Chief Officer's Office. Small and square, the deck is patterned with scuff marks from heavy boots and squashed cigarette ends. A wooden bench against the wall waits patiently for something to happen. Usually a card game in the middle of the night or an exchange of money in a plain envelope. Sometimes it is used to sleep on. An empty paint drum, dented and battered, has been promoted to a waste paper bin. The one issued by Drake Line had been stolen three trips ago.

The local Security guards assume command here, rifles slung lazily over their shoulders. Drinking coffee, smoking cigarettes, picking their teeth and dozing off when no one was around during the grave yard watch. Dock workers on the scrounge come here too, looking for food, cigarettes, sweets, chocolate, newspapers, pens, pencils, old rags, anything that didn't move.

"Need dunnage. Planks. Wood." Jeff takes the letter from the Mission and puts it to one side. "To secure those pipes for Valparaiso. They slipped in that rough weather."

The baffled, dark eyes gaze back at him as if he were asking for gold ingots.

"No planks. No wood. Nothing." He manoeuvres the tooth pick until it is fast between two front teeth. "Weather to Valpo will be good. Trust me. No Pilot for two days."

"What!" Jeff swings round in his chair, his eyes fixed on the tooth pick. Then he turns back to his desk gritting his teeth, staring down at the stowage plans. No good getting on the wrong side of the Landing Agent. He can make or break a stay in port. And he's desperate to use that mobile phone. He can see it peeping out of the top pocket of his shabby jacket. He must get through to Linda. She would be sure to be home now.

"No Pilot! Why?"

"You know, Mister Blossom," the Landing Agent picks up the stowage plans, wafts them and tosses them back on to the desk.

"Bloxham," Jeff's eyes are on the tooth pick again.

"You know. They have problem. With locks at Gatún. And as well there's an increase in fruit traffic waiting to come through. How you say, backlog. That's why delay." He turns his head sideways and spits out the tooth pick. It lands near a bright orange lifejacket slumped in the corner near the wooden bench. "Have to

3

wait. Two days." He snorts and Jeff thought he was going to spit.

"Two days?" Jeff slams his hands down on to the desk curling them into two hard balls. He takes a deep breath. "Nothing we can do about it, is there? Suppose we missed our slot because we were late."

2

In spite of the delay transitting the Canal the *Welland* is now a hundred miles south of the Equator, skirting the coast of Ecuador and approaching the broad estuary to the River Guayas. Jeff had used the Landing Agent's phone again but hadn't been able to get through to Linda, leaving him with a ragged anxiety that would not go away.

He wanders past the main console and pauses at the radar station alive with its myriad of orange fireflies darting across the screen and then he goes to the chart table to check the position.

It is oblong with a polished teak surface. Dark green curtains are bunched on three sides but at night they are closed to ensure that the Bridge is in total darkness. The chart table then becomes a stage for plotting the course as the *Welland* steadily pushes through the dark oceans.

Overhead racks bulge with volumes of maritime publications and below the table wide drawers hold Admiralty charts for all the navigable waters in the world.

Jeff pores over the map spread across the table like a damask cloth. It shows the River Guayas weaving its way like a broad, white ribbon to the port of Guayaquil.

Viewed from the wing of the Bridge this river is a filthy, steamy pig's breakfast of flotsam and jetsam. Thirty miles of it with nothing but mangroves and swamps for as far as the eye can see. It's a nightmare to navigate. In fact, the entire west coast of South America is a nightmare.

He sprawls across the table, his long fingers caressing the scar, an L-shaped gash like a miniature railway line skirting the bottom lip and sweeping up the left side of his cheek. It's just over a year since the attack and the memory has faded but sometimes, standing on the wing of the Bridge in the still of the night, he would see the jagged end of a bottle coming at him in that crowded bar.

Landfall can never come too soon for the *Welland* and after twenty five days at sea she had sidled into port, made herself comfortable at Berth 3 and spewed the exhausted ship's company down the gangway to fend for themselves.

He and Billy Lloyd, the Chief Engineer, had tanked up before going ashore that evening and after a full circuit of downtown Cristóbal they were in the Big Bamboo, a sleazy little bar not far from the ship, waiting to transit the Panama Canal.

They had sailed together, on and off, for years and in those days of high octane living Billy had rescued him from a number of challenging feats. Climbing over the roof of the Roman Catholic Church in Liverpool at two o'clock in the morning. Carrying a statue of a naked female from the Plaza Colón to the quayside in Antofagasta. Lifting a decorated saddle from a huge stuffed elephant in the window of an Indian restaurant in New York.

He'd never been alone in these forays ashore. Well, they weren't really forays. They had been therapeutic excursions to let off steam after weeks of living in thirteen thousand tons of floating metal. There had always been a gang of them dissipating the excess of adrenaline and testosterone coursing through their veins.

The Big Bamboo is a run-down two storey building in a street just off the Plaza. It stands between two shops. One had a window full of saucepans and brooms and buckets. The other window displayed rows and rows of shoes and trainers for men with big feet.

Both shops are closed when The Big Bamboo is open.

The name had been spelt out above the entrance door with pieces of bamboo but some had been pulled off by drunks, some had been stolen by children and some had just dropped off. The notice now spelt *E BI BOO* but seafarers had no problem finding this little bar not far from the waterfront. It is their first call for a heart-starter after leaving the ship and their last hazy recollection before going back on board.

6

Jeff was on the threshold he knew so well. Order another drink and step across that frontier leaving behind his problems. His worry about Linda. There had been no reply when he used the Landing Agent's mobile. His worry about Tom. The same Landing Agent, the same mobile phone, the same worries came around each voyage like a merry-go-round he couldn't get off.

The steady drinking had eased the frustration and he had felt pleasantly anaesthetised squinting at a little pink plastic model standing on a shelf between the bottles at the back of the bar. It was a naked man, no more than six inches tall with shiny black hair and a shiny black moustache holding a shiny black bowler hat in front of his groin.

He could see it all as clearly as if it had happened yesterday. The room. Thick with smoke and heady with cheap perfume. The light bulbs nestling in frilly red lamp shades that looked like crepe paper flowers sprouting from the walls. Men shouting and singing and waving their arms about.

But some of the ship's company were sitting around the jumble of tables, pensive, leaning forward, elbows on knees, studying the sawdust on the floor littered with matchsticks, cigarette ends, toothpicks, husks of nuts and glistening pools of spit, their thoughts slipping away, far, far away to their homes, their wives, their lovers on the other side of the world as they slipped into alcoholic oblivion.

The low hum of voices filled the room, pierced from time to time by the raucous cackle of women. They were draped along the bar, edging their glossy bosoms between the men, flashing smiles and tossing their thick hair impatiently.

Some were leaning against the wall at the back of the room, laughing, chatting, lighting each other's cigarettes. And some were lolling in chairs, flaunting their long brown thighs and long brown legs.

Music that sounded like a saucepan full of boiling spoons vented itself from a ghetto blaster on a shelf at the back of the till. At the end of the bar a faded green curtain sagged across a doorway.

Billy stood away from the bar scratching the curly cake frill of hair that decorates his bald pate. Pitch black eyes survey a world that holds no problems for him, not even in the engine room when a piston had fragmented in the middle of the night nor when a careless Engineer nearly decapitated himself on a lathe. Jeff envied the man's unruffled life. At home a sturdy little sofa of a woman kept his bed safe.

All of a sudden there was a whirring sound. Something had activated the little plastic model on the shelf. Jeff narrowed his eyes and saw the naked man slowly raise the bowler hat and a little shiny pink penis popped up. Then there was more whirring as the mechanism ran down and the hands returned the hat to his groin.

"We should take one of those back for the Old Man." Billy pointed with his chin.

"Wouldn't know what to do with it," Jeff eased his willowy body sideways and scrutinised the room. Through the haze of smoke he watched a tall, ungainly woman come in. She was wearing a bright orange sweater that gave her boobs all the attention they deserved. A tight black skirt sheathed her skinny hips. Thick, dark hair was cut in a fringe and fell to her shoulders.

She paused for a moment just inside the door, caressed her left thigh and adjusted the small black handbag across her shoulder. Then she edged between the tables to join some friends in the corner.

"Standard stuff." Jeff picked up his drink. It had done its work and he was convinced that this was the only place to be on a Tuesday night several thousand miles from home when he really just wants to talk to his wife, better still to be at home with her and Tom, but he wasn't going along that road tonight, not after the hassle with the Landing Agent.

"Did you manage to get through?" Billy pushed the two empty glasses towards the barman who was taking a quick swig from a glass behind the till. "Same again, please."

"No answer. Don't know what the hell Linda's up to. She might have gone to visit her mother. What's the date?"

"Look. Over there." Billy pointed to a small set of cards propped against the bar mirror. "Just to remind everybody, as if they cared in here!"

"Might be half term." Jeff took a long draught of beer. "Out here the world could have come to an end and we wouldn't know, would we. Did you get through?"

"Yes. Got a good line. Everything's OK. But she's on another diet. As far as I'm concerned she'll do as she is."

Suddenly there was a commotion and the woman in the orange sweater slapped the face of the man sitting opposite her. Then weaving through the maze of tables she made her way to the bar pausing in front of Jeff. The face was attractive as only faces can be attractive after three weeks at sea and a skinful of drink.

She inched closer and he held the glare of the aggressive eyes that meant what they said. They said that the world is unfair and that somebody owes her something. Join the Club, lady. The world *is* unfair. It's time I was Captain. It's time I was Master of my ship.

He turned away staring into the mirror at the back of the bar surprised his blond hair looked ginger under the harsh lights. He could see the arched back of the woman in the orange sweater as she stooped to reach for something on the table.

Then he heard the splinter of broken glass and turned just in time to see the jagged end of a bottle coming at him through the haze of smoke. A cold, sharp pain scored his cheek. He put his hand to his face and felt warm liquid running down his chin.

Still gripping the neck of the bottle, the woman in the orange sweater stepped backwards, tripping on a table leg sending glasses and ash trays crashing to the floor. She fell flat on her back, long legs in black fish net tights flailing the air. Her wig bowled across the floor gathering sawdust until it became wedged between two chair legs. It looked like a bird's nest.

Jeff stared down at the spiky crew cut hair, the burning eyes, the scarlet lips then his eyes went to her skirt. It was ripped from hem to thigh showing orange bikini panties neatly pinning back penis and testicles.

Men were shouting and yelling and the women were pushing and shoving all around him. Then a big, sweaty man in a dirty white shirt was at his elbow.

"Come. Come. This way." He flicked aside the faded green

curtain and Jeff followed him along a short passage into a dimly lit room that smelt of garlic.

He slumped into a rickety cane chair and leant forward with his elbows on his knees as spots of blood dripped on to the lino. The floor began to move slowly, first one way then another until it was spinning like a top. His stomach heaved, his head was full of cotton wool and he sank into a hot, black bath.

Billy Lloyd had got him to the American Hospital in Cristóbal and they had cleaned the wound and stitched it.

"There it is," the tall, bony man in the white coat passed a mirror to him. "Best we can do."

"It's hideous." Jeff frowned into the mirror. "It's so red and swollen. What a mess!"

"The swelling will go down. The stitches will be removed." The voice was dull but dignified. "Everything will be OK."

The doctor's confidence had not been misplaced. By the time the *Welland* docked in Southampton the wound had healed and the scar had settled into a perpetual one-sided smile after hours of massaging, fondling and scowling in front of the mirror.

By pulling back his closed lips ever so slightly in the manner of a middle-aged actress, the smile absorbs the scar. Not many people ask how he got it but when they do he tells the truth. But he didn't tell Linda the truth.

He had been in bed watching her at the dressing table, her peach negligée falling from her shoulders as she smoothed the brush across her silky brown hair. They had just made love and she had just faked an orgasm. Why, when he had been away for three months? Perhaps she was tired. Perhaps it was Tom. He'd been playing truant again.

Perhaps it was his mother-in-law. She was there, on the doorstep, every time he got voyage leave. She and Linda had come to this arrangement shortly after Tom was born and the ritual had become routine. She would take charge of Tom to give him and Linda quality time together. A good idea but he wanted to have his wife, his son and his house to himself, thank you. But he kept quiet.

"Darling, what happened?"

10

"Well, we were in this lousy storm. Just off The Azores. Notorious for its ferocious winds."

"The Azores!" Linda turns and fixes him with her bold brown eyes. "I wouldn't have thought it was stormy there."

"Oh yes, we had to divert and sail between San Jorge and San Miguel. More sheltered."

"Darling, it's no good throwing these names at me. Why did you divert?"

"I've just told you. We were in this violent weather and we had to protect the cargo. I was on inspection and this sheet of glass caved in."

"Oh, darling," she dropped the hairbrush and hurried back to the bed, caressing his cheek. "Will the scar fade?"

"Don't know."

The scar has not faded and will not fade but Linda has never mentioned it again.

Management in Southampton accepted the story but the bad news is that his promotion to Captain had been pegged. Again. He's sure it's on account of this escapade which he had done nothing to incite. Just minding his own business at the bar. That's what made his blood boil. Not spotting a fucking pansy when he saw one.

Landing members of the ship's company for hospital treatment is a costly business in any port but he had been able to return to the ship before transitting the Panama Canal. He hadn't missed an hour's duty and God knows he worked day and night to keep the *Welland* ship-shape. And he'd been in more trouble when they arrived at Puerto Chacabuco, south of Valparaiso. They had to load zinc concentrates at the inner port of Seno Aysén. Quickly.

The bay is deep and clear of dangers but it is a hell of a place to berth a ship. The weather is so unpredictable. Sudden squalls blow from a ravine on the southwest side of the bay and the Pilots advise that because of the strong squalls vessels should not remain alongside longer than was necessary. So everything is done at break-neck speed.

It had been Jeff's rotten luck that a sudden squall *did* blow up and a mooring rope snapped. No crew member had been injured but it mutilated one of the dogs prowling around for food. It was old and mangy but it didn't deserve to be cut through by a mooring rope.

The loss of the rope had to be recorded in the Log Book, of course. Ship's gear is expensive and Management said that he should have been more vigilant in checking the tension of the mooring ropes when discharging cargo.

He'd been signed off the *Welland* and posted to the sister ship, *Witham*. This had not been a problem. In fact, it filled him with hope. Every officer knows that promotion often entails a change of ship and a long, unpopular voyage. The *Witham* was bound for Bombay, Calcutta, Colombo, Mombasa under the command of Captain John Griffin, reputedly the best Captain in Drake Line's fleet.

A hoary bear of a man on his last voyage. There were shoes to fill, gold braid to be awarded. It was a good sign and Jeff could endure all the delays and diarrhoea that such an itinerary brings to the long-suffering ship's company. He was sure he would get his promotion when they docked at Southampton. He didn't and here he is back on the *Welland*, still Chief Officer, still worrying about Linda and Tom.

In his most despairing moments, when Linda whinged, when Tom played truant, when his mother wrote imploring him to come ashore to save his marriage, he did just wonder if he would ever get command of a ship. Stand on the Bridge and give the orders, Master of all he surveys.

It's no good his mother sticking her oar in. She means well and is only being helpful but he would rather she kept out of it. And she had quite enough to do taking care of father and his failing heart. Since they lived near Bristol she was too far away to do anything but offer advice.

He runs his fingers over his cheek again. He does this often for no particular reason but usually when he is deep in thought and alone. Branded for life. The good news is that women love the scar. They kiss it. Caress it. Demand to know how he got it. On

12

safari in Africa? In the Amazonian rainforest? In a car crash on the M3? Fighting off a pirate attack in the South China Sea?

Women are such romantics. Anyone could have guessed that he'd been in a brawl. But that was just the point. He hadn't been in a brawl. He'd been minding his own bloody business.

But come what may, knock him back, peg him down, defer his promotion, he was going to be Master. Linda is waiting for the announcement. So is Tom. How much longer would he have to wait? He got his Master's ticket seven years ago and had served his penance year in, year out and he didn't want to be scrambling around the holds of a ship for ever. In fact, he was Master of everything on board *Welland* minus the gold braid. He had to make all the decisions that his prat of a Captain was paid to make.

He studies the map again but sees nothing as the memories trek along the well-worn route, searching for the answers. Swallow the anchor. Go ashore. Get a job. That voice was there again.

Relief Master in that car ferry between Barry and Dublin would have been a useful entry in his Discharge Book and good for his marriage. A valuable step up the promotion ladder. Owned by a Greek company, registered under the Cypriot flag with Greek sailors and Cape Verde Islanders as Oilers. The interview went well.

"Yes, sir," Jeff sat at the cluttered desk in a stuffy office that smelt peculiar. He decided it was a mixture of sweaty socks and flatulence.

He crossed his legs, leaned back in the uncomfortable chair and met the weary eyes of the Personnel Manager. A fat, untidy man with thinning grey hair and a big beer belly. He explained that it was a short run with generous leave and a good salary which meant that he would be home with Linda regularly and they would be able to lead a more normal life instead of the endless months crossing the oceans of the world, missing her too much to find any relief for the immortal longings at the ports of call.

He signed on the dotted line but when he reported for duty he was not at all happy with what he found and refused to accept cargo that wasn't fit for shipment. Lorries with loads badly stowed that would have shifted once the ship started to roll. The Manager

13

fired him for refusing to sail when a Force 12 was predicted in the Irish Sea but he knew the real reason was because he wouldn't carry dodgy cargo.

After that sacking he went to Universal Marine. They wanted relief Masters for oil rig moves. Conditions were good. A day's leave for each day aboard and normally on board for two weeks at a time. If the rig went abroad the company sent the family and the pay was good.

"But darling, that's so exciting." Linda had been enthusiastic. "And Tom will be able to learn a new language. Imagine it!"

Yes, it had sounded good but it didn't work out. Linda changed her mind at the last minute but gave no reason.

There was always something to deny his longed-for command. A mooring rope snapped, a fucking transvestite had a go at him, a fight in crew quarters had to be reported. There had been damage to Company property. It wasn't his fault that the Oilers got pissed on some filthy concoction they had made themselves but he was blamed because he was in charge.

Instead of being Master he is still Chief Officer on thirteen thousand tons of floating metal loaded with cargo that needs constant supervision and checking to make sure the bags of sodium sulphate for Puerto Limón have not slipped. That the ropes holding the bundles of lorry wheels for Callao have not slackened. That the drums of newsprint for Valparaiso have not rolled.

Then there is the worry of the dangerous cargoes. Good paying and not to be refused. Caustic soda, lead compounds, paint, resin, hydrogen peroxide. The developed world is delivering chemicals and pollutants to countries where no chemicals or pollutants have ever been used before. These so-called developing countries welcomed 'progress' by the shipload.

He presses a button on the screen of the small grey box in front of him. It flickers. Then he presses another and another until it shows Greenwich Mean Time. Eight fifteen. At 7 Coleridge Avenue Southampton, Tom would be on his way to school and Linda would be on her way to Mass. A sense of alarm sweeps through him. A quickness of fear. Linda.

When they decided to marry she knew that he would be spending time on the oceans and in the ports around the world, away for months. She didn't bat an eyelid at the prospect of dealing with frozen pipes in the middle of winter whilst he was a grease spot in Djibouti. No, everything was fine. Just perfect.

But it wasn't perfect. He'd expected a little more eagerness during this port turnaround. But there had been precious little of that uncontrollable passion of the honeymoon in The Seychelles.

Of course there is a simple way to rescue the marriage. Swallow the anchor. The voice is there again, clear and challenging. He rattles the pencil on the edge of the chart table. Its needle-sharp point snaps off. He picks up the smidgen of lead and rolls it between his thumb and forefinger. Go ashore.

"Of course we won't have so much money. Things will be tight. And Tom won't get as many goodies..."

They are in the bedroom. Tom had gone with his Nana to the cinema. With an empty house, an inviting bed and at least three hours of peace, he was disappointed that they'd been unable to recapture the excitement they had once shared so spontaneously.

"Tom's got a roomful of games and gadgets, darling," Linda is pulling on her Levi jeans.

"Yes, but you know as well as I do just how much pressure these kids are under. To get the latest big name gear." He watches as she tugs on the zip and the jeans mould around her slim hips.

"We'd manage," she drags a cream sweater over her head, "but it's up to you darling."

She always leaves it up to him. And he didn't remind her that there are all the other things that Tom needs. Swimming, bicycles, videos, computer games. And clothes for a rapidly growing boy.

And that is as far as the conversation ever gets when he considers swallowing the anchor. He straightens his back and yawns at the tangle of wires next to the screen, the paper punch, the spectacle case belonging to the Captain, the pile of manuals. His eyes sweep across them all. Calm down. Voyage leave next trip. Things will be different.

He presses the button to bring the global position back to the screen. The large white chart spread across the table glares up at him but he's lost interest in the calculations. He picks it up with his finger tips as if he were hanging out a wet tablecloth and places it carefully in the drawer below the table.

It will be several hours before they enter the longest river on the west coast of South America and he doesn't want to be reminded of that mosquito-infested haul up the estuary. Time enough to worry about the River Guayas and its hazards. Those long streamers of growing kelp. A sure sign of danger and never to be passed through if they can be avoided. And the unlit fishing vessels. And the long rafts of balsa wood that float down river at night.

The door to the Bridge opens and a young man pauses then decides to come in. A mop of light brown hair tumbles around a moon face that always seems pleased about something.

Jeff glances at him without raising his head. It's unnatural for anyone to smile so much but John Bailey, Radio Officer, is imperturbable. If the ship were sinking he would still be smiling that inane smile.

"Old Man not here?" He hands over the piece of paper.

"In his dayroom, I think," Jeff read the telex. "Oh, my God. That's all we need."

3

Captain Peter Pycroft is in his day room standing in front of the window on the starboard side, hands slotted in his reefer pockets, gazing at the ocean. There is not a bird nor a vessel in sight just the sea gliding past the ship taking all his thoughts with it leaving his mind empty.

Moving to the forward window he can see the Bo'sun in the foc's'le standing near a seaman sweeping up bits with a dustpan and brush. He raises his eyebrows and turns away, puckering his moist pink lips.

He sweeps his podgy hands across the television set. It is clamped to the bulkhead on top of a chest of drawers by a broad piece of webbing and some brackets. Next to it is a music centre, also clamped. A pile of cassettes has slithered to the deck with the ship's rolling, forming a miniature staircase on the mottled green carpet.

A settee is pushed back against the bulkhead and in front of it is a long low table on which stands a plate of chocolate biscuits, an empty glass, and an ash tray full of cigarette ends.

Sniffing disapproval he struts past it, waddling like a pigeon, slowly, his head moving and jerking. It is a square head that twitches a lot on a short neck.

"It's time Dowse was here," he said to the plate of chocolate biscuits.

Three arm chairs pitted with cigarette burns sulk around the table as they wait for the next parliament. This is where they all come. To his dayroom to sit in his easy chairs, to eat his chocolate biscuits, to smoke his cigarettes, to drink his Scotch and to hold forth.

The session might be with the Pilot - delay on sailing anticipated. The Landing Agent - no spare containers available. Customs Officers - surprise search at some godforsaken hour. Immigration Officers - extra copies of the crew manifest. Port Health - ditto. Never satisfied. But Bloxham is his man. There isn't a problem that man cannot solve. But Bloxham is due for promotion and that worries him.

If the worst comes to the worst he could speak to Charles Paling the General Manager of Drake Line. Peter had met him when he made a voyage in the *Ryma,* Drake Line's prestigious cruise liner, shortly after the death of Mrs Paling. He remembers that voyage well. Serving as Senior First Navigating Officer on the *Ryma* Peter had been included in the cocktail party circuit in the Wardroom, a much coveted invitation for special passengers. They were usually the 'socially-prominent' selected to enjoy the facilities of Naval officers for recreation, dining and drinking.

He had got himself a gin and tonic and edged his way into the crowded room buzzing with the low drone of voices. Standing below the portrait of the Queen he scanned the talent on offer. Not a lot to interest him then he heard a conversation going on next to him.

"Perhaps if he turned round we can see for ourselves," the female voice was self-assured.

He turned to face a group of men surrounding a tall, angular woman. In fact, she was skinny. Her aquiline nose was a fraction too big but she had stunning bluey-green eyes, almost turquoise, and thick auburn hair that seemed a little out of control. And there was something magnetic about that ringing voice.

"Peter Pycroft. How do you do?" He offered his hand.

"Hello, I'm Denise Paling."

He took the cold, bony hand and stared into the questing eyes. "Now what did you want to see for yourselves?"

But her acquaintances had melted into the throng and they were alone. The conversation romped along and after several more gins he discovered that she was dedicated to golf.

"And I can't stand politicians. They just like to hear their own voice." She went on, "and do-gooders. Do they ever do any good?" The question trilled in the smoke above their heads.

Denise Paling, daughter of the General Manager of Drake Line, wore no wedding ring.

A year later they married and settled in a mock Tudor house, much too spacious for them, in a leafy avenue on the outskirts of Southampton. He encouraged her golf and social-climbing. It was good for her while he was away. After ten years of marriage they remained childless, a fact that neither disheartened nor heartened either of them.

He continues his pacing around the day room waiting for Dowse to come then he takes a chocolate biscuit and moves over to his desk. It is screened by tubs of exotic plants climbing up wooden trellis made by the Carpenter. Some had green rubbery leaves, some had feathery palm fronds, some are as delicate as ferns. They all thrive as they roll across the oceans in all weathers. Never get seasick, never complain, never get drunk. He loves his little arboretum. Behind this jungle he can sit at his desk, secluded from the rest of his dayroom.

An enormous tapestry covers the bulkhead at the back of his desk. It is beautifully woven in shades of beige, cream and brown and depicts a small town on a hillside. The spire of the church dominates the quaint houses and narrow streets leading to the Market Place. This luxurious wall hanging reinforces his impression that he is living in a penthouse. A world of his own and quite unrelated to the reality of a general cargo ship with twenty two crew members and three passengers.

He drums his plump, white fingers on the desk then studies them thoughtfully. Yes, if the worst comes to the worst and Bloxham's name comes up for promotion he would have a word with his father-in-law. He doesn't want to use his father-in-law but he needs Bloxham here as Chief Officer but even Bloxham can't help with his worst nightmare. The arrival of a passenger at his door with a complaint.

But it's the 'professionals' that he has to watch out for. They work their way through the cargo ship companies, building up a head of steam when they get on board, persuading other passengers to complain that the bread is stale, that the serviettes are too small, that the apples are bad, that the milk is watered. Writing letters, taking photos.

To avoid damaging publicity the company give them refunds, rebates, free trips. These professional complainers do very nicely thank you. And they give him diarrhoea.

A sea of invoices, crew wage calculations, telex messages and weather forecasts ebb and flow around the computer. He shuffles them into a pile and rummages for the passenger manifest. Three of them, round trip.

Joy Galbraith, 76 years, and her sister Violet Galbraith, 75 years. Dodging the English winter. They argue a lot. He's heard them from the wing of the Bridge and Dowse says they are always nagging each other in the cabin. And they like to drink.

The Slop Chest is the *Welland's* own little supermarket. Call it a shop. Call it a canteen. It is called all sorts of things these days but in sailing days it was the Slop Chest where ready-made clothes were issued to sailors. New trousers, Guernseys and other items of clothing. String, rope and anything else needed to keep a ship sailing.

Now it sells bottles of whisky, gin, vodka, brandy, beers, Coca-cola, Seven-up, Fanta, wine, cigarettes, toothpaste, shaving soap, peanuts (salted) and chocolate bars all purchased through the Landing Agent in port at the best rate possible. The Galbraith sisters get through a lot of gin asking for the Slop Chest to be opened when they know that it's only open every Friday at six o'clock in the afternoon, except in port.

He runs his finger down the manifest to the next name. Fiona Meredith, age 35. A bit young to be on a cargo ship. Why isn't she on the QE2 joining in that razzle-dazzle?

He reaches for a paper clip and straightens it. Is she going to work her way through the Crew List? His men can do better than that in any port along the west coast of South America. Is she an alcoholic? He tries to bend the paper click back into shape but it snaps. Is she a junkie?

They've been at sea for three weeks now and there has been no suggestion of anything. Drink, drugs or sex. She keeps herself to herself. Always punctual for meals. If the passengers are late for meals the overtime bill hits the fan and bang goes his budget. But for his money he would rather have another twenty foot container sitting on deck. Passengers are a pain in the arse. Containers do not complain.

"And the ultimate… the ultimate…" Peter Pycroft's high-pitched voice now fills the dayroom as he spits the words on to the calendar swaying from a rubber band. "Complaining about the smell of fish meal at Iquique. Huh! The major port for the loading of fish meal on the west coast of South America and these idiots complain about the smell. What do they expect? Chanel No. 5?"

He is surprised by the timbre of his voice and glances towards the door. No one has heard him. His eyes go back to the manifest then he throws it down and strides to the forward window. Passengers agitate him. Make him nervous. But so far these three have not complained about anything. The Blue Rinse Twins could argue until we dock at Southampton and Ms. Meredith, well…

Solid footsteps clatter down the companionway from the Bridge and he scurries back to his desk. The footsteps continue along the alleyway to his door. It's the Chief Officer with a piece of paper in his hand.

"Scuse me sir," Jeff hesitates in the doorway. "Message from Head Office."

"Come in." He takes the telex and reads it. 'Suspected cholera outbreak in Peru. Please confirm you have 5,700 tons steel girders, 1,600 tons sodium sulphate for Callao. Advise discharge plans.'

He fixes his suspicious blue eyes on the scar on Jeffrey Bloxham's left cheek. His father-in-law had told him about the pane of glass that had caved in during a storm. Rotten luck. He reads the telex again.

"Is that correct?"

"Yes, sir."

"It will have to be discharged." He straightens out another paper clip and prods his blotter with it. "What are we going to do?"

"It could be sent overland. By lorry." Jeff watches the plump little fingers fidgetting with the paper clip. "They've got that splendid Pan American highway with hardly a vehicle on it. The odd local bus, a dead condor here and there. You can go like the clappers for hundreds of miles. M3 eat your heart out."

Peter glares at his Chief Officer. Feeder the cargo. Of course. The Agent can organise a fleet of lorries.

Arranging his hands behind his back he paces the length of the dayroom, eyes on the carpet, head bobbing up and down somewhat annoyed that he hadn't thought of solving the problem with the cargo himself. Once again he has been upstaged by Bloxham and he needs to distance himself from the towering figure standing near his desk but in the darker reaches of his mind he knows that come what may he must hang on to this Chief Officer and, besides, no one will know whose idea it was to trans-ship the cargo by road from Guayaquil in Ecuador along the magnificent Pan-American highway to Callao in Peru.

He stops in front of the window, then turns slowly. "Yes. Good idea. It could solve the problem. I'll talk to Southampton."

4

Bert Dowse moves around his small pantry in a final inspection after clearing up breakfast in the Officer's Mess Room. He wipes the stainless steel draining board, caresses the two taps and then turns to check the cupboards above the work counter.

They are full of dinner plates, side plates, jugs, cups and saucers, mugs, tumblers and a spare jar of coffee hidden at the back of the big salad bowl. No joke to come off watch and find the coffee jar empty. He checks that there are plenty of tea bags in the Jacob's cream cracker tin. Clean towels hang from pegs near the door.

He puts the bread bin back in its usual place. It should be flush against the bulkhead with the bread board in front to stop it sliding off in bad weather. Next to it is a half empty jar of blackcurrant jam. The Second Officer likes to eat jam with a spoon from the jar. Bert discovered this quite by chance one day when he had been doing his tidy up. The Second Officer barged into the pantry and started opening and shutting the cupboard doors looking for something.

"Can't find the jam."

"I'm waiting for more from the Stores." Bert watched the frantic search.

"Thank you. Good for constipation, keeps everything moving." The Second Officer took an apple from the bowl, rubbed it down his faded denims and was gone crunching his apple.

Bert had never heard of this before but word got around and now everybody wants to eat jam with a spoon from the jar.

A sneck and hook has been welded on to the side of the fridge door so that it doesn't fly open in bad weather. He peers inside. There is some salami, three slices of ham, a sliver of cheese, tomatoes from yesterday's salad, milk and two of last night's puddings that now look like dog mess.

Sometimes passengers eat everything in the fridge leaving nothing for the men coming off watch. But these three women are like bundles of sticks and don't eat enough to keep a sparrow alive but Lipstick Lulu gets up his nose. She will mess about with the bread rolls, breaking them and taking the middles out and leaving the crust on her plate.

The crew and passengers come here at all hours to look for something to eat or drink and some just come to see what's going on. Nothing much goes on in this little pantry sandwiched between the Mess Rooms and the Galley.

He straddles the doorway and his tired blue eyes sweep over the two round tables with their white table cloths. Salt and pepper pots are refilled. Serviette holders replenished. Floor swept. Satisfied that all is well he hitches up his sagging trousers with his elbows and singing through his teeth, ambles along the short alleyway pausing at the open door of the Crew Mess Room.

It's a bit smaller than the Officer's Mess and has two oblong tables. The blue plastic tablecloths make it look like a transport café. He's amazed what a difference a white tablecloth makes. Then he steps into the Galley next door.

It is spotless and can match the kitchen of any prestigious hotel anywhere in the world but nothing can compare with the heat generated in this vital little area of a working cargo ship.

Mid-Atlantic is a challenge juggling with boiling pans in a Force 10 gale but once in the tropics it's an endurance test.

Large hotplates radiate heat and the stainless steel work benches shimmer. The steady rhythm of the ship's engines conduct a percussion of spoons and pans and ladles swinging from hooks. Shiny fat cauldrons begin to simmer and splutter and good, wholesome smells permeate the air.

Bert marches over to the port hole and adjusts the old cardboard box. It had once contained cartons of dried milk but now serves as a wind funnel to capture every whisper of a breeze from the River Guayas.

"This bloody heat will kill me," he wipes his brow with the back of his hand and turns to the man squatting on a stool in front of a bucket of potatoes.

Dinty Lee, Assistant Cook, is on his second bucket. His long, melancholy face is dominated by a sharp beak of a nose, his hollow cheeks droop and the weary eyes have receded into their sockets. Wisps of hair like strands of black knitting wool wander across his domed head. He looks as if he's come back from the grave to finish his work.

Bert sinks his heavy frame on to the stool next to him and reaches for the knife poking out from under a mixing bowl. Then he plucks a potato from the yellow bucket.

"Don't have to bother," Dinty sniffs. "Nearly finished. He'll be waiting for you topsides…"

"Bugger him. He can wait." Bert slices the peel off the potato with expert precision and drops it into the large pan. He'd served his apprenticeship in the Galley and decided it wasn't for him. It was all these bloody potatoes. Never ending. Just when he'd got to the bottom of the last bucket Cook would go into the storage room and come back with another one.

So Bert had great sympathy for Dinty Lees. He'd been there. Done that and opted to sign on as Steward but he always gives Dinty a hand after clearing up the Mess Rooms before going topsides.

"Should get one of them machines." Bert drops another potato into the pan. "Do you remember when we had that Time and Motion joker on board?"

"Yes, I do. Waste of time he were," Dinty squints against the smoke from his skinny cigarette. "Prancing around in his pin-striped suit."

"He were to decide whether Drake Line should invest in spud machines. Huh! Was in his sack most of the trip." Bert straightens his back with a groan. "Seasick. Didn't care a bugger about the

25

potato bashing. And when he wasn't seasick he was hung-over."

"Came down here twice," Dinty perches his cigarette on the edge of the stainless steel table top.

"Well, those spud machines didn't peel 'em, did they?" Bert wags his knife at Dinty. "Whacked 'em around in a drum till they were no bigger than bloody marbles. Then he reported that the machinery was too expensive and that hand-peeling the potatoes should continue. I say fuck the Time and Motion bugger."

Bert had been used to other things. He'd been Captain's Tiger on the *Ryma*, Drake Line's luxury cruise liner and soon came to terms with the goings-on in those rarefied uplands. It was a cushy number. Plenty of overtime, no questions asked.

All those passenger cocktail parties and next morning discreetly returning lost valuables. A diamond ear-ring, a gold bracelet, sometimes a ring, a wrist watch. It was amazing how careless women are after their exciting experience and they never thought to look under the bed before they left which is where he found most things.

Then there was the constant stream of officials at the ports of call. Immigration, Customs and Port Health. Not forgetting the Landing Agent who knew everybody and could fix anything.

Before arrival in port Bert had to haul out the extra bottles and cigarettes and chocolates and biscuits and soap from the bonded stores before they were sealed on entering territorial waters. The goodies were important and the clearance of the ship could be influenced by the Captain's largesse so it all had to be ready. If he didn't cough up the officials would find something wrong with the ship's documents or demand extra copies of the forms. Sailing would be delayed and all hell would be let loose waiting for Pilot, tugs, not to mention the mayhem caused by the late arrival at the next port of call. No, Bert always got the goodies out in readiness.

He used to watch it all from his pantry next to the Captain's dayroom and he would never have believed where bottles of Scotch and cartons of cigarettes could be hidden on the human frame.

He saw the bulging briefcases, the lumpy jackets, the stiff arms and the padded socks as they clumped down the gangway. And it was just the same here. On this little tub full of cargo. So he just kept his mouth shut and did what he was told.

But then the bottom fell out of his world. His wife was mowed down by a drunken driver in broad daylight on her way home from shopping. On Christmas Eve. Jean. Constant and cosy and comfortable. His safe harbour. He still felt that ache, that yearning when they came past Calshot Spit. He used to be home within half an hour of signing off. Home to a decent cup of tea, home for a beer with the boys and home to his own bed, with Jean and all the banter from his son.

Now she wasn't there when he docked and she would never be there when he docked. And a year later Keith wasn't there when he docked. Keith couldn't handle it, went off the rails. His wife gone, his son gone - well, not gone, just not around. Coming back to that empty house had dredged him dry, hollowed him out till there was nothing left.

But Bert found his consolation in the rum bottle. Rum was cheaper than Coco-cola in the Caribbean. Fill your boots. And he did and it had cost him his job on the *Ryma*.

He'd gone ashore with a gang of shipmates drinking at Bar Shango in Port au Prince. Somebody had spiked his drink and the next morning he'd woken up in an alleyway between heaps of stinking rubbish with a strange sensation in his lower abdomen. A mangy dog was sniffing his private parts.

He yelled and waved his arms, scaring away the animal. Looking down he was horrified to see that some bastard had robbed him, stripped him and left him wearing only his underpants. His shoes had been stolen as well and he was standing in dark brown smelly mud.

"For Christ's sake, what the bloody hell?" Bert's voice echoed.

"Are you there?" A voice called.

A figure lurched along the alleyway. It was Jacko, the Carpenter and he, too, was barefoot and in his underpants."We're in a right bloody pickle," Bert stood hands on hips staring at Jacko. "Let's get out of this hellhole. We must find the Agent's office."

"Like this?" Jacko looked down at his dirty feet.

"No option. Let's just hope we don't get picked up by the Police."

The Landing Agent listened, made some notes, went into the back office and produced laundered shirts and denims for them both as if seamen were drugged, robbed and stripped every night. He explained that the *Ryma* had sailed this morning and they were now registered as Distressed British Seamen in Haiti and would have to wait for a ship to Europe.

Luck was on their side. A cargo ship, the *Ruby Bay*, docked the next morning and they were on their way back to Southampton. He got a Decline to Report stamp in his Discharge Book and that meant the end of a seagoing career. No shipping company would ever accept a crew member with a D.R. stamp. So Bert took his Discharge Book into the garden shed and burnt the page bearing the stamp. All the personal details and signatures and the ships he had sailed in were scorched but still legible.

He filled in a form, sent it off to the Registrar-General of Shipping in Cardiff with a letter explaining that the Discharge Book had fallen into the fire. After filling in more forms and telling a few fibs a new book was issued and he was back at sea on a cargo ship. Deep sea and long voyages. That suited him. When Jean was alive he didn't want to be on the other side of the world counting the days to docking but now the *Welland* and his shipmates had become his home and his family.

He signed on as Assistant Cook but when his chance came to be Steward he willingly swapped peeling potatoes for mops, dusters and diatribes from a hung-over Captain.

He has plenty to do cleaning stairways and alleyways, Captain's and officers' quarters and passenger cabins, serving food in the Mess, but he likes to give Dinty a hand with the last bucket of potatoes.

"Only three bloods this trip," Bert makes the statement for no reason at all.

"No trouble. So far." Dinty tosses a potato into the large shiny pan. "But them two sisters argue a lot. I was out there having a smoke and I heard such a ding-dong. At it hammer and tongs they were. Up there. On the passenger deck. Don't know what to make of the other one. The glamorous one." Dinty rolls another miserably thin cigarette and lights it. "Dock this afternoon. What's the betting they all get mugged."

"Guayaquil is a bloody free for all, ain't it." Bert throws another potato at the pan but it misses and rolls under the work bench. "And I'll bet the Old Man will want his usual tonight. Any road on, we can go to the Mission for a bevy or two when we've finished."

Bert pushes the knife under the mixing bowl and goes to the locker near the door. He hauls out his red plastic bucket full of dusters and air fresheners and rolls of toilet paper.

"That's it then. I'm off. See ya later."

*****

In Cabin 314 Fiona Meredith is studying the street map of Guayaquil. She hasn't decided yet about going ashore. The warning words of the Captain hover in the distant reaches of her mind. When she had taken her money for safe keeping he had said what a previous Captain had said on a previous trip.

"Come in, Mrs Meredith. Please sit down." A clean-cut, handsome man stares at her with vacant blue eyes that belong more to a youth than a man in his mid-forties. A lock of brown hair falls across his forehead. She suspects that he encourages this wisp of wayward hair. It gives a hint of much-needed recklessness in a face that is not lived in. There is no history to read here. No traumas, no loss, no love, no heartache has left its mark. It is almost mask-like with its waxy, fair skin and straight nose.

He is sitting at his desk behind a thicket of plants. They have been trained to climb up a wooden trellis in front of his desk. Others sit in tubs and urns. She is amazed they grow so well in such a stuffy atmosphere.

"You should not go ashore alone. It is quite dangerous. There are youths, junkies, drop-outs." He is bent over his desk prodding the blotter with a paper clip. "Child beggars, abductions, muggings, knife attacks. And never travel alone in a taxi…" He throws down the paper clip and leans back in the swivel chair, fixing her with those round vacant eyes.

"Oh, please don't be concerned. I've never had a problem yet." She smiles and can see that he is nervous of smiling people. "You know, Captain, recently there was a murder in a quiet residential street not far from where I live in Southampton. *A murder!"* She leans forward, emphasising the word. "No one is safe anywhere in the world. No one." She folds the flap of her suede leather bag and rests her clasped hands on it. "So please don't worry about me. If my number comes up, well there's nothing to be done about it, is there?"

After all, Paul's number had come up. And who would ever have expected that? The silent question forces her momentarily to the edge of the abyss. She takes a deep breath, her eyes on the paper clip on his blotter. No, she must not go there today. She must remember why she is here, sweeping away the emptiness and filling the gaps with new sights and sounds and…

"You know, I like being amongst the poor. Exploring the culture of poverty. It's a world apart from the one we leave behind with those shopping malls and supermarkets. Temples of consumerism. Imagine! There are whole aisles of dog and cat food for sale. And out there…" she points to the port hole with her chin, "out there children scavenge on stinking rubbish heaps to find something to eat. The world has gone mad."

He is fiddling with that paper clip again, uneasy with people airing an unsolicited opinion but she continues, "I find great peace of mind here in South America. Perhaps it's that massive backbone of the Andean mountains that gives the people such qualities. They're so different, so resilient, so friendly. That's the reason why I make these voyages."

Fiona smiles at her lie. Her unadulterated lie. That is not the reason she makes these voyages. The reason she makes these voyages is a secret. So far the secret is safe in spite of that dreadful woman's nosey parkering.

The Captain pouts his thick lips, raises the neat eyebrows but makes no reply as he pushes her money wallet into the large brown envelope, seals it and passes it to her.

"Sign please. Across the seal."

Since that first encounter she had watched him, always polite but on guard. Good-looking, presentable but there's something about him that she can't quite reach, can't analyse. The gold braid on his sleeves is quite new and she decides that he must have been promoted recently. But in spite of his gold braid he is not familiar with confidence. Hesitates too much.

She folds the street map. The rhythm of the ship's engines is lulling her into idleness. The gentle vibration is soothing, reassuring. It is there all day and all night and she feels at ease as this brave little ship pushes its way through the oceans, taking all that the mighty Bay of Biscay can heave at her then a few days later she rides every crashing wave around The Azores before gliding through the Mona Straits into the Caribbean. She then edges through the Panama Canal into the Pacific with an escort of flying fish.

Yes she's a plucky little ship, the *Welland* with a personality of her own. Sleek and lean and grey she appears to be longer than five hundred feet with three masts, five derricks - he had explained that they are loading cranes - and three holds. She had watched the crew pampering her, painting her, tending to her bruises, tidying her rigging and keeping her heart beating steadily through every storm. In fact, they make her into quite a coquette flirting with the oceans, displaying in the ports.

After Paul... that's what she had done after Paul... not knowing what she could do after Paul. She chokes back that lump in her throat. After Paul nothing had existed and the terror of the abyss was still lurking, waiting to strike her ice cold every time. But she had to move on, she had to escape the silent horror of the abyss. And she had to find out where she should move to.

Her sister Joanne, had suggested a cruise but Fiona cringed at the thought. All those passengers, and having to listen to all that boring high-flown humbug, the ego trips at the cocktail parties and dining table. The innate desire to belong to a group. The herding instinct. No, she could not face that but she did find what she needed at the end of a telephone. Her second telephone solved the problem of loneliness, emptiness and brought her intelligent conversation, social evenings. Yes, it had been that telephone and then last year she had found the holiday she needed. She had chosen the *Witham*, sailing across the Indian Ocean under a deep orange moon in an indigo sky. This year she had chosen the *Welland* to South America.

These little cargo ships have transformed her outlook and life has taken on a totally different temperament. So different to living ashore where everything is taken for granted even on her telephone. Here at sea nothing is taken for granted. Ships are at the mercy of the wind, the weather, the officials on arrival in port, the delays on departure. Two different worlds existing in parallel time. Only thirteen thousand tons, so he had told her, which isn't very big when you think of some of those luxury liners.

And that bad weather had kept those two elderly passengers in their cabin. Sea-sick. No inquisition for three days. Now, they would have been more at home in a cruise liner than this little working ship but then they, too, probably have their reason for choosing a cargo ship.

Of the two she liked Joy the most. She was more balanced, more wholesome. Violet was dogmatic and so irritating with her incessant probing, endless questions. Fiona didn't want to have a row with her but if she pushes too hard she will probably flip her lid and let her have it.

She looks at the map again. It's a long taxi ride into the centre of Guayaquil but worth it for the Tea Salon and its chocolate cake. And there was that market she'd been told about where she can buy woven rugs from those seriously good-looking men who don't know how handsome they are with their rugged copper faces, their wide smiles, their sturdy bodies that withstand a lifetime of high altitudes and hard work. They speak to each other in Quechua, the language of the Inca, their ancestors. It is fascinating just to listen to them. And there is that Art Galley at the top of Calle 9 de Octubre. Yes, the long taxi ride is worth it.

The dock gates are some distance from the ship and there are challenges the moment she steps down the gangway. In Puerto Cabello she had been accosted by a group of young boys. Six or seven of them. All barefoot wearing faded shorts, their skeletal rib cages like shiny brown barrels.

"One dollar," The grubby little hand grabs her wrist.

"You want man. Beeg," another boy puffs out his cheeks and cups his hands in front of his groin jumping up and down. "Beeg, beeg man. Good fuck."

That's television for you, thought Fiona. They see naked white women doing acrobatics on a bed with naked white men.

"Where do you live?" She ruffles the boy's wiry black curls.

"Over there," he points to a cluster of shacks beyond the perimeter fence. A jumble of old wooden doors, battered oil drums, black plastic bags and sheets of galvanised iron bear no resemblance to a home.

"We come to shine shoes," the same boy beams at her. His two front teeth have been broken in exactly the same place cutting out a perfect triangle.

"No, he doesn't," a bigger boy elbows his friend out of the way. He has silvery streaks across his thick, crinkly hair. It reminds her of a Christmas decoration but she can't think why. "Never shines shoes."

"Oh," Fiona isn't at all sure that a handful of passengers would expect to have their shoes polished. After The Azores everyone wears sandals or flip-flops.

"He does dirty work."

"What dirty work?" she asks.

"He does Mafia work." The smallest boy blurts out.

"You mean drugs?" She scans the eager, smiling faces.

"No, dirty work," the boy with the silver streaks yells at the top of his voice as he belts into the little one, hammering his head with both fists.

This causes an immediate scrum and fists rain blows all over the lean, brown boy until he falls to the ground between two rusty oil drums.

An old man appears from the cavernous depths of a warehouse

and shuffles towards the fighting boys. His skin is like brown leather and years of humping sacks of coffee beans have taken their toll. His spine has collapsed and now he is bent double, eyes on the ground as if he were looking for something.

"What's going on, *niños?* That's enough. Be off with you. Leave the Señora alone." He forces the writhing bodies apart and clips the ears of the biggest boy.

"*Anda!*" he calls over his shoulder as he ambles back to the warehouse, still searching for something on the ground.

The taxi driver had told her that these are the children of the prostitutes and they steal anything. Leather bags, straw bags, cloth bags, handbags that women wear over their shoulders. All bags have straps and you just hold each side of the bag and yank it down with both hands. The strap breaks, the bag is yours. And you never know what you will find. There might be something to eat, something to drink, sometimes a watch, sometimes a camera. Money. A lipstick.

And there are rich pickings from other bags, too. Passengers think they are safe carrying plastic bags from Marks and Spencer or Tesco or Asda but these rascals have X-ray eyes and with the sun shining it's easy to see a camera or watch glinting next to an apple and a bottle of water.

They are good at picking pockets, too. The gringos are so careless with money. They have too much of it. They fold dollar bills and tuck them neatly into top pockets of shirts, slide them into trouser pockets, push them into the back pocket of shorts. The boys are so quick, their touch is so light, so delicate the owners don't know that anything is missing until they are back at the dock gates fumbling for their shore passes.

"Come on now, boys, *basta*," Fiona produces a packet of biscuits from her zip bag. "Here. Share these."

The boy who had started the fight grabs it and pelts off at top speed along the quayside with the others galloping after him.

They can run very fast and are as agile as monkeys. From a vantage point high on the Bridge Deck, waiting for the ship to sail, she had watched them scale the cranes, barefoot, and disappear into the tall metal hoppers, sliding down inside to scoop the spilt flour into small cloth bags tied round their waists with string leaving both hands free for the perilous climb out of the hopper. Then they scrambled down the iron framework of the crane back to safety on the quayside. They risked their lives for a handful of flour to take home to their families. They are slick, quick, crafty and clever. And they are doomed from Day One.

She folds the map and puts it in her deck bag. Heavy footsteps clump along the alleyway and the Steward appears in the doorway carrying a red plastic bucket.

"Good morning, Bert. Do come in." She shuffles papers together and then reaches for her sun hat.

She likes Bert. His plump, mottled cheeks are like crushed anemones, his beer belly must have taken years to cultivate and his gentle, pale eyes seem not to have a care in the world. He's a good man to have in a ship with his placid acceptance of life.

"I'll leave you to get on in peace," she grabs her deck bag. "See you later."

The deck is deserted and she blinks against the sun on the white superstructure and feels an excitement with the vast expanse of sea and sky. Out here there is no room for arrogance, no need for riches or property, no greed, no poverty. Just the sea, this boundless sea, ignoring the irrelevance of the human race crawling across the face of this planet. And yet it is needed to perform all these things. Conveying people in luxury liners, cargo in ships, daring feats by yachtsmen. All challenging its world of unfathomable mystery.

It lifts her from the melancholy that overwhelms her at home and dead waves fascinate her. She had never heard of them but he'd explained it to her after that storm south of The Azores. He said that dead waves make the ship appear to stick in the water, behaving sluggishly, making little headway. It's a bit like the life she lives since Paul. Behaving sluggishly, making little headway.

Now the oceans are giving way to this seething river flanked by steamy swamps. The air is full of midges dancing around her head. She pulls her hat down to the bridge of her nose and leans on the boat rail. Canoes are slicing through the soupy waters and a rampaging motor boat rudely disturbs the peace, roaring to a climax that never comes. It disappears into the swamps and the wash settles into calmness again.

Just below the Bridge two butterflies are basking on the dazzling white superstructure. One is bright yellow and the other is blue and black. She moves to get a closer look but they sense her presence and slip into the sun. Her eyes go to the Bridge and she catches a glimpse of him as he steps into the wheel-house. She waits a moment in case he comes outside again. He doesn't, but his sorcery has registered and she feels a spasm where she always feels a spasm when she's near him. She hurries down to her cabin.

*****

Back in cabin 314 Bert siss-sisses through his teeth. It isn't a song, just a nice little rhythm. He reaches for the waste paper bin full of little packages. Mrs Meredith wraps all her rubbish in old newspaper. Apple peelings, banana skins, orange peel and it means that there is never any smell in the cabin. She's a nifty one. But why on earth does a woman want to come all this way on her own? Don't make no sense. Not to have company but she doesn't care a fig about going shore alone but then he'd seen more women travelling alone than men travelling alone. You'd think it would be the other way round.

He'd been in the Captain's night cabin the day she came to leave her money and had heard her telling the Captain that she was interested in poverty. Bugger me! Poverty! Why would anyone be so interested in the miseries of the poor. They're always with us. That's what his mother had said years ago. Alright the charities and do-gooders are always at it and everyone talks about the third world and poverty but the rich don't care a bugger. They sign a cheque here, sign a cheque there so they can sleep nights.

He puts the waste paper bin back under the table with a grunt and hitches up his trousers with his elbows.

But there's no stopping Mrs Meredith. Off she goes, down the gangway and back she comes with not a hair out of place and an armful of flowers.

She keeps herself to herself. Just polite conversation with the Blue Rinse twins at the table in the Mess. They're a bloody nuisance. Especially Lipstick Lulu. Always quizzing, a real nosy parker. Never let's up. Bert could smack her in the gob for being such a pain in the arse but he has to hand it to Mrs Meredith. She keeps her cool and deals with all that Lipstick Lulu dishes up.

Sissing through his teeth he makes up the bed, puts a new roll of toilet paper on top of the bathroom cabinet, polishes the mirror over the wash basin and closes the door of her cabin although she's told him he can leave it open.

Some passengers lock their door every time they step outside the cabin even when the ship is hundreds of miles from the nearest land. It's a bit over the top, not trusting the crew. She's tidy and methodical and her cabin never takes long. Soon he's next door strapping up the Chief Officer's cabin. Well, you can't call it a cabin. It's like one of them penthouse suites that cost an arm and a leg on the *Ryma*.

A spacious dayroom with potted plants, settee, a long low table, easy chairs, desk, phones, television, music centre, fridge. The lot. Not quite as big as the Captain's pad. You have to hand it to Drake Line. They look after their deep sea crew.

To the left of the door beyond the faded green brocade curtain is the night cabin. They might have left a bit more room to get round the bed. But it didn't put off the nocturnal visitor to the Chief Officer. Yes, this Chief worked hard and played hard and the devil take the hindmost and so say all of us, Bert sisses through his teeth as he wallops the pillows.

And he's seen the way this Chief scrambles around the holds then he strides along the quayside checking that the gangway is not ranging, checking the Security police are doing their job. At any rate the crew know where they stand with him. When there's a problem the Chief Officer is the man to find.

He picks up the oily gloves and puts them inside the yellow hard hat and lodges it on the peg just inside the door. Then he hauls the crate of empty beer bottles into the alleyway.

The Captain's dayroom is one deck up. It is deserted. He scoops up the chocolate biscuits from the plate on the low table and puts them in a plastic bag. He'll give them to the kids on the dock when he goes ashore. He empties the ashtrays, wipes the top of the table, then he waters the plants.

The Old Man is very particular about Kew Gardens. Spends hours caressing the trellis work, inspecting the rubbery leaves. If Bert could have his way he'd chuck the lot over the side. He's forever picking up dead leaves and bits that drop off in bad weather.

After that rough night near The Azores, the whole caboodle crashed. Soil all over the carpet, splintered trellis, broken shoots and he found a plant pot under the table. Such a bloody work up.

He pushes everything back into his bucket and clomps down the stairs. As he passes the cabin of the Blue Rinse Twins he can hear them arguing. He smiles and continues on his way down to the Galley.

5

"Can't hear. What did you say?" Joy Galbraith is stretched full length on her bed flicking through The Economist. The Captain had sent it to their cabin the day after sailing.

"I said…" her sister calls from the bathroom. "I said… I think she might be a prostitute."

"Who?" Joy pushes the magazine away.

"That woman. Travelling alone. You know, in the cabin at the end of the corridor. Mizz Meredith."

"Oh, her! Well, she'd have to travel alone because there's only one double cabin and we've got it. And it's one of the best cabins we've had isn't it?" Joy didn't wait for a reply. "I like that long table. And the settee with its back to the wall."

Violet steps out of the bathroom, slapping sun tan oil on to her bony arms. "It's not a wall. In a ship it's a bulkhead. And the ceiling is the deckhead. And the floor is the deck."

"Oh alright," Joy flicks opens The Economist. Violet is being pedantic and worse, she is looking for an argument. "Yes, we're lucky this trip. We've got much more space and it's much lighter with these two windows."

"Remember that ghastly container ship we went on? All those generators humming night and day." Violet's skin gleams as she coaxes more oil into her cheeks.

"Don't remind me. Twenty four thousand tons of copper in the hold! What a sell-out that was! Vibrating and rattling day and night. It was like living in a fairground."

"But," Violet stretches her neck as if she were about to sing.

"That woman's too young to be in a cargo ship. And travelling alone."

"Nonsense. We've met younger ones. Don't you remember those young women who were going back-packing in Nicaragua? And that weirdo woman. Collecting shells. So she said. And then there was that handsome German. Para-gliding in Colombia." Joy keeps her eyes on her sister hovering in the bathroom doorway. A green satin robe is slipping off her thin brown shoulders exposing folds of deflated breasts, hanging like bags of bird seed.

They were both as wrinkled as walnuts after more than half a century of sun worshipping. Joy is a year older than her sister but many people think they are twins. They are the same height, five feet eleven inches tall but shrinking by the year, with straight backs, long legs, big feet and a slow, dawdling walk. Each has a classical straight nose and a sharp jaw line with nothing to droop. The grey curls are rinsed with a blue tint painting an altogether bizarre picture with their mahogany skin and sapphire blue eyes.

They do look alike but astute observers are able to distinguish them because of their makeup. Violet plasters it on. Joy uses very little. Standing side by side they look like an advertisement for some 'before and after' product.

"Well, she's not very forthcoming at the table is she? At breakfast she just sits there toying with her bowl of cereal. I mean, she avoids my questions. It's the same every meal time."

"Clearly she doesn't want to talk much. She's got her own reasons. I quite like her. Seems somewhat surprised about everything, the way she tilts her head to one side. It's that pert little nose. And those freckles. I find her quite charming and you should leave her alone." Joy swings her long legs off the bed, puts her elbows on her knees and cradles her head with both hands. "You're too nosy."

"No, I'm not."

"Yes, you are. It's embarrassing at the table but you won't shut up. And that hair's natural, you know. Ours used to look like that didn't it? Short and curly and brown."

"I don't want to be reminded of how things *used* to be. Besides she's young. I think she's a bit of a mystery. Probably got something to hide."

"Oh, don't be so ridiculous Vi, really. I can't cope with you today. I've got a headache."

"Serves you right if you've got a hangover."

"I said 'headache' not 'hangover.'"

"You should keep away from the crew parties. They're all hardened drinkers."

"No, they're not." Joy flops back on to the bed, "I've never seen any crew member drunk. I consider it a compliment to be invited. Why should they bother with us old maids?"

"You tell me!" Violet swipes lipstick across her mouth.

"Well, they're here. They're intelligent human beings and we're all in the same boat..."

"Ship." Violet squeezes her lips into a thin red line.

"Alright, ship." Joy gets to her feet but wobbles back on to the bed. "You should have gone. It was great. These are good, honest, hard-working men. And at this stage of the game I'm going to accept every invitation that comes my way."

"Beats me why any man wants to spend his life tossing about in all this water. And as for crossing Biscay. Madness!" Violet's voice pierces the quiet cabin. "And they do it year in, year out."

"So do we." Joy hugs her knees.

"Yes. But only once a year. They're doing it all the time."

"And it makes them different to the men ashore. I always think these are *real* men. It's the spirit of adventure. The questing." Joy punches the pillow and leans back on it. "'The ever present mystery of infinite time and space out there'..."

"Here we go again," Violet stands in front of the port hole scrutinising her face in a mirror shaped like a pink heart.

"Wait a minute. It's coming." Joy holds her forehead. "Another quote from one of your books."

"I think it's Albert Camus. 'Individuals grow old and lonely and their pathetic little preoccupations are out of all proportion to the sea and desert…"

"Thirty years in a Library and for thirty years I've listened to gems of wisdom that you've stolen from some high-minded genius."

"'…those ever-present symbols of the mystery of infinite time and space.' "That's it." The row was definitely coming and Joy didn't want a row this morning. Not with this thick head.

She'd been the only woman at last night's party in the Bo'sun's cabin. He had invited all three passengers. Violet refused to go and Fiona Meredith was nowhere to be found. There were Stewards, Engineers, Deck Sailors, Deck Officers, Electrician, Cook and Assistant Cook. She would never had believed so many people could get into such a small cabin. They were sitting on a settee along the wall, in chairs, on life jackets used as a cushion on top of the waste paper bin, squatting on the floor. A transient crowd changing all the time as they came on and off watch. She noticed that those going on watch were not drinking alcohol.

She couldn't see where the music was coming from but as the evening wore on the singing drowned it. Wonderful singing with a resonance, a power, ringing through that crew cabin. Close your eyes and it could have been a church choir or a choral concert.

She liked the Bo'sun. Tall and willowy with the stealth of a wild animal, cautious with energy, wasting nothing. His doleful, weather-beaten face was neither agreeable nor disagreeable. Neither handsome nor ugly but distinctive. His back was slightly bowed with the years of heaving against the winds, pulling ropes, pilot ladders and gangways. He created a frisson in her that she hadn't sensed for years.

"Why should a woman like that make a voyage like this?" Violet questions the reflection in the pink heart mirror.

"Oh, for heaven's sake, Vi. Leave it alone. She's probably asking herself exactly the same question about us. Two old maids going to South America to get mugged and robbed."

"Ah, but we shan't get mugged and robbed shall we," Violet frowns at the yellow teeth in the little mirror. "I shall have to decide about them soon."

"What?"

"My teeth. Whether to spend all that money on having them whitened. If we do well this trip I shall get them done." She purses her lips again. "But I still think she might be on the game."

"Well, I don't care a fig. She can do it from the top of the flag-pole for all I care." Joy smoothes her aching head with the palms of her hands. "I can't imagine these men forming an orderly queue for a bonk when they can get all those dark-eyed beauties ashore. 'Ay, yay, Ay yay…have you ever kissed in the moonlight…'" Joy broke into song. "Do you remember Carmen Miranda? I thought she was fabulous."

"You shouldn't use that word," Violet shoots a glance over her shoulders.

"Which word?"

"Bonk."

"Why not? Everybody else does." Joy strokes her cold toes. "Come on…get real…get a life…"

Vi rummages for her eyebrow tweezers. "We shall never know. Need evidence."

"Well, Vi, you can spend the rest of the trip finding out. I really don't know why it bothers you so much. Live and let live, I say. Nothing to do with us. Your trouble is…" Joy stops. If she said what the trouble is there would be one hell of a row. Violet's problem is that she is still encased in puritanical armour and only very occasionally does she allow fragments to be chipped away.

The widower who ran the Social Club was frisky enough to attempt it. So was the family butcher, also a widower. Joy remembers her sister's passion for Tony Muncaster. He joined the Paratroopers, and Violet never saw him again. A German sniper got him as he floated down on his parachute at Arnhem. His mate, who survived, said it was just like shooting ducks. Those men didn't stand a chance. It happened to hundreds of thousands of them leaving hundreds of thousands of women to wail and wilt or get on with their lives. That's Violet's trouble. She won't let go. She has sucked on the raggy remnant of grief for so many years that she's become addicted to it. It's her pacifier, her raison d-être, her excuse for remaining as Tony had left her. Eager, sexy with a promise of a wedding ring.

The Tax Office where she worked had done nothing to obliterate the yearning. Day after day she scribbled on forms, ticked boxes, sent letters to men and women who simply tossed them into the waste paper bin.

Joy had decided that the Tax Office and everybody in it aided and abetted the sterility of her sister's life, hanging bits out to dry, sympathising with her, massaging the pain. She had been inconsolable at the D-Day Commemorations and howled her eyes out for Tony Muncaster.

She glances across at Vi filing her nails. Always titillating herself for the big affair she never has. All this lipstick, all this sun tan oil, all these preparations for attracting a partner. Violet wants to say 'yes' but always says 'no'.

"Time for a gin," Violet drops the nail file into the tartan bag, puts it back in the drawer and pulls a bottle from the bottom of the wardrobe. "I do hope Mrs Little has checked the immersion heater."

"Oh, stop prattling. She will have got your letter from Rotterdam."

Joy and Violet Galbraith wintered abroad every year and they made two check lists. Violet was responsible for the electricals. Everything unplugged and switched off. Joy did the water, window locks and keys.

"You really should loosen up Vi. Every year you think of some darned thing that you've left switched on and every year Mrs Little writes to tell you everything is OK. I'm surprised she bothers with us. I don't know what we'd do without her. Being away all this time. We wouldn't find anyone else to keep an eye on things. Not like she does."

"You just have no sense of responsibility. That's your trouble." Vi puts two glasses on the table. "Mother was always chiding you about it."

"That's not true." Joy's eyes blaze. "If I had no sense of responsibility how is it I ended up as Chief Librarian and you didn't move an inch from your mountain of assessment forms in that...that constipated Tax Office."

"Ha, ha!" Violet pours gin into her glass. "But I ended up with a bigger pension." She held up the gin bottle. "More for you?"

"True. But I don't let immersion heaters take over my life. We're on the home stretch, you know. A little more tonic please."

"Don't you dare mention age..." Vi gives the cap on the gin bottle a vicious turn.

"I didn't. It's no good waiting for better days. This is it!" Joy collapses on the bed again and reaches for The Economist. She really isn't in the mood for a row this morning.

Violet is standing in front of the settee, clutching her gin and tonic watching her sister lying on the bed pretending to read. She's right, of course, but she isn't going to admit it. We *are* on the home stretch. The trouble with Joy is that she always has to have the last word. It had got worse after mother died, blaming each other for imaginary short-comings and an abundance of 'if-only's'.

Mother had been the stabilising influence. The anchorage they had both needed, the warning voice that had kept them on an even keel. Now they have adjusted to the empty chair at the dining table, the empty chair by the fireside but they still argue.

And last night Joy had gone to a crew party. Mother would have had a fit but then, mother would have had a fit about many of the things they are now doing. Like wintering abroad, not to mention...

Joy has always been a loose cannon where men are concerned but she envies her ability to fascinate them. Yes, fascinate would be the word. She has something that men like. They flock around her. And there had been that affair with the married man. Thank goodness mother never got to know about it.

So when they received their retirement presents, a carriage clock for Violet from colleagues at the Inland Revenue, and a set of Encyclopaedia Britannica for Joy from fellow librarians, they had settled into a routine sharing the financial responsibility of running the house, the shopping, Bridge parties, sorting out jumble at the Oxfam shop, Church committee meetings, ending the year carol singing at Christmas outside Asda.

They used to travel on cruise liners until Ben, their milkman, suggested they might enjoy cargo ship travel. He'd spent years at sea in the Merchant Navy and knew the ropes.

No more cocktail parties. No more bingo. No more cabaret. No more boring 'Travelling Alones' parties. Good old Ben. He'd brought a new dimension to their predictable daily round. And lots of money. It financed their annual escape to the sunshine.

Violet leans forward, narrowing her eyes at the large picture on the bulkhead above the settee. It depicts the head and shoulders of Marlene Dietrich in a low cut silver lamé dress with an atomic bomb exploding from the top of her head. "Don't know what to make of this Captain. He's too good-looking to be true."

"Looks like an overgrown schoolboy with those blank eyes. Saw him on deck and you'll never guess what he was wearing! Khaki shorts. Flapping around his knees. He looked quite ridiculous." Joy is clutching her glass with both hands. "I think he's wobbly."

"What do you mean 'wobbly'?" Violet screws up her eyes until Marlene Dietrich is a shiny blur.

"I mean... Well, shifty. He always looks away. You can't get anyone's measure if you can't look into their eyes, can you?"

"No. But I still think he's good-looking." Vi sips her gin slowly, one hand on her hip as she gazes at the picture.

"Arrogant," Joy spits out the word. "And it doesn't look as if anything's happened in that face since the day he was born."

"But he knows his job and that's all that matters. We've never had a night boat drill before, have we? That got everybody on their toes." Violet kneels on the settee to peer closer at Marlene Dietrich. "She's got no eyebrows at all. But that's a beautiful woman if ever there was one."

"It was the Chief Officer's idea."

"What was?"

"Night Boat Drill."

"How do you know?"

"I heard him giving orders to the Second Officer. If you ask me I think *he* runs the ship."

"You could be right. And you'd think the Captain would smile a bit more often."

"Probably got nothing much to smile about. Domestic problems. Nagging wife. Unruly kids." Joy rolls the mouthful of gin around, savouring it. "Now that Chief Officer!"

"Chief Mate," Violet sinks on to the settee folding her legs underneath her.

"He's the Chief Officer…" Joy places her glass on the bedside cabinet and hauls herself into an upright position.

"Chief Mate. That's what they call him." Violet wafts the hem of her satin robe with her painted toe nails.

"Yes, but I saw the crew manifest when I went to the Radio Room." Joy stands up for a moment, changes her mind and slumps back on to the bed. "He's Jeffrey Bloxham, Chief Officer, aged 35. Next time I go I'll get a copy then perhaps you'll believe me. Anyway, he's a dish. Wonder how he got that scar?"

"It's quite deep." Violet drains her glass and reaches for the bottle of gin.

"Well, I like it. Mocking the world for what it did to his handsome face. Now that's what I call a lived-in face. Let's have one more before lunch." She held out her glass. "We can sleep it off this afternoon. And we must decide where we're going to buy."

"I like the man in Guayaquil. Pedro." Violet puts the gin bottle back in the bottom of the wardrobe. "I wasn't too sure about the one in Cartagena. A bit risky."

"They're all risky," Joy swings her legs to the floor. "Never forget it."

"Do you think she'll want to go ashore with us?" Violet stands in front of the open bathroom door, turning her head to preen in the mirror above the washbasin.

"Who, Fiona? Stop worrying about her." Joy reaches for the bright blue cardigan at the bottom of the bed.

"You won't need that. It's going to be very hot then you'll start complaining about having to carry it. And we don't go ashore with anyone, do we?"

"No. We can't take any chances whether we're doing business or not. She'll know how to take care of herself."

Violet empties her glass and wanders to the porthole. "Oh, good. They're rigging the pilot ladder. Come on, let's go for lunch."

6

Jeffrey Bloxham is on the starboard wing of the Bridge gazing at the ramshackle wooden huts on stilts at the water's edge less than a hundred yards away. They are the huts of the prawn fishers, the *camarones*. A pathway meanders into a wilderness of swamps and in the distance the mountains rise out of the green spongy lowlands.

The heat is heavy, pressing on his head like a lead weight. Last night he and Billy Lloyd had cracked too many bottles of beer and chased them with a double Scotch but the session had done nothing to blot out the concern about Linda. He needs to talk to her. To know that she's alright. That Tom's alright. Soon they will be docking in Guayaquil and he should get a phone connection during the port turn around. It will take at least two days to discharge the cargo. Steel rods and machinery and several twenty foot containers and as they are now in mañana country it will probably take longer.

Butterflies hover around the superstructure in flashes of blue, black, yellow, scarlet. Living confetti. Then he sees a flock of wild duck rise from the swamp and curve away in a wide arc until a thin black skein trails across the sky.

The *Welland* entered the estuary of the River Guayas in the early hours and is now creeping past the hulk of a sunken cargo ship. There are few warning signals in the river but mariners know where to position their ships to avoid this mass of rusting metal.

He scans the wreck. The Bridge is garnished with plastic bags, strips of grey cloth and what appears to be a pair of faded green shorts. Broken tree branches lodge between the boat rails. An old red shirt flaps in a tangle of kelp wafting across the wheelhouse. The bloated body of a dog is trapped against the anchor chain.

The Pilot told him the wreck has been there for forty years and no one is going to pay for its salvage. He hears footsteps. Captain Pycroft is at his elbow.

"Pilot at 1400."

"Good," Jeff follows him into the wheelhouse. With a bit of luck the Landing Agent will have the shore gang ready to get the cargo discharged and he may, just may, be free this evening.

It's more than ten kilometres from the maritime port to downtown Guayaquil and that was a long way to go to get mugged and robbed.

"Go and get your meal," Peter Pycroft is at his side again, hands clasped behind his back staring at the bow slicing through the muddy waters.

"Yes, sir," Jeff puts the binoculars on the chart table, scoops up his dirty gloves and clatters down the stairway, hating Peter Pycroft with every fibre in his body. 'Go and get your meal'. He whacks his gloves on the door frame as he steps into the cabin then throws them on to the carpet just inside the door. 'Go and get your meal'. Not 'Would you like…' or 'long time since breakfast…'

He takes a bottle of beer from the fridge. This is his second voyage under the command of recently promoted Peter Pycroft and he'd quickly learned that the man dithers about like a brainless chicken. How the hell he could be given command was beyond Jeff's comprehension.

"No, it isn't." He tosses the cap from the beer bottle into the waste paper bin. "You know how he got command. He married the daughter of the General Manager. Simple! He married the boss's daughter."

Jeff had chosen the daughter of an Air Force Officer and there was no one to give him a hand up the promotion ladder but one day… One day he'd get his command. He would be Captain. At the moment he has no choice but to take orders from this piss artist who fiddles and farts about and could never decide what colour to whitewash the church. So, he would go and get his meal like a

50

good little boy.

But there are compensations. Cargo passenger lists don't offer much in the way of Rest and Recreation for the crew - that is to say, sex. Retired school teachers, retired bankers, retired professors, retired bakers and retired candlestick makers, boring the daylight out of him and bumming around for free drinks.

Passengers are just a pain in the neck but this slip of a woman is something different. She had been a passenger on the *Witham*, travelling alone, just over a year ago. He'd been transferred from the *Welland* to the *Witham* for a grand-daddy of a voyage, through the Suez Canal and Indian Ocean. He didn't know whether this posting was because of his encounter with the pane of glass that caved in or whether it was the mooring rope that snapped at Seno Aysén or whether it was preparatory to his promotion. Time will tell.

Since sailing from Southampton there had been more than the usual number of cock-ups. After getting alongside in Hamburg they had lost the anchor. Without warning it had gone to the bottom of the harbour and created the biggest bloody workup anyone could imagine. The Chief Engineer, the Bo'sun and his team had worked all day heaving that spare anchor, all five and a half tons of it, from the forward hold up on to the deck and into position. Sailing was delayed and overtime is expensive. Don't hang about in Hamburg. But Management couldn't pin this one on him. Oh, no! But someone should have reported that worn anchor chain.

After Mombasa they had been in the Indian Ocean en route for Sri Lanka when a deck sailor reported sick. Suspected appendicitis. The condition of this nineteen year old deteriorated rapidly. Telexes were flying to and from the ship and then Head Office instructed the *Witham* to proceed to the nearest port. Victoria in the Seychelles, the smallest capital in the world, huddled against the side of a hill. And there they were, stranded.

Jeff had been supervising the landing of the seaman to hospital and was surprised to see the *Witham's* one and only passenger coming down the gangway. Since sailing he'd been too busy with the cock-ups that were jinxing this trip and his only contact with this passenger had been a nod and 'good morning' in the Messroom, a nod and greeting on deck and here she is, standing in front of him.

This was the closest he'd been to her. A confusion of chestnut curls tumbled over her head and around her ears. The freckles on her face looked like gold dust in the bright sunshine. Petite and slim, her compact body was honed and charged with a controlled energy.

"Will you be going ashore today Chief?"

He noticed she had a space between her two front teeth. Lucky, they say. She took off her sunglasses and stared at him.

"Probably. There's no cargo to discharge. We didn't expect to be here. This is an unscheduled call."

"Can we go together?" she tilted her head and smiled at him. "My name's Fiona Meredith and I'm harmless." She twirled her sunglasses around.

Surprised at her almost brazen suggestion, he held the wide, wanton eyes for a moment too long. They were hazel eyes with a hint of despair, a hint of sadness. He looked away quickly scanning the deserted quayside for space, for time to think quickly about this unknown female, travelling alone on his sturdy little ship who wants to go on a jaunt ashore with him. He rarely went ashore in any of the ports. Never had time. Always busy. Always problems.

He cleared his throat. "Why not? There's nothing to be done until we get the report from the hospital. And the name's Jeffrey Bloxham. Jeff to you." He glanced down at his dusty boots. "Give me a few minutes to clean up."

Then he was at her side, showered and changed at the bottom of the gangway. "What would you like to do?"

"Get away." She was twirling her sunglasses again.

"Alright." Jeff could see a tall man wearing frayed shorts and a torn blue shirt lolling against his battered taxi parked at the entrance to the dock gates whittling at a piece of wood.

"Hullo," Jeff waved to him and signalled to him to come over. Fiona spoke to him in French but his patois was difficult to understand and they settled for fractured English. His name was Henry and he would show them many good things.

Soon they were clear of the hustle and bustle of the streets and shops and climbing to the woods high above Mahé.

Henry parked the taxi in a clearing just off the main road. "Come. Follow me."

He led the way along moist, green tracks hemmed in by a blaze of exotic bushes and ferns.

"That's the coco plum, and there behind it, cinnamon tree. Smell!"

They followed him along the path.

"Vanilla tree and over there, bread fruit." He waves his long brown arm. "And this," he paused, "this is pitcher plant. Very clever. Fools nature. Catches insects in that cup for food. See."

Jeff was walking behind Fiona, his eyes ranging from the shapely legs to her firm little bottom in the cropped blue jeans. And he noticed she wasn't wearing a bra.

Henry was a few yards ahead of them.

"Come," he beckoned. "Follow me."

They tramped through clumps of long grass, weaving and bending to avoid the young saplings.

"Look!" Henry pointed to a low-growing tree with slender horizontal branches armed with short spines. Small downy flowers clustered around the short leathery leaves.

"But what is it?" Jeff moved closer to touch the leaves.

"Careful!" Henry barred his way. "No touch. Strychnine tree."

"You mean…" Fiona moved to Jeff's side.

"The Calebassier du Pays - Strychnos annae." Henry beamed his regiment of teeth at them. "Poisonous. All of tree poisonous. And look. Here. More." He led them along another path, damp and soggy underfoot.

"Look!" An enormous wine-coloured flower must have been two feet in diameter. It was monstrous and looked like a huge deformed rose growing inside a huge deformed cabbage.

53

"It's a giant aroid. Smell very bad, very bad." He steps away. "Stuns flies. How you say, knocks them. Very bad smell."

"Phew! It's disgusting," Fiona held her nose.

Jeff stood with hands on hips staring at the unusual growth. "You certainly know your plants, Henry."

"Oh, yes," Henry grinned. "Come. We see more." He led them back along the path to the taxi.

"Now I show you red bananas. Other side of the island," he explains. "We go now."

"Red bananas, really? I had no idea there were red bananas." Fiona turned to Jeff. "We must see them."

Jeff pulls his wrist watch from his shirt pocket. "I'm sorry. We don't really have time. I must check on the hospital."

Henry was now throwing his clapped out taxi between the cyclists, hooting cars, rattling lorries and coughing buses weaving between men pulling hand-carts laden with fruits and vegetables. He pulled up in a narrow opening at the shopping centre near the harbour.

"Plenty good things," Henry stuffed the dollars into a tiny pocket inside the waistband of his shorts then he folded his long brown legs into the cab. "OK Goodbye. Good luck. Next time, red bananas, yes," and the battered old taxi disappeared into the frenzied streets.

Jeff pulled out his wrist watch again. "Let's go and get a bite to eat. We've got time. Over there perhaps. The Sunfish Restaurant."

It was one small room with slim waiters moving silently between little square tables. He led her to a window seat and after a brief scan of the menu they settled for Seychelles fresh water prawns.

"Henry certainly knew his flora," she swept off her sunglasses and put them on the gingham table cloth. "And did you see? He was barefoot. Walking in that jungle. Barefoot!"

"Yes. I didn't notice until we were looking at that weird cabbage thing."

"It's been fabulous." She was a little unsure as to whether he shared her view. His mood was difficult to read. Pleasant and friendly but there was some reticence about him. Perhaps he was worried about the poor sailor in the hospital all these miles from home.

"Yes," Jeff toyed with his glass of lager. He knew it was fabulous, he knew it was exotic. He knew it was like no other place on this planet. But *she* didn't know that this is where he'd brought Linda for their honeymoon. His fingers fidgetted with a small round stain on the gingham tablecloth.

The chatter in the restaurant faded away and he saw Linda in her blue beach coat that tantalisingly stopped at the top of her bronze thighs. They were stretched out on the beach watching the sun wrap itself in a deep orange cloak of satin before slipping into the Indian Ocean.

Yes, this is where all the promises had been laid out, placed like jewels along the white beach, rinsed by the aquamarine sea, hidden amongst the coral reefs where they had snorkelled.

"We'll have two children. A boy and a girl. What do you think?" Jeff sifted sand across her bare thighs.

"That tickles. No, let's have three. For luck!"

"Alright. But we'll have to manage with the old car until…"

"I know what you're going to say,' Linda pulled him down and kissed his forehead. "Until you're promoted. Until you're the Captain of your ship."

"Yes. And we'll stay in Coleridge Avenue for the time being. And I promise to swallow the anchor when you want me home, for good." All planned. All decided. All settled. Here in paradise.

Twelve years later they had one son, Tom, and he was a problem. Jeff felt that Tom would not be a problem if he were at home with him, leading a normal life. Doing all the things that boys did with their fathers. Not as big treats every time he came on leave. Quit the sea and get a job ashore. But he and Linda had gone through it all time and time again, coming out by the same door as 'in they went'.

Linda had crashed the car in Tesco's car park and it had been replaced by another second hand Vauxhall. And he had not yet been promoted. He is not in command of a ship. He is not the

Captain.

But he isn't going to dwell on his domestic worries. Not here. Not today. He gives his glass of lager a little shake. He's going to enjoy this compensation. Fiona Meredith, widow, she had explained, which he already knew from the ship's manifest. He looks up without moving his head.

"It's time I got back." He empties his glass quickly. "We should know something about the seaman by now."

"Yes, we don't want to be stranded here. Or do we?" Those wandering eyes flash a message and a mischievous desire upsets his equilibrium.

Impulsively, he blurts out the suggestion. "What about a night-cap. Later. To celebrate our fantastic communion with Mother Nature today?"

She picks up her sunglasses. "Sounds like a good idea."

He holds her gaze and once again he feels control slipping away from him. "I'll give you a ring. Should be clear by ten o'clock. After the Pilot's gone."

On board he discovers that the deck sailor will have to remain in hospital and will be repatriated to the United Kingdom when he is fit enough to travel.

"What a place to be a Distressed British Seaman!" Jeff is counting the longshoremen standing by the bollards ready to cast off. Captain John Griffin is leaning over the boat rail watching the men dismantle the gangway. He is a grizzled, brooding man with a head of bushy grey hair, steely blue eyes, and a command presence to be envied by any officer.

"Oh, there'll be a cargo ship homeward bound to pick him up, sooner or later." He half-turns. "If he gets lucky there might even be the QE2."

It's nearly half past ten when Jeff gets down to his dayroom. They had sailed on time, the pilot has gone, he is now showered and changed. Stepping back from the bathroom mirror he touches his scar. Bet she asks how I got it, they all do. He frowns and wanders across the dayroom to his desk then picks up the phone. She answers straight away and before he can get up from his chair there is a light tap on the door and she steps inside.

He is startled to see her looking so glamorous. She is wearing a tailored kaftan in pale turquoise, much the same colour of the sea that caresses the beaches of the Indian Ocean. It has long sleeves and a deep V neck. On her feet are white fur mules. They look like kittens.

This afternoon, on those narrow, squelchy footpaths in the steamy undergrowth she had looked like a teenager in her cropped jeans, her check shirt and floppy sun hat. And he is surprised that she's so punctual. Once again he's been caught off balance by this enigmatic woman.

"What about a drink?" he went to the fridge to compose himself. "White wine, red wine, gin, scotch?"

"White wine please."

She moves to the settee, slowly, catlike and sits down, compactly folding her legs underneath her.

With his back to her he watches through the long, slim mirror at the back of the drinks cabinet. Yes, there is something feline about her. Quiet, wary, on guard. The slit of the kaftan bares a pale thigh gleaming like a fish. He pours the drinks and carries them to the coffee table then he lowers himself into an easy chair wondering why she has chosen a work-weary little cargo ship visiting remote, run down and obscure ports for her holiday. He doesn't have to coax the answers from her. They come fluently, smoothly, without embarrassment, without faltering.

She raises her glass and winks at the wine. "Shoulder the sky and drink your ale." I think it's from a poem. Well, that's what Paul and I did. He was a pilot. My husband. I was Air Hostess with Meridian Airlines. Those were the days and we thought they'd never end. Shouldering the skies all over the world."

"What happened?"

"Well, I was on leave. Paul was on a long haul flight to South America. It was November. The phone rang. It was the Personnel Manager. Said he would like to see me but gave no hint as to why." She puts down her glass of wine and keeps her eyes on it. "I thought it might be a social visit - we knew him and his wife -

although he knew Paul was away."

She untangles her legs, stands up, and stares down at the carpet. "He came...he came..." she falters, "he came to tell me that Flight 213 captained by Paul had crashed into a mountainside in Ecuador." She walks slowly to the port hole and gazes into the black round space. "Ninety six people on board. No survivors."

"The Safety Board Investigation Report stated that it was difficult to imagine this experienced and competent pilot attempting to pass over an 8,100 foot peak at 7,500 feet." She is talking to the black space of the port hole. "Was something wrong with the altimeter? Was it human error?" She's still staring into the black round space of the porthole as the questions haunt every corner of the dayroom.

Turning she walks back towards the settee. "We used to joke about his transference of numbers."

Now she is looking down at him, holding the steadfast gaze of the questioning blue eyes. "I remember when we stayed in this hotel in Singapore. The receptionist said the room allocated was No. 53. Paul took the key and off we went but we couldn't open the door so we went back to Reception. They confirmed that we had had been allocated the correct key. It was for Room 35 and we had been on the wrong floor! Is this what happened in that cockpit? I will never know. None of us will ever know." Her voice is a whisper as she perches on the arm of his chair.

"If you lose the love of your life, that's that, finito and it has to be accepted." She kicks away first one furry kitten and then the other.

"When you enjoy life and living and all that a happy partnership brings to that state of affairs, and when all this is taken away..." her voice peters out.

Outside, below the porthole, there is just the gentle swish of water against the skin of the ship, the distant hoot of a vessel, a vehicle revving away, men's voices as gangways are hauled into position. The world is getting on with its business but here, in this room, she needs to be drawn away from the abyss of terror that is waiting for her.

"You know, life seems like a lighted room, full of people, books, music, conversation. Stretch out an arm and put your finger through the wall and you find that it's only paper thin. The shrieking dark comes whirling in, through the hole, and in a second everything - people, laughter, music - is whirled away in tiny meaningless fragments. Into the abyss." Quickly she reaches for the wine glass on the low table. It's almost empty. He eases it from her fingers and goes to the drinks cabinet.

He feels himself slipping into her space. Her snare, her trap. Whatever it is, he's being drawn into it and he cannot resist.

"Of course my mother, my sister Joanne, and my friends were all there doing everything possible to take away the torment, the pain. They were so kind it made me weep with self-pity as they tried to fill the empty space with dinner parties, invitation to Cowes, to the theatre. You know, all the normal things. But things were not normal. And the hardest thing was to convince myself that Paul would not be ringing again. Would not be on leave again. Would not... I'm sorry," she drinks quickly. "Do forgive me. All these negatives that have filled my mind since..." She swirls the wine around her glass.

"The weeks and months ambled by ignoring me, so I decided to move from our home in a leafy lane in a village in the New Forest. Too many ghosts. The past will not come back."

He watches as she saunters across the room, turns and comes back to stand in front of him.

"I chose an apartment in Southampton. Much smaller than the house. With a different view. But you know, it is just as empty. The shapes of the rooms are different, the kitchen is oblong and not square, the living room is smaller, more compact. I changed around the bedroom completely. The decor is different, the colour scheme is different. Paul was a traditionalist so I went minimalist. To ease the pain."

She wanders across to the black port hole again. "But it's the same emptiness. The same emptiness," her voice is in despair. "Paul was not there. His death left me wandering around a bleak landscape and a bleak apartment. So bleak that nothing whatever matters. That's the interesting thing I've learned. Life is so intense for many people. They worry about things that do not warrant so much concern. I find that nothing matters anymore. I've lost the most important person in my life. My imperfect, lovable Paul. So it doesn't matter whether I eat or sleep. It doesn't matter whether I do this or that. It doesn't matter what the news is telling me on radio or television. Nothing at all…matters." She speaks slowly. "Strange isn't it, when our whole life is chock full of things that matter."

He keeps his eyes on her but does not interrupt. It is almost as if she were acting on a stage, in a play, a tragedy, quietly speaking her lines, moving in a planned circuit around the dayroom.

"So, I decided to get away. To try and find something that mattered again. A beggar boy on the docks, an old woman in the gutter trying to sell things that nobody wants." She is now at the back of his chair then she moves round to look at him, fully relaxed in the easy chair. "Do you remember what Herman Melville says at the beginning of *Moby Dick*? Like Captain Ahab I found myself growing grim about the mouth with nothing to smile about. So… I decided to make a voyage to the unknown on board a cargo ship."

"So you exchanged that bleakness for an endless ocean that is almost as bleak. So what's the difference?"

"But the ocean isn't bleak. It's so powerful. I love the solitude and space and mystery of it all. The sea, especially at night. The sky so dark, the stars so bright. And the storms, when they come, are just awesome. The fury, the huge waves pushing and pounding, the demented wind, the anger, the confusion but most of all the power! And we are powerless. Absolutely powerless. Just mere mortals living out our life span and the oceans roll on… Byron had something to say about it but I can't recall it for the moment."

She is now at the other side of the dayroom. "And the dead waves. Your explanation during the Bridge visit was interesting." Her fingers tap the wine glass giving the impression of nervousness but this young woman is calm, composed and in control. "Do tell me more about dead waves."

"Well, there's not a lot to tell really." He shifts his position and gives his glass a little shake. "No one really knows what's down there. There's a lot of research on the movement of water. Waves have been observed at the boundary between light and heavy water. That is to say, between warm and cold, high-salinity water. In old sailing accounts these waves were mistaken for sea monsters which were holding back ships."

"Well, it's like me and my life. Behaving sluggishly and making little headway. But here I am." She is tapping her wine glass again, watching him from the other side of the dayroom and vowing not to tell him the truth. The truth about what really happened after Paul…

There is a pause and then she asks, "What's the name of your wife?"

The question stuns him.

"Linda."

"And your children?"

"One son, Tom. Twelve years old going on thirteen." He takes a deep breath to recover from the unexpected question and decides he isn't going to tell her that Linda and Tom are a constant worry to him. That his mother interferes from a distance, that Linda is quite happy to abdicate her responsibility to her mother who spoils the boy rotten. And he doesn't tell her of his concern for the state of their marriage. The dreadful dilemma of being away for months on end. Burst pipes, car repairs, blown fuses, school holidays to fill, and the way his wife copes with all of this so well… and alone. And she also has to cope with his absence from her bed. He doesn't say any of these things.

She puts her glass on the table and moves to his side.

He is aware of her closeness, the energy, the magic and then her arms are around his shoulders and she is swamping him with kisses on his forehead, eyes, ears, cheeks.

She breaks away. "And this is my very last question." She traces his scar with her cool fingers. "How did you get this?"

"We must go somewhere else for that story."

"Good." She held his cheeks and traced the scar with her finger then she kisses his lips again.

He scoops her up and carries her to the bedroom, kicking the curtain aside with his foot.

That night they ran amok creating havoc with every nerve, every muscle, every sigh in their bodies until they were spent. Lying back, with her asleep in his arms, he is wide awake thinking about this dynamic, energetic, grieving human being trying to come to terms with loss. How does one come to terms with it? Drink, drugs, brain washing, do-gooders, well-wishers. This woman took to the mighty oceans to find solace and peace and tranquillity and here she is, in his arms and he has a wife, a son and a crumbling marriage to add to the mix.

The only answer comes from the steady throb of the *Witham's* engines and the silky swish of the Indian Ocean below his port hole. He is content. Revitalised and reluctant to succumb to the fatigue that is luring him away to sleep.

Since that magical day in the forests of Mahé, Fiona Meredith has become an integral part of his existence. She is firmly placed in the jigsaw puzzle of his life. No forcing a match, no bending, no twisting of the pieces. She fitted perfectly.

Fiona has the wherewithal to do exactly what she wants with her time and money so she has booked passage again and here she is on his ship again.

Her apartment is just as she had described it. Modern, minimalist, and dare he say it…empty. Nothing has happened in it. To be a home it has to endure the happiness, the sadness, the strife, the peace. It is empty and it tortures him.

It is less than three miles from Coleridge Avenue and he is able to visit during his voyage leave with strict instructions to phone before he plans to comes. Linda never questions why the simple problem with the car has taken longer than anticipated and accepts that he gets held up chatting with this fellow Master Mariners after the meetings.

He is surprised that she has two phones. Living alone with two different phone numbers. He has never asked but assumes it is for her security and perhaps she had to have a separate phone when she was flying.

And for his part. Well, he has no strategy. He has a job to do. He has a wife and he has a son. Both need him and he needs them.

Now, here he is one year later, still Chief Officer of the *Welland*, alongside in Guayaquil and about to go and get his meal as the Captain ordered. Dock labour organised for a night shift. An engineer will be here tomorrow morning to look at the satellite connection and Mr Modesto, the Landing Agent, has promised to find that empty container. But tonight he would be with Fiona and not one step nearer to solving the emotional conflict of the eternal triangle.

7

Joy and Violet are on the deck below the Bridge as the *Welland* glides through the river passing the mangroves and clusters of rickety wooden huts on stilts. Beyond them acres and acres of swamps creep up to a ridge of mountains, shimmering in the heat.

"Look!" Joy is watching through binoculars. Over there. Fishermen."

Three agile young men climb down the wooden slats of the ladder and slip into a canoe tethered to the stilts of the hut then one of them turns and helps an old man to climb in. A woman as thin as a twig follows him and they sit side by side amongst the bundles and bags.

Several larger canoes, full of jabbering children, are already

midstream.

"Where do you think they're going?" Violet squints against the sun. "Those children."

"To school."

"Don't be stupid. How can they be going to school? In these swamps?" Violet snaps.

Joy decides not to answer. Violet wants a row. She can tell by the tone of the 'don't be stupid' but she isn't going to take the bait, Not today. They are arriving in port and she will not allow Violet to spoil shore leave. The different sights and smells invigorate her after so many days at sea and the people are fascinating to watch. Often they are doing things that people do at home. Shopping, drinking coffee, smoking cigarettes, gossiping but some of them are doing things she's never seen before.

Last trip she'd been sitting on a bench in the shade of a tree in a precinct full of street vendors and shoppers. Vi had gone to find the Post Office. A few yards away a young man wearing a torn check shirt and baggy grey trousers was trying to attract an audience. Two bulging brown paper bags hanging from his trouser belt. Soon he had gathered a group of inquisitive shoppers around him. He untied the string of one of the paper bags dangling from his waist and pulled out a bundle.

It was a grey squirrel. Small, thin and its fur was quite wet. He dropped the squirrel on to the pavement and kept hold of the string fastened around its tail but it was so dazed it could hardly stand. Then he pulled out another bedraggled squirrel from the other paper bag and held it out to the crowd.

"Two soles." He pleaded with the onlookers but no one wanted to buy squirrel.

Joy couldn't take her eyes off his lean, bronzed face. He had inherited a noble profile that had come down through the centuries to give him a distinction he could never have dreamed of as he tried to sell squirrels in the precinct.

Another time she had watched a man bent over an old car tyre cutting the rubber into pieces to make a pair of sandals. You just never know who or what you'll see so she's not going to let Vi sabotage the day with arguments.

"Well?" Violet has a big question mark in her voice.

"Those children will be going to school." Joy keeps her eyes on the canoes moving swiftly through the water. "Remember when we hired that Land Rover to take us into the rain forest and we came across a school in the jungle. Miles from anywhere. Children must walk along paths to get there. So it's not such a stupid answer."

The *Welland* eases past the line of ships at anchor. All waiting for Pilot and a berth. Then the silver water tower comes into view as they turn on the knuckle towards the quay.

It is swarming with bare-chested boys wearing scruffy shorts and no shoes. They are offering cardboard boxes full of bananas. A team of Inspectors has examined and measured and rejected the fruit. They do not meet the European Union Directive standard so the Inspectors toss them into the filthy water lapping around the ships. The boys dive in and clamber out with an armful of bananas placing them on the quayside before diving in again to bring out more. Then they put them in the discarded boxes and sell them."Two dollar one box. Only two dollar." The boys are waving their spindly arms, pushing and shoving each other, calling up to the crew and passengers on deck. "Chip, very chip."

"Just think," Violet stares down at the noisy throng on the quayside. "Less than two pound sterling for 40lbs of bananas, In Price Rite we pay 60p for three! It's disgraceful. It's those European Union Commissioners."

"Here we go," Joy keeps her eyes on the boys guarding their boxes of bananas. Vi is getting steamed up about Europe again. Her favourite punch bag and a diatribe about Europe is the last thing she wants today. "Really, I don't understand why you get so worked up." She glances sideways at Violet. "There have been two World Wars Vi - and we survived the last one, remember. The only thing to do is join the Club."

"Huh! Join the Club!" Violet's indignation is drowned by the din of the fork-lift trucks rampaging along the quay. "Some Club! Full of our failed politicians who get on the gravy train to Brussels when they're thrown out of Parliament! All those meetings and summits and jamborees and junketing. All those limousines. All those bodyguards. They're all at it with their public contracts and kickback schemes. The system has institutionalised corruption. That's what's happened in your "Club.""

"Oh do be quiet, Vi. There's nothing we an do about it," Joy walks away and stands under No 2 Boat to shelter from the sun.

"That's the trouble. We don't know what goes on, do we?" She moves to Joy's side. "Do you have any idea?" She doesn't wait for an answer. "And those photographs! All jockeying for position, preening, straightening their ties, adjusting their shirt cuffs. What *do* they do with all those photographs? Where do they put them , for heaven's sake? And who pays for it all?" She answers her own question. "We do. It makes me boil to see so much money and time wasted. It's a scandal. But it won't last. It'll end up bankrupt."

"Well…" Joy opens her mouth but Violet is unstoppable.

"And they never achieve anything except another mountain of paper to translate." Vi slaps her hands on the boat rail. "Do you remember when they ordered all fishermen to wear hair nets and carry condoms on board? Huh! The Danes soon told them what to do. And they did their best to kill off Wensleydale cheese."

"Well, one thing is certain," Joy must close the subject otherwise she's going to get Europe all day. "It will ensure that such events never happen again. No more wars." After all, the war had claimed Violet's man but she wasn't going to say that. Not today.

"Like to bet." Vi takes off her sun hat and wafts it across her face.

"Oh, please calm down. It's no good getting into a lather." Joy slips the binoculars from around her neck and winds the strap into a bundle. "We're going ashore and we've got to stay focussed. Come on, let's go and get ready."

"Well, down there those kids are fishing bananas out of that stinking water because those European Union Clowns say they're not straight enough. Straight bananas! Barking mad. They're all barking mad!"

"Oh shut up."

Footsteps echo on the deck.

"Hello, good morning." Fiona takes off her sunglasses but puts them on again. "I've come to see what's going on. Love to watch the docking, don't you?" She moves towards the boat rail. "Bargains in all Departments, down there," she points to the group of youths huddled on the quayside with their bundles and battered suitcases. "And bananas."

Crew members are doing a brisk trade. They don't pay the two dollars. They give the boys soap, biscuits, cigarettes and sweets.

"Yes," Violet said, "we were just talking about the bananas. Two dollars a box and we pay…"

"Oh, look," Joy interrupts. "Gangway in position. Good." She turns to Fiona. Those sunglasses suited her. Probably very expensive. "Are you going ashore?"

"No," Fiona leans away from the boat rail, arms rigid. "I hope to go tomorrow. But it all depends on the cargo loading, doesn't it? What about you?"

"Oh, yes. Violet looks directly into the sunglasses and sees her own distorted reflection. "We're going."

"What are you going to do? Shop?"

"No," Violet pulls on her sun hat.

"Yes. Well, yes and no." Joy rectifies the contradiction. "Nothing in particular."

"Oh, look! That must be the Agent," Fiona points to a man with a black briefcase hurrying up the gangway, two steps at a time. Three other men with briefcases follow him.

"That's a good sign," Violet takes off her sun hat again. "We'll soon have our shore passes."

"Yes, we'd better go and get ready. See you later. Enjoy yourself." Joy calls over her shoulder as she leads the way down to the cabin.

"There you are," Violet swipes lipstick around her lips and shapes them into a withered rose bud.

"What do you mean 'there you are'." Joy reaches for a straw bag in the bottom of the wardrobe.

"She's not going ashore. What on earth is she going to do on board. In port?"

"Really Vi. Don't you ever listen? She told us. She might go ashore tomorrow. And does it matter? It's her business. If I remember rightly she didn't go ashore in Buenaventura either."

"Well, I've said all along she's a mystery."

"And I've said all along that you can spend the voyage solving it. She's never so much as hinted that she wants to go ashore with us. And we wouldn't go with her if she did, would we?"

"No," Violet pouts her scarlet lips. "Did you notice? She's wearing a wedding ring. Haven't seen that before."

"She always wears that ring." Joy shakes out the red straw bag with the squashed red flower on the side. It has two long plaited straw handles that go across her shoulders and hangs below her bosom. A mugger would need a sharp knife to cut it from her. "Shall we dress the same today?"

"Yes, let's wear the blue cotton."

"It confuses them. They don't know who to mug first." Joy chuckles. "And it's my turn to carry, isn't it?" She rummages through the bottom drawer and pulls out a pair of sleek elastic control panties. Kicking off her sandals she struggles into them. "Phew! I'm going to be hot."

"It's always hot wearing them. We needn't take the camera," Violet holds it at arm's length.

"But there might be something of interest…"

"In Guayaquil there's nothing of interest except Pedro." She throws the camera on to the bed.

"That's not true," Joy grabs it. "All that magnificent architecture I didn't get a picture of the equestrian statue inn Plaza Centenario last time."

"Leave it here. We've got enough to concentrate on without worrying about a camera. And you know you've got to do the hablaring with Pedro. His English is quite good but we don't want any misunderstanding, do we?"

"Oh do stop wittering Vi."

"Can you remember where he lives?"

"More or less. We'll take a taxi to the Malecón. Need to be over towards the Old Town. And remember… It's dangerous there."

"I know it is." Violet fishes out her make-up bag and checks her lipstick in the little mirror again. "Everywhere is dangerous. Let's go and see if the shore passes are ready."

"No. We must wait. They'll bring them as soon as they're issued. You know that." Joy fidgets with the elastic knickers. "We mustn't

bother them. For goodness' sake sit down and keep quiet."

Vi drops the mirror into her make-up bag and sits on the edge of the bed. Her eyes fixed on the picture of Marlene Dietrich.

"El 245 Section B," she announced.

"What on earth are you talking about?"

"Size tolerances. Bent bananas. Just remembered the European Union regulation. L 245 Section B. Issued on 20 September 1994."

8

Fiona flicks off her sandals and climbs on to the desk under the window to secure the port locks. Now they are in port it is the responsibility of passengers to make sure their port windows are closed. Thieves can scale the skin of the ship with a grappling iron and rope that's what he had told her.

She stays on top of the desk peering down at the busy scene below. It is over an hour since the *Welland* was tethered and the dockside is teeming with men. Some are standing around in groups, smoking, spitting, scratching their heads, Others are sitting on wooden pallets waiting for the hatches to be opened so that they can start unloading the cargo.

At the bottom of the gangway several youths have laid out their wares. Music from a tiny cassette player balanced on the edge of a bollard is rasping out its tune as they argue and push and shove each other.

All the bananas have been sold and now they have other merchandise to offer. One young man stands at the side of an open battered suitcase. Cigarettes, chewing gum and ball point pens are displayed. Another painfully thin young man displays bulky sweaters and T-shirts on a black plastic bag spread on the ground and a plump young man wearing a red woolly hat is adorned with small colourful cushions suspended by string across his shoulders. There is something for everyone but Fiona doesn't think the sweaters will go too well in this soaring heat and she can't imagine why crew members would buy cushions but these vendors know their markets.

Lorries are revving and shunting and reversing. Fork-lift trucks buzz up and down the avenues of containers. Mangy dogs amble around, pausing to sniff at the corner of every gantry, the plastic bags, empty cigarette packets, unconcerned about the mayhem all around them. Sleek, shiny cars speed along the dockside carrying officials to the different ships waiting for clearance. Then she sees him standing near a battered old lorry thumbing through a sheaf of papers, chatting to a tall, grey-haired man at his side. This must be the Cargo Superintendent he's told her about. He comes to the ship to synchronise information with that held by the Chief Officer on board. All cargo has to be stowed in its proper place in the correct hold in the right order for unloading at the destination port. That's what they will be doing now. To Fiona it seems like one big nightmare for getting the wrong cargo in the wrong hold, even the wrong ship. She watches them disappear behind a large grey container.

Then two tall figures pick their way down the gangway. Joy and Violet Galbraith are off on their jaunt. One thinks they are going shopping. The other one said 'no' they are not. More arguments! They are wearing identical blue dresses and white sandals which make their feet look enormous.

Slowly they stride across the quayside heading for the comparative safety of the warehouse wall as trucks bleep and swerve around them.

Strange couple. Forever squabbling. At breakfast, lunch and dinner they always seem to goad each other into some verbal affray. She can tolerate Joy but Violet is a frustrated, interfering old busy-body and she is curious to know what event in her life can have left her so sour.

She has been quizzing and questioning Fiona for weeks and it's getting to her. She might just put a stop to it. Tell her everything. Well, nearly everything. Tell her that she had been married for eight years to a man who could raise her to fever pitch every time he touched her. Tell her that together they had soared through the skies by day and night. She, pandering to the whims of passengers while his blood pressure oscillated in that little den of sophisticated technology in the cone of the silver bird. How they had loved it all! The flights, the snarl-ups, the delays, the stop-overs, the exotic restaurants, the luxurious hotels, yes, most of all the hotels.

Then, staring into Violet Galbraith's blue eyes she would explain that her husband was dead. Yes, she might just say all this. Have a show down. And then she might not. Keep her guessing. It's none of her business.

Fiona keeps her eyes on their tall, straight backs until they vanish from view beyond the warehouse. She's glad they've gone. Heavens knows what they do. They never come back with bags of shopping or souvenirs. They'll probably get mugged. They're both carrying bags and her little dock friends love to snatch bags.

She jumps down from the desk and wonders what to do next. She is waiting. Always waiting. Waiting for the milkman. The postman. She used to wait for Paul to phone.

"I'm down, lover, be with you soon." He was on his way.

She would wait for him to swerve into the drive at great speed and shower gravel over the flower beds. The car door would slam and then she would be in his arms. She would press the button on the answer phone, wait for the red light and they then would go upstairs.

But it's more than two years since... since Paul had telephoned. That hollow yearning sweeps through her again. It's like a bleak, cold wind chilling her heart until it seems not to beat, drawing her to that abyss. She must get a grip. She's here. She's safe. She glances round the cabin. So neat. So tidy. Quite luxurious. Drake Line look after their few passengers. And now she is waiting again. Waiting for him. He matters and she thought she had convinced herself that nothing matters.

He has mattered since the moment she set eyes on him shortly after she boarded the *Witham* last year. He had been in a hurry clattering down the companionway just as she was coming up to the Bridge deck. Turning sideways to allow him to pass she had to do a double take. The sun on his thick, fair hair, the determined set of his jaw, the energy of the lean body. For a moment, a fleeting moment, so fleeting it almost escaped her, she thought it was Paul and almost called after him.

Since that close encounter she had studied him from behind her book. From behind her sunglasses. From behind her newspaper, scrutinising every mannerism, his walk, the quizzical furrowing of the brow. Every gesture.

The way he would transfer his weight from one foot to the other. Everything about him reminded her of Paul. His voice and that announcement once they were airborne.

'Good afternoon, ladies and gentlemen. This is Captain Meredith. Today…"

It was unsettling. Paul in the flesh and blood again. Impossible. Paul had been in that pilot's seat when it crashed into the mountain. Yet here he was. The only difference being that Paul now had an L-shaped scar on his left cheek.

But this man scarcely noticed her. A polite greeting. A door held open for her. She might as well be invisible. That was, until they arrived at Mahé in the Seychelles.

At breakfast the steward had told her the news. "Didn't expect to be here, Miss. Bit of excitement today. Never know what's round the corner, do we? We've got a sick crew member."

"Oh, what's wrong with him?" Fiona spread honey on her bread roll.

"That's the trouble, Miss. We don't know. Need a doctor. Need a hospital. That's why he's being landed."

Fiona took up a vantage point on the Bridge deck to watch the shore officials and doctor bustling about on the quayside. Four crew members emerged on to the deck with a stretcher held aloft to keep it level as they stepped slowly down the gangway to the open doors of the ambulance.

He was standing alone, hands on hips, staring at the ambulance as it disappeared through the dock gates. Without hesitation she clattered down the companionway to the gangway and then she was at his side suggesting that they go ashore together.

Later, back on board they had drunk wine, laughed, danced and made love. Wild, uninhibited, urgent. It wasn't until she got back to her cabin at four o'clock in the morning that reality challenged her.

She had been in the arms of a man whose full name she did not know, whose age she did not know. In fact, she knew nothing about him yet she felt she knew all there was to know about him. His mannerisms, his mood, the way he speaks to her. Everything seems familiar. She's sure she has known him for years. He looks and acts like Paul. He moves like Paul. It excited and alarmed her and finally, overwhelmed her until sleep carried her away from her catharsis.

Tonight she will be with the man she had propositioned on the dockside in Mahé. But this man has a wife called Linda but she could never put a face or personality to Linda. And this man has a son, Tom - yes, that's his name. A family doing all the things that a family does.

During the years of flying she and Paul knew they had forfeited the possibility of a child. They had discussed it endlessly but pressurised cabins and three breakfasts in one day through different time zones played havoc with the natural cycle of the human body. There was never any sign of a baby. So they accepted that it was to be just her and Paul inexorably moving toward the day when they were grounded, when they would no longer 'shoulder the sky' together. Now she must shoulder it alone. It was unbearable.

Now, in Southampton it is possible to meet with careful planning. Once in a while they could have dinner together. They spent precious hours at her flat and since she is not looking for a husband no one is at risk.

Only she is at risk. She hears the little voice reminding her that she is edging towards a bleak landscape, alone. So, shoulder the sky. Nothing matters.

*****

Joy and Violet are in a clapped-out taxi roaring along a dual carriage way towards the city centre. They are sitting side by side in the back seat with its torn yellow plastic cover. There is no door handle, only a length of string tied to a bit of broken metal. The windows are wide open and the heat is scythed by the speed of the car and bleeds on to them as it veers from one lane to another, weaving between the buses and container lorries, slamming on brakes when revving the guts out of the exhausted engine.

The driver is young and handsome and reckless. After a very dodgy manoeuvre, just a whisker away from being crushed between a lorry and a bus, he glances over his shoulder grinning at them.

"Good. OK." He smiles at them through the driving mirror.

Violet grips the piece of string on the door handle. "Look where you're going."

"It's no good picking an argument with him. He doesn't speak English." Joy sinks back into the seat and keeps her eyes on the number plate of the lorry in front. It is lopsided and may fall off any minute.

Soon the taxi turns off the dual carriage way into quiet, tidy streets lined with swanky white houses, safe and secure behind high walls and ornate wrought-iron gates. Scarlet frangipani and geraniums cascade from the balconies to the courtyards below.

Then it squeals sharp left and suddenly affluence gives way to poverty in the blink of an eye. Shacks and hovels line the streets. Old women are sitting in doorways, old men are staring into space smoking weedy cigarettes and children are scrambling over the heaps of rubbish, prodding and poking the crumpled newspapers, the rotting fruit, the drink bottles and the Coca-Cola cans, looking for anything they could eat or drink or sell.

They are now driving through the open market with fruit and vegetables piled high on the stalls and there is a sickly sour stench from the rubbish in the gutter creeping through the open windows of the taxi. A right turn takes them on to a broad avenue and now they are trapped in the main body of downtown traffic full of gleaming limousines and rattling buses, bumper to bumper.

Office blocks tower over the waterfront, their mirror windows reflecting the Pacific Ocean a few yards away and then the taxi screeches to a halt at the Malecón. The young driver turns and gives them a stunning smile.

They pay him and walk past La Rotunda, the spectacular monument of Jose de San Martin and Simon Bolivar. It's made of marble and ornately carved. If you stand on one side and speak to the marble column the words echo around the semi-circular wall to your friend standing on the opposite side of the monument. Not every visitor knows this but an old man had explained this to Violet and Joy last year.

"Shall we do the echo again?" Vi drops the change into the bottom of her straw bag. "I love to hear it. So clever."

"No, Let's go." Joy leads the way through the gardens past El Pirata towards Pier 5. "This way."

"Are you sure?"

"Yes. This is where we need to cross. Then it's right, then left." They continue through the maze of alleyways until they arrive at a small plaza with slippery bluish stones.

"Over there," Joy points as they cross the plaza and enter a crudely-paved street. Three children are chasing a dog in the middle of the road. It is wearing a yellow band round its neck but they can't catch it. A plump middle-aged woman in a long black dress is sweeping the pavement in front of her house. She pauses, leans on her broom and watches as Joy and Violet stride past in their blue dresses and large white sandals, then she continues to sweep.

A man is hunched on a stool outside a closed shop with metal concertina doors. In front of him is a wooden crate he is using as a table. It is covered with bits of leather, a tin of nails, a jar containing glue, a sharp knife and a hammer. He's working on the heel of worn-out boot and doesn't even glance up as Joy and Violet make their way past him.

Ahead they can see a bouquet of balloons floating above a small table on the pavement. A green and white striped sheet forms a canopy and a child wearing faded blue shorts is teasing a kitten with a fluffy toy mouse.

"Here we are. This is it." Joy pauses outside the house and studies the trestle table piled high with goods for sale. Cigarettes in an open box. In this part of Guayaquil they buy one cigarette at a time. Boiled sweets in colourful wrappers glisten in another open box. They, too, are sold singly. Envelopes and sheets of writing paper. All sold singly. Pencils, ball pens, batteries. Birthday cards. First Communion cards.

A bunch of over-ripe bananas, two apples past their best, a mutilated pineapple and some squashed grapes are stacked in one corner of the table. All garnered from underneath the stalls at the fruit market.

"Hello, good morning," Joy uses her best Spanish.

The young boy pushes the kitten to the ground and it streaks down the passage at the side of the house. He blinks his wide, startled eyes at Joy then he put his right hand behind his head to scratch his left ear and smiles.

"Just look at those beautiful teeth. And I bet he's never been to a dentist in his life." Joy adjusts the straw bag. "Is Señor Pedro here?"

"Si," and the child scampers off down the passage.

Immediately he returns followed by a big man who darkens the space in the passage. He has massive shoulders and an enormous belly sags over brown trousers that rely on a narrow leather belt. His large, round head is personalised by tiny, crumpled ears sitting in a frill of greying hair. A thick, black moustache thrives under his nose.

"Ah, good morning, how are you?" He offers his big, hairy hand first to Joy and then to Violet. "Good. Glad to see you. Come this way."

Joy and Violet follow him along the passage through an open door on the right into a living room that smells of peppery stew.

The furniture has been re-arranged since the last time they were here. The black sofa is now in front of the window. A life-size doll in pink tulle sits in a chair next to the sideboard. A false fireplace occupied most of the opposite wall. On a small table near the sofa is a television set. Cardboard cartons are stacked in one corner next to what appears to be a folded invalid chair.

There are family photos on the sideboard, pictures of weddings and christenings and First Communion brides. A large glass vase of dried flowers perches close to the edge of the sideboard.

A porcelain image of the Virgin Mary stands in the window next to a yellow plastic duck. There is another Virgin Mary on a small ledge. This one is more colourful and there is another, dressed like a doll, suspended from the door lintel.

A plump lady comes from the kitchen wiping her hands on a towel. The years have padded her square face and several chins rest in a thick neck. She is wearing a spotless white pinafore over a floral dress.

"You remember my wife, no?" Señor Pedro beams.

Mrs Pedro comes forward. Quick, knowing eyes dart from Joy to Violet and then back to Joy. "Please. Sit. Coffee, no?" And with a smile that confirms where the teeth of her son have come from she goes back into the kitchen.

Joy takes the chair that is offered and glances around the room again. It suffocates her.

Señor Pedro opens a side board cupboard and pulls out a small brown paper package.

"The same as last time, no?" he sucks on his teeth, leaning closer to Joy. He's been eating garlic.

Mrs Pedro carries a tray with a dish of home-made biscuits and four coffee cups.

There is a scuffle in the doorway and the little boy rampages across the room, pushing past the sofa, screaming at the top of his voice as he chases the kitten *"Ven aqui... ven aqui... espere."* It disappears into the corner behind the cardboard boxes.

"The same price?" Joy plunges her hand inside the low collar of her dress and pulls a wad of dollar bills from her bra.

"Of course," Pedro counts the money, pausing from time to time to lick his thumb. "That's it. *Gracias.*" He shuffles the dollar bills together and hands them to Mrs Pedro who pushes them into a pocket inside her pinafore.

Joy picks up the brown paper package and glances across at Violet. *"Vamos."*

"Take care," Pedro warns as he leads them down the passage. "In the street, you know."

"Don 't worry. We will. Thank you for the coffee.."

Joy waits until Pedro , Violet and Mrs Pedro are ahead of her in the passage then she hoists up the skirt of her dress and stuffs the package inside her elastic control panties. She does not see the little boy standing behind her watching with his wide, startled eyes.

9

Captain Peter Pycroft strokes the leaves of the plant. It has grown at a disturbing rate and is showing signs of becoming a small tree. He presses his finger into the soil. Quite moist. Dowse has remembered to water it. It should have flowers. White flowers with crimson-tipped stamens like a feathery brush but there is no sign of even a bud.

If it does become a tree he will take it home to Denise whether she likes it or not. She isn't keen on plants. They always die on her but, as he has explained many times, they need care and attention and she doesn't even notice when they are nothing but a shrivelled up twig.

He ambles over to the starboard window and gazes down at the scene on the dock. "That estimated time of departure is a bit ambitious," he speaks to the window, massaging his hands behind his back.

"There's tons and tons to be loaded yet but they're going to work all night, so the Agent said. Should only take twelve hours. Impossible to know but Bloxham will have it all under control."

He shrugs his shoulders and turns away, stroking his hands down his chest as he walks the length of the dayroom. The officials have gone. It's Saturday and they want to get home to their families. He's given them all their goodies and they've marched down the gangway satisfied after all the discussions and arguments.

The cost of shore labour, the cost of the cranes and fork-lifts, the cost of victualling. And the Agent going on and on about the empty container needed for homeward bound. He must find one. He knows where they are and if he doesn't, he should. He goes back to his desk and jots a note on his pad to tell Bloxham to chase it up, make sure we have it before we sail.

So no there's nothing for him to do but relax. The *Welland* would not be going anywhere tonight. Bloxham is staying on board and will be available for any emergency. He shuffles the pile of official forms until he finds the letter. Air mail, posted ten days ago. From Denise.

He unfolds the flimsy pages and reads the solid, square handwriting. Like Denise it knows where it is going and takes up all the space venturing right to the edge of the page. She had bought a new coat in the sales, she had played Bridge at the Golf Club three times last week. The Course was closed. Water-logged.

She had been to a cocktail party given by the Lady President and she had worn her diamonds. Denise loved those diamonds. He'd given them to her shortly after they were married. He remembered the occasion well. They had just got home from a very liquid party celebrating his father-in-law's birthday. The champagne had flowed and they had opened another bottle before they went to bed.

She always tells him when she has worn the diamonds. The ring is worn on every possible occasion and sometimes she wears it when playing a foursome, depending on who she is playing with. The necklace and ear-rings have to wait for a Command Performance. The Annual Dinner Dance or a London theatre weekend.

He flicks to the next page of the letter. There was a leak in the passage next to the garage and she'd put a bucket to catch the water. The fridge light had gone off and when she put the car away she'd got a teeny bit too close and scraped the garage doors.

He tosses the letter on to his desk and snatches at the paper clip, twisting and bending it until it snaps, then he cleans his left ear with the rounded end. He wanders back to the window. The scene below drifts into a mist. He can't concentrate on anything. Not the cargoes being loaded, the empty container nor the leaking roof in the passage, nor the repairs needed to the garage door. He needs Denise.

He glances at his wristwatch. Half past five. Then he picks up the phone and rings the Galley.

"Dowse."

"Yes, sir."

"I'll have the usual tonight. Nine o'clock."

"Very good, sir."

*****

Bert Dowse slams down the phone. It misses its cradle and falls, swinging on its cord above the well-scrubbed deck of the Galley.

"Bugger him."

"What's wrong?" Dinty is washing the saucepans.

"The Old Man," Bert crushes his cigarette on the sole of his shoe. "Wants the usual."

"Well, this is Guayaquil. You might know he'll have his usual." Dinty hangs the last saucepan on its hook. "Allus does."

"I say bugger him." Bert goes to the store cupboard. Measures a bowl of flour and brings it to the large baking board. He scoops lard from another bowl and begins to make the dough..

"Did he say what time he wants them?" Dinty fishes under his apron for his tin of hand-rolled cigarettes.

"Nine o'clock." Bert is up to his elbows in flour. "We'll still have time to go to the Mission. Pity I didn't make them earlier. But you never know where you are with the bugger If I'd made them he probably wouldn't have wanted them."

"He takes some reckoning, he does," Dinty lights his cigarette and frowns at the smoke. "How the bloody hell does a fellow like that get command of a ship, eh?"

"Depends who you know, don't it?" Bert swishes a fly from his face leaving a smear of flour under his nose. "Well, I'm not wasting cream on him. Besides it's as hard as rock in the freezer. I'll use the same as last time. I've got some in my cabin."

An hour later, one dozen buns have been pulled out of the middle oven and left to cool. Cooked to perfection with a light golden glaze. Standing next to the tray of buns is a large aerosol canister.

83

Bert and Dinty are sitting side by side on the stools, feeling no pain. They have been drinking steadily whilst the buns baked. Bert drains his glass, gets to his feet and selects a large, sharp knife. He whirls it above his head.

"Wha hey…" and then slices each bun diagonally cross the top. "Here we go, 'here we go, 'here we go…"

He grabs the aerosol, throws it from one hand to the other then he squirts into the slash he's made on each bun. "It's a waste of bloody good shaving cream but…" He takes a spoon and, singing through his teeth, titillates the cream bulging from the buns. Then he reaches for a clean cloth from the linen drawer and lays it across the tray.

"Off topsides. With these. Shan't be long. Then we'll foot it to the Mission. Here we go… here we go… here we go…" And Bert waltzes across the Galley singing through his teeth with the tray held aloft as if he were presenting a boar's head at a banquet.

*****

After leaving Pedro, Joy and Violet walk back along the Malecón to La Rotunda.

"Let's go to Casa Dorita," Joy is longing to adjust the package in her panties. It is chafing her thigh.

"Good idea," Violet is slowing down. "Can't take this heat."

Casa Dorita is just off the main street beyond the plaza. It's a Western-style Department Store on four floors. The café is at the top and you get there by escalators as far as the third floor and then there are just a few stairs to the entrance.

"One thing about this place," Violet hangs on to the banister pausing to suck in air, "it's nice and clean."

"Yes. This loo is the best we've ever found. Do you remember that one in Puerto Sucua?"

"Oh, my goodness, don't even want to think about it. More like a cow shed."

"Here we are." Joy pushes on the door and hurries into a vacant cubicle. "The package feels heavy today. That's better." She joins

Vi at the wash basins. "And this elastic is so tight. Suppose that's why they're called control panties. Enough to strangle the life out of you. Let's go and have some tea and then get a taxi."

As they step out of Casa Dorita a taxi pulls up, a lumpy lady festooned with shopping bags heaves herself out and they climb in. Soon they are roaring along the dual carriage way to the Marine Terminal.

"Get your shore pass ready, Vi, and remember to stay calm. No arguments. In fact, don't say a word unless he asks you something."

They pay the taxi driver and stride slowly up to the dock gates and wait at the small window of the booth.

The policeman, a heavy soporific man, doesn't get up from his chair. He glances at Joy then Violet then shapes his mouth into a wide, dark cavern and yawns, waving them through with a nonchalant flick of his hand.

"Easy-peasy," Vi pushes her shore pass back into the bag. "But you never know where you are with these jokers. Sometimes you just get waved through, sometimes they all but strip you.. The youngest ones are keenest. Looking for promotion. Suppose it all depends what time they came on duty. He's probably about to finish his shift." She fans herself with a tissue. "Watch out!"

Fork-lift trucks are skimming around in a frenzy, lorries are roaring along the broad road between the warehouses, a pack of scruffy dogs mooch about, noses to the ground disappointed to find nothing but empty Coca-Cola bottles and beer cans. Groups of men and youths are lounging around the gaping doors, watching the two women.

They approach the *Welland*, swarming with dockers and crew from, bow to stern and wait for an overhead crane to swing out of the way. They trudge up the gangway, step by step, gripping the rail, then they cross the deck and labour up the stairs to the passenger deck. Footsteps follow them. It's Bert Dowse carrying a tray covered with a cloth.

"Stand back, Vi. Man in a hurry."

"Thank you ladies." Bert squeezes past them.

"What've you got there?" Violet lifts a corner of the cloth. "Ooh! Look, fresh cream buns. Can we have some?"

Bert accelerates up the last few stairs and is well ahead of them.

"Sorry Miss Galbraith," he calls over his shoulder. "You wouldn't like these." He lowers the tray and disappears through the door marked 'Officers Only'.

"Now why wouldn't we like a nice fresh bun?" Violet rummages in her bag for the key to the cabin.

"You've just had the biggest piece of chocolate mocha cake imaginable…"

"Well, he doesn't know that." Violet pushes open the door.

Joy throws her bag on to the bed and pulls out the brown paper package waving it above her head. "We've got it. We've got the gear for Ben."

"Well, I want a cream bun. I've a good mind to go down to the Galley and get some."

"Oh forget the buns." Joy hoists up her dress, wriggling to peel off the elastic knickers then throws them across the cabin. They land on her bed. "What a relief." She reaches for a pair of cool, white cotton panties and pulls them on. "And now…now we have to get it ready for Southampton."

"That's an awful fiddle." Vi is struggling out of her blue flowered dress. "The worst part of the deal."

"Yes, it does take time but it has to be done and we know it works so the sooner it's done the better. Come on, let's have a gin. Ben will be pleased."

10

Barrio Nortino nudges up to the dock gates and wire fencing of the Maritime Terminal at Guayaquil. The settlement is a huddle of wooden houses in shades of blue and green and pink. Most of them have a porch and they all need a fresh coat of paint. The streets are not paved and in the rainy season you are ankle deep in mud.

The main street boasts a small store built with wooden planks, black plastic bags and sheets of galvanised iron to protect it from thieves. Opposite there is a tavern, Bar El Bosso, for drinking, playing dominoes, arguing, fighting and sometimes killing. Bodies are buried at the edge of the river.

The people of Barrio Nortino live in a cacophony of noise from tinny radios and crackling television sets, most of them stolen from the gringos, punctuated by shouting, singing, crying babies and barking dogs.

The estuary is a short distance away. It's the dirtiest part of Barrio Nortino. Several large conduits, broken in places, carry sewage into the river and the banks are littered with garbage, human faeces, beer bottles, condoms, broken beds and rotting pieces of wood.

But the people of Barrio Nortino come here for fishing, for bathing, for love making and when hungry to collect snails and crabs. And they breed pigs here because of the abundant supply of garbage.

Lorinda lives in a house in an alleyway off the main street. The faded blue paint is peeling off in little curls creating the impression that the walls are adorned with blue flowers. The house has five rooms, all of them rented. She rents two on the ground floor, a living room and a bedroom.

She is sitting on the edge of her bed, preening into a broken mirror. It used to be a square mirror but is now a triangle after falling to the floor. Above the bed is a framed picture of the Virgin Mary. It hangs lop-sided but she has intentionally not touched it. A reminder never to see that man again, ranting and raving and cursing. Of course, he'd been too drunk, but it was a gamble she took. They're often too drunk but not this one. He had clouted her with the pillow, it had missed and dislodged the picture of the Virgin Mary. She is convinced that it would be unlucky to straighten it.

Leaning into the mirror, she purses her glossy lips. She is pleased with them. She's quite pleased with herself altogether. Huge almond eyes that are almost black, flash at her. She knows her eyes are her best feature, very slightly Oriental but that's because she knows how to pencil the eyebrows.

She decides to wear her gold satin blouse with a wrap-over front cushioning two soft shiny gold balls that are her beautiful breasts. Well, she's always being told they are beautiful. The black knee-length tailored skirt is slit at one side and as she moves a smooth brown thigh guarantees a second glance. A little gold bag in the shape of an envelope on a chain hangs from her left shoulder. Her secret weapon that has come to her rescue more than once. If a client gets rough she knows exactly how to twist and swing that chain.

But tonight it's a gringo and he'd be easy. Not greedy like the locals. Once they mount there's no getting them off for their measly ten dollars. And often with a gringo you didn't have to take your clothes off. And he sometimes doesn't even take *his* pants off.

She's pleased Señor Modesto had sent that message via young Rubio. Five years old, a thin, energetic shoe shine boy. He is also an accomplished thief, an efficient drug-dealer and a good-natured messenger. Rubio is the son of Felicita, one of her many friends here in the barrio and the result of a liaison with a Swedish Captain.

Perceptive blue eyes, gift from the Swedish Captain, shine from his dark, inquisitive face.

"Meet el señor Modesto tonight. Dock gates. Ten o'clock." Rubio recites the message as he leans on her door, wiping his forehead with his arm. "It's hot."

Lorinda goes into the bedroom and scrabbles for fifty cents in the bottom of the biscuit tin on the bedside cabinet. It holds her curlers and jewellery. She takes a can of Coca-Cola from the cupboard below and sends Rubio on his way with a finger to her lips. He winks and runs off along the road. She knows that fifty cents ensures his silence.

Señor Modesto was kind to her after her father died five years ago. They had been evicted from their dingy little rooms on account of rent arrears. Her mother and younger sister moved to the country to live with Aunt Taqui at Paguacho. But Paguacho is a one horse town without a horse. Lorinda decided to stay put, renting two rooms in Barrio Nortino near the Maritime Terminal. She knew that Señor Modesto had good contacts, meeting the ships and crews and she is convinced that one day she will be out of this life, away from these sweaty, heaving, grunting men but until that day comes…

Señor Modesto is punctual. He tucks his briefcase under his arm and nods to the dock policeman who yawns and waves them through the gates. She teeters along in her high-heeled shoes, the gold straps nipping her toes.

The wide dock road is flanked by warehouses with sliding doors regurgitating lorries from their black depths. Groups of men loll against walls of the buildings, smoking and chatting before returning to their back-breaking job of humping sacks and loading pallets.

They turn a corner and she can see the ship a few yards ahead. It's long and sleek and grey crouching in the water, succumbing to the clamour on deck. Lights from the cranes and derricks twinkle and glow and flicker giving the ship a carnival aspect.

Men are everywhere. Swarming over the open hatch covers, waving their arms and shouting as they signal to the crane operators. Some are sitting on bollards, some are slumped on piles of wood and coils of rope, smoking, and some are standing in small groups, doing nothing.

The tall gantries straddling the railway lines on the quayside look like monstrous spiders from outer space grabbing containers and dangling them in mid-air before dumping them on the flat bed lorries lined up underneath. Then their tentacles reach out again, clawing the dark belly of the ship, probing for more containers.

Orange lights on high concrete posts bathe the docks. Lorinda is glad of these bright lights when going home in the early hours. Men are working night shifts but there are prowlers and drunks and you can't see what's going on behind the stacks of containers.

She follows Señor Modesto up the gangway, clinging to the wobbly metal rail, stumbling in her uncomfortable shoes as she steps on to the deck.

A figure is hunched on a stool in the shadows. It's the Security Guard, fast asleep. His log book, recording all times and visitors to the *Welland,* has slipped from his fingers and is spread open on the deck, the light breeze from the river playing with the pages, flicking them over and then back again. She is tempted to pick it up but decides against it. She doesn't want to waken the Security Guard.

Señor Modesto steps into the alleyway and strides past the Chief Officer's Office then he's climbing the stairs quickly and she follows with her eyes on the frayed turn-ups of his shabby brown trousers. They need a stitch. And his shoes need heeling.

They are now in front of a door. A letter box on the wall is overflowing with pieces of paper. He taps once and the door swings open.

"Ah, good evening. Do come in." Captain Pycroft stands aside and she follows Señor Modesto into the room.

She's been here before and it's just as she remembers. Spacious and luxurious and light and three times bigger than her little two-roomed apartment. And all those beautiful plants. That's what she will have one day. When she is out of the life. A big room full of green plants.

Señor Modesto puts his briefcase on the low table and signals to her to sit down. She chooses an easy chair under the port window.

The Captain perches on the edge of the settee and Señor Modesto squats next to him. He opens his briefcase and pulls out a handful of papers and begins to speak in English, too quickly for her to understand.

Her eyes drift from the television set to the music player and the drinks cabinet. Next to it, on top of the fridge, is a tray covered with a white cloth. She leans into the back of the chair with a comfortable sigh. It's going to be one of those nights. Easy money.

"Good, that's it then," Señor Modesto is on his feet and shaking hands with the Captain. He glances at Lorinda, nods and is gone.

The Captain clears his throat, shuffles the papers together and takes them to his desk behind the wall of plants. Then he comes and stands in front of her staring with his bulging eyes. She gives him her standard smile, unblinking.

"How have you been?" And before she can reply he moves to the fridge. "What will you have. Scotch, gin, wine?"

"Wine please." Lorinda slips the gold bag from her shoulder. She's dying for a cigarette but she remembers that this gringo doesn't like people to smoke although there is an ash tray on the table. She must wait and see if he invites her.

He places the glass of red wine in front of her and stares at her again with those large empty eyes.

"Excuse me a moment," and he hurries across the room with his short quick steps and pushes through the curtain to his bedroom.

She sips the wine and helps herself to a chocolate biscuit. He always has a plate of biscuits on the table but he never eats them himself and never offers them. She finds it strange to have chocolate biscuits and not want to eat them. She hears a drawer open and close. Then she hears some rustling of clothes and then he sweeps the door curtain aside and stands, arms outstretched, smiling at her.

He's wearing khaki shorts that cover his knees. And nothing else. No shirt, no socks, no shoes. A clean white sheet is folded over one arm. He flaps it open and drapes it carefully over the settee.

"That's better," he empties his glass. "Time for another. How's yours?"

An hour later Lorinda is dancing alone, barefoot, to the music of Pedro Infante. It's an Argentinian orchestra and one of her favourites. The wine has relieved the boredom of giving this idiot his kinky thrills and she feels happy and relaxed dancing and swaying to the music. She wreathes and wriggles around the leafy plants, bumps into the easy chairs and sashays across to the door curtain whisking it across her shoulders.

The Captain is stretched full length on the settee, flat on his back in his underpants, his feet poking the air like slabs of ridged concrete. His shorts are in a crumpled heap on the floor near the door. He just rolled them up into a ball, aimed them at her and missed.

She had plied him with drinks and tried to get him to dance. After all she is here to please him but he's now so boozed up he can't even stand. She's not sure whether he'll fall asleep before the buns in which case she'll take the money and the buns.

"Start now," the voice seems to come from under his chin. His head is resting on a cushion at the end of the settee and he is watching her through floating, watery eyes.

"With musica?" Lorinda waves her glass spraying wine over the carpet.

"Yes." He clasps his hands on top of his head, closes his eyes and smiles.

She goes to the tray, removes the cloth, swirls it above her head and slings it across the room. It lands on one of the thick, green plants and reminds her of washing spread out to dry. She slides her little finger across one of the buns and sucks it. Just like last time it tastes of peppermint and disinfectant. No point in saving any of them to take home.

"Ready?" She steps back towards his desk with a bun in one hand, bumping into one of the plants. It topples over spilling soil on to the carpet. Quickly she grabs the plant, stands it upright and scoops the soil back into the pot. He doesn't see what has happened, his eyes are closed, his mouth open. Then she takes aim. She's good at pelting. As children they had to be good at throwing stones and sticks, anything they could find to scare off the dogs, to scare off the rival gangs snooping around their sheds and alleyways and sometimes they pelted the police.

She throws the cream bun across the room and it lands between his nipples. The cream splays across his chest and on to the sheet.

"Again."

This time she hit his left elbow and the squashed bun rolls under the settee.

"More," he is writhing from side to side. Another one bounces off his chest and on to the wall. And so it went on until there is only one left.

He is splattered in cream with bits of bun in his hair, on his chest, his underpants, his bony white legs.

Lorinda is dying for a cigarette. She could sneak into the bathroom and have a quick drag but she decides to wait. A large bit of bun has landed in his glass which he has placed on the carpet at the end of the settee. She picks it up, goes over to the drinks cabinet and selects a clean one. She isn't sure whether he's drinking Scotch or gin so she sloshes in a good measure of each, pops in some ice and goes back to him.

He grabs her wrist and pulls her down towards him. His eyes are like tadpoles moving around slowly in opaque pools. "Feed me."

She supports the back of his head as if she were giving a patient a drink of water. He swallows greedily then his head falls back and he is gasping for air. Ever so slightly alarmed, she stares at him and the empty glass.

She goes to the music centre, turns over the Pedro Infante tape and dances across the room, grabbing the last bun on the tray and aims it. He groans, rolling his head from side to side.

Between sips of wine she sings along with Pedro Infante, *"No se cabe el mundo cuando un amor se va..."* turning with delicate little steps into the bedroom. This is it. He'll be a goner any minute now. She tugs the blanket off the bed, goes back to the settee and drapes it over the Captain.

She hums as she pushes her feet into her shoes, arranging the gold straps around her toes so that they won't pinch. Then she tips the chocolate biscuits into her gold bag and glances at the settee.

He is fast asleep with his head on one side, mouth open.

Bits of bun are scattered around the room so she collects them up and tosses them into the waste paper bin near his desk then she goes to the bathroom, dampens the towel and wipes the cream off the carpet, dumping the towel in the waste paper bin.

A twenty dollar bill is tucked underneath the telephone. As she stuffs it into her bra she catches sight of a bunch of keys partly covered by a pile of papers. She grabs them and tip-toes to the door.

Pausing in the deserted corridor, head cocked, she listens but all she can hear are the dying strains of Pedro Infante *"cuando un amor se va…"* coming from the Captain's room.

There is not a sound in the ship, just the distant echoes from the dock. Men's voices, revving lorries, fork-lift trucks bleeping. Quickly she locks the door and drops the keys into her bag. There is a good market for keys in Barrio Nortino.

11

Jeff is in a deep sleep in a warm, satisfying world. Fiona's world of contentment where she knows how to obliterate her pain and sorrow to bring them together in the here and now. No past, no future. Just the now which, as she says, is all we've got. But something is drawing him to the outer edges of this world. Something is trying to lure him away.

There it is again. He raises himself on to one elbow. Her mop of curls is a tangle of spun sugar on the pillow. One arm is thrown above her head, the other rests on top of the sheet. She appears to be just thinking. About a conversation, or a book she has read, or perhaps some music she is remembering but she's sleeping without a murmur. And for some perverse reason, with not a pang of guilt, his thoughts go to Linda.

He had used the Landing Agent's mobile this afternoon but there had been no reply. Where was she? Is she alright? Does she have problems? And Tom. He wants to speak to Tom. To hear the clear, ringing voice of his son. What has he been doing? Camping, football, fishing. Soon he'd be home to do all these things with him but he is at his wit's end to know what is going on at Coleridge Avenue.

His thoughts drift back to his last leave. He had suggested dinner at a swanky hotel. They had arranged for Jason to stay the night so that he and Tom could play their computer games, watch the approved videos and Father Michael would check that all was well at No. 7 Coleridge Avenue during the evening.

Jeff never goes to church so he doesn't know how good or bad Father Michael is with his ministry but there is no doubt that he is popular with families, especially the children.

That night Linda had been dutiful in their love making. Dutiful. Being in love is not a duty. It's an inexplicable emotion that no one in the world has ever been able to define properly. No one can issue a permit to be in love. Or issue an extension to that permit. Or rescind it. He sensed that she had been acting. Something is wrong and it disturbs him deeply.

He glances at this woman, here at his side. She has engulfed him. Captivated him. Lured him into her space and he has now become part of her space. He stares at the sprinkler in the deck head above him. It looks like a tiny gold filigree lantern bathed in the orange glow from the lights on the dock outside. The lorries have quietened. The fork-lift trucks no longer bleep. The drivers will be having their meal break.

Then he hears it again. He shoots out of bed, rushes through the curtain and grabs the phone on his desk.

"Third Officer, sir. Sorry to disturb you, sir, but we have orders to sail."

"What?" Jeff spat into the phone.

"We're about to sail, sir. I've tried to raise the Captain. Must be ashore. Pilot on board, sir."

"Bloody hell!" Jeff grabs his hair. "OK. I'll be right with you. Get everyone on stations."

He yanks on his denims, pushes his arms into a check shirt, fastening the buttons as he bounds up the stairs to the Bridge.

The Third Officer is pacing the chart room, staring at the deck, his thin, tense body leaning forward with each step. His shoulder length hair is swept back into a pony tail held in place with a rubber band and he boasts a sparse black beard in defiance of his perceived youthfulness. Jeff is surprised that such a weedy young man can grow so much hair but he's a good officer and that's all that matters.

The Pilot is sitting in the Captain's chair. It is dark red leather with box sides, comfortably upholstered, like a raised armchair on a swivel. He is staring ahead, sipping coffee and Mr Modesto, the Landing Agent, is near the echo sounder, smoking a cigarette.

"Sorry about this Chief," the Pilot shakes hands.

Jeff recognises Captain Rodriguez Ferrero, one of the best pilots in Guayaquil. A hefty man with broad shoulders and a body tapering into quite remarkably small shoes. His square head grows a thatch of black hair now streaked with grey which teams up with the bristly moustache. An aquiline nose and chiselled jaw line ensure that his every command is obeyed.

"Need the berth," he leans back in his chair sucking on a gold tooth. "We proceed west to Punta Punta in Rio Guayas and drop anchor until 10.00 hours tomorrow morning."

"Then we shall finish the discharge and loading," Mr Modesto chips in, squinting against the smoke from his cigarette. "Shore gang ordered. Estimated time of Departure 1900."

The Pilot nods agreement.

"Very good, sir," Jeff goes to the tray on the table near the flag locker, pours himself a mug of coffee and turns to the Third Officer. "Have you checked the Captain's cabin?"

"No, sir," the Third Officer avoids Jeff's eyes and stares straight ahead at the stern of the *Ponce de Leon* which arrived a few hours before them.

"Well go and check it." Jeff barks. "We can't sail without a Captain. And find out how many crew remain on board."

"Yes, sir," he hurries from the chart room.

Jeff goes out on to the wing of the Bridge and leans over the rail. The shadowy figures of the Bo'sun and his men are moving about in the fo'c'sle head. Longshoremen are waiting at the bollards ready to release the ropes forward. There is a crackle from his two-way radio.

"Second Officer, sir. All ready astern."

"Standby for orders." Jeff slots his radio into the holster across his shoulders "Thank Christ for that. Ready astern but there must be a lot of crew ashore."

"Don't worry," Mr. Modesto waves his cigarette. "I've alerted the Dock Police. They will explain to crew that the ship will be back at berth tomorrow morning."

A tug on the port side hoots mischievously. Jeff strides across the chart room and out on to the Bridge again. The Pilot is at his side.

"Ready?"

"Yes… but… we're waiting for the Captain." Jeff pulls back his lips and clenches his teeth. It screws up his scar.

Footsteps rattle on the stairs, the door of the chart room swings open and the Third Officer bursts in.

"No reply from the Captain's door, sir, and no answer to his phone."

Mr Modesto clears his throat, takes another cigarette and lights it.

"How many crew on board?" Jeff turns to the Third Officer.

"Fifteen, sir."

"Bloody hell. Six adrift, seven with the Captain. All ashore and probably legless by now." Jeff looks into the deep-set eyes of Captain Ferrero. They are alert eyes that have seen a thousand ships and a thousand dockings and a thousand near misses with the pirates and narco-traffickers in this perilous river.

"Can't wait. Must go with this tide." He wanders to the wing of the Bridge and spits over the side. "Take command."

"Yes, sir." Jeff turns to Mr Modesto. "The gangway's going."

"Yes. I'll meet the ship tomorrow. Shore gang will be waiting." The cigarette waggles between his lips. He offers his long, bony hand first to the Pilot and then to Jeff. Grabbing his briefcase he scuttles down the stairs past the Captain's dayroom and arrives to find that the rails have already been dismantled so he steps down the swaying gangway using the side of the ship for support.

Orders are given and the chant is taken up as voices crackle. From the wing of the Bridge Jeff watches as the ropes are released on the forward and aft bollards. The *Welland* sidles away from the quay, tugs nosing her through the inky waters, turning her gently. The river glistens with lights from the small boats, the large boats, the fishing boats and the canoes.

It isn't the first time Jeff has performed these duties but it is the first time he has done them as Master and the adrenaline surges through his body. He feels good. The cool night air is refreshing, the moon is high in the sky over Guayaquil and the *Welland* is moving, responding to the engines, co-operating with the tugs. And he is in command.

His eyes skim the water for the unlit fishing boats and rafts in the river. Just bulging shapes. They are a menace. But the biggest nightmare is the possibility of pirates boarding. They bring their canoes alongside the ship without a sound and tether knotted ropes over the boat rail with a grappling iron. Then they scramble on board, their bare toes gripping the knots in the rope. Sometimes they brandish machetes. Sometimes they wave guns. These men are desperate and trigger happy and the ship's company don't stand a chance looking down the barrel of a gun. Chances of survival are strongest if the pirates carry machetes.

Captain Ferrero comes to his side, scanning the river he knows so well.

"Don't worry. Attack unlikely," he is chewing a tooth pick. "We're too close to port."

"Do you think so?" Jeff studies the face of this confident man, surprised that he has read his thoughts.

"*Si,*" he removes the tooth pick. "need more darkness than this. Too many lights. Too many boats. River's too busy here. They prefer their ships to be anchored off the jungle so that they can lose themselves in the swamps quickly."

Soon the river broadens, the lights are fewer and at last Captain Ferrero gives the order to drop anchor. The pilot launch has followed and is now standing off the starboard side of the *Welland* amidships.

Jeff strides to the chart table, picks up a pen and writes in the Log Book. Then Captain Ferrero is at his side, reading the entry. "03.25 hours Chief Officer Jeffrey Bloxham assumed command of mv *Welland.*" That is correct. He reads on. "Vessel left Berth 3 at Maritime Terminal, Guayaquil at 03.45 16 March 1997 and proceeded to anchorage at Punta Punta, Rio Guyas arriving at 04.10 hours under the pilotage of Captain Rodriguez Ferrero."

"*Bueno*, that's it." He watches Jeff sign the Log Book then shakes hands, gathers up his pilot's bag and follows the Third Officer down one companionway after another.

Jeff watches from the wing of the Bridge as Captain Ferrero strides along the weather deck and down the pilot ladder and into the waiting launch.

He returns to the chart table and stares at the entry in the Log Book. Yes, here it is. Signed Jeffrey Bloxham, Master of the *Welland*. And yes, he is in command until Captain Peter Pycroft gets back on board.

Southampton

March 1997

12

"He's leaving now," Linda is standing at the bottom of the stairs her eyes on the thin layer of dust between the banisters.

"Tom! Come and say goodbye." She waits but the door at the top of the stairs remains closed. "Tom. Do you hear me?"

She shrugs her shoulders and goes back to the lounge. It is light and airy, with an oatmeal carpet draining the magnolia walls to off-white. Newspapers and magazines are neatly stacked on the small octagonal table near the window. On the other window sill is a huge cut-glass bowl filled with pot-pourri. Scorched by the sun it now smells like dried hay.

The settee is across the room with two easy chairs covered in terra-cotta brocade facing each other near the fireplace. The curtains match the three-piece suite adding to the boredom of symmetry.

The dark mahogany cabinet in the corner silences the television and it isn't allowed to say anything until the two polished doors are opened. A carriage clock sits in isolated splendour on the marble mantelpiece and a large rubber plant seems discontented in the corner.

All together the lounge has the disciplined air of a show house on a moderately up-market estate. There's a lot of open space giving the impression that nothing ever happens in here.

"He's playing that wretched music," Linda shrugs her shoulders again and flops into the easy chair near the fireplace. Another bowl of pot-pourri, just as dry and dreary, guards the stack of artificial logs in the cavernous hearth.

A man is sprawled on the settee studying a bunch of keys dangling from his nimble white fingers. "You didn't give me an answer, Linda."

"Well, you know," she bit her bottom lip, "it's quite difficult. I mean, about Tom." She gets up quickly and moves to the settee sinking into the cushions at his side. Their thighs are now touching. She looks into his glistening purple eyes then gently touches the quiff of flat, black hair falling across his forehead.

"Why is it difficult? We were quite safe last time. No one knew."

"Yes, but…"

"But nothing. I'm giving Tom instruction." He tosses the keys into the air and catches them. "Why should you feel guilty about that?"

"I suppose you're right." She's twisting the rings on her left finger. Jeff had put them there and she had been blissfully unaware of their significance until Michael arrived in her driveway.

He'd been making his introductory call at No 7 Coleridge Avenue eighteen months ago. Hot and flustered she had been struggling to open the garage doors. They had jammed before and Jeff had promised to fix them before he went back.

"Here, let me help you." The voice was young, clear, eager.

Turning she locked on to those eyes. Purple, almost black. They might have been menacing if he hadn't smiled. She watched him tackle the mechanism on the garage door, marvelling at his head of hair. Dense black in the sun, expensively layered over his ears into a profile that made her melt.

"There we are. Needed a bit of brute force." He scans the doors then turns to her. "I've come to introduce myself. Father Nolan.

Michael Nolan. Is it Mrs Bloxham?"

"Why, yes, of course. Our new priest. Welcome to St Bernard's." Linda meets the treacherous eyes again and the world moves an octave. "Would you like a cup of coffee? And perhaps you'd like to wash your hands. I didn't realise the doors were so messy. Please come in."

Two months later she melted into him completely. The respectable Mrs Bloxham entertaining Father Michael, priest of this parish, with Jeff, her husband, on the other side of the world. She feels faint at the thought of anyone knowing that in addition to dinner at No. 7 Coleridge Avenue there was something else. That something else being of such moral consequence, of such shame that her heart somersaults into her throat, choking her. And, of course, her mother knows nothing about it. Fortunately, she lives several travelling hours from Coleridge Avenue.

In her bouts of anxiety Michael is able to convince her that no one will think anything about his visits. He and Tom are good friends and he often has lunch or dinner with parishioners, takes tea with the elderly ladies, gives instruction to the boys. He has to do a lot of socialising, part of his job, he says. Nothing to worry about.

She finds his cavalier attitude difficult to juxtapose with his job. But every assignation, every stolen hour takes her right hand to her left hand to contort and fiddle and twist and agitate those rings, sometimes until her finger is quite sore.

"Of course, I'm right. Now stop worrying. Shall we say the same time then? On Saturday." He rattles the bunch of keys then he's smiling, showing off those magnificent white teeth. He's good at smiling. He's expected to smile at everyone but only when they're alone like this can she really call the smile hers.

Michael Nolan carries his clean good looks around with him as an optional extra but his face says very little to the world at large. She realises that nothing much has happened to him during the past thirty three years. He'd told her about his doting mother, about a father he'd never known who had provided a modest private income. He'd given up his job as physical training instructor to study theology, had been ordained and here he is at St Bernard's.

And he's so good to Tom with visits to the swimming pool, football matches, camping. Michael willingly gives up his precious free time when perhaps he should.... well, she doesn't really know what else he'd be doing since he has no wife and family.

Footsteps thump down the stairs and a young boy rushes into the room leaving the door wide open. Tom Bloxham is a miniature version of his father. Lean and energetic with long, loose legs and long, loose arms and a shock of thick fair hair.

He stops dead in his tracks as wild blue eyes garner the scene and come to rest on the man sprawling on the settee.

"What've you been doing?" Linda reaches for his hand.

"Watching. Wasn't very good." Tom walks backwards until he sinks to the floor in front of the easy chair near the television cabinet.

"Father Michael says he'll take you swimming again next Tuesday," Linda shrugs her shoulders. As a child it had meant not agreeing with her mother, not agreeing with her father, defying her sister. Don't. Can't. Won't. Shan't. But those days are long past and now it means nothing. It's something she does regularly and for no reason.

"Oh, brill," Tom's quick eyes dart from his mother to the man staring back at him. "Can Jason come as well?"

"Of course," Michael heaves himself out of the settee and waits for Linda's approval.

"Well," she plumps up the cushion Michael has squashed. "It will depend on Jason's Mum. But just behave yourselves, OK?"

She knows that Tracey will not be a problem. She agrees to everything Jason wants to do. It's one child less to argue with. Jason has two brothers and a father whose job takes him away from home and he knows every inch of the south coast from Kent to Cornwall. Tracey and Linda have a lot in common, coping with children, caring for children, solving household problems and discussing their absent husbands and lonely nights.

Tom has no brother and a father on the other side of the world so she is glad that Tom has Jason as a pal even if they do get into more than their fair share of scrapes.

104

The biggest worry had been when they were accused of vandalising the school bus but that was amicably resolved thanks to Michael's intervention. And only last week they'd tried to buy a six inch knife in a hardware shop. The smart young assistant asked enough questions to frighten them off.

Shop-lifting. How else could Tom have come home with those Quality Street chocolates? The most intense questioning revealed nothing. A wall of silence from Tom and Jason. Jeff knows nothing of these escapades. No point in telling him since there is nothing he can do all those thousands of miles away. It isn't fair to give him that anxiety. There are other things Jeff doesn't know and once again she twists the rings on her finger.

"Must go." Michael slots his hands into his trouser pockets and stares at the carpet for a moment as if trying to remember something. "Bye Tom."

Linda leads him through the hall and opens the front door.

"See you Saturday," he whispers.

Tom has put on the television and it's blasting out a screen full of frenetic teenagers waving and shouting at a pop concert. The girls are throwing their heads all over the place whirling their long fronds of hair round and round like Catherine wheels. The boys in scruffy T-shirts and baggy trousers, are mimicking the demented guitarists and drummers. Lights flash. Faces and hands zoom into the camera and out again.

"Now that's enough Tom. I will not have that clatter in here."

"Why not," but he's already lost interest in the teenagers and is flicking through the channels. He stops on a nature programme. Two impalas are copulating.

Linda snatches the remote control from him and switches off the television.

"Oh, Muuum," his lower lip drops. "They're making more babies."

"The whole world is making more babies. That's what makes it go round." she is plumping up the cushions on the settee again. "What would you like to eat?"

"Burger and chips."

"Please?" With slender fingers she hooks strands of fine brown hair behind her ears.

"Yes, please." Tom reaches for the remote control again and goes back to the nature programme. It's an underwater scene of fishes, like a big silver wheel turning on the screen. "Jason's coming and we're going for a bike ride."

"That's alright. What time?" she calls from the kitchen.

"Now."

"Then he won't have had anything to eat will he?"

"No." Tom moves closer to the television screen, his eyes glued to the bulge of fishes swirling and twirling in a huge bait ball. "They don't live long. Fishes."

"No. Pity." She stands in the doorway of the lounge struggling to open a burger pack. "Many of them are very beautiful," she went back to the kitchen and opened the pack with a knife.

"When's Dad coming home?" Tom watches a whale, its great bulk gliding through the water separating the fishes into darting silver arrows.

"In about three weeks." she calls over her shoulder. "That's if they don't go somewhere else?"

"Why do they go somewhere else?"

"For the cargo. I don't know why." Linda reaches for two plates.

"Will Dad be Captain when he comes home this time?"

"Don't think so. Can't hear you properly Tom."

"He told me he'd be Captain soon." Tom is now standing in the kitchen doorway.

"Yes, but he'll have to be promoted here. In England. By the management. He's the Deputy now."

"No, he's not. He's the Chief Officer." Tom fidgets with the door handle. "Not the Deputy."

"Same thing. But it won't be long. You'll see. Please don't do that."

She reaches for two glasses. Jeff should be here to answer these questions. About cargo ships. About promotion. About impalas copulating and fishes spawning. But they'd gone through it all before. Time after time. Jeff to come ashore and get a job. But what job, for heaven's sake? And the money? There's nothing to match his salary as Chief Officer with Drake Line, and soon he'd be Master and she would be Mrs Bloxham, wife of Captain Bloxham.

But…if he did come ashore then he'd be here to take Tom swimming, to play football, go camping. Tom and Jason were lucky. They had a good time doing all these things with Father Michael. She's glad Michael is around to give the boys treats. .

There was a loud banging.

"That's Jason." Tom was at the kitchen door.

Linda took the pan from the hob. "You smelt burger and chips, didn't you?"

Everything about Jason is square from his jaw to his stubby hands, to his solid chest, to his legs that seem like rough hewn logs. His untidy curly hair always needs brushing and he usually has holes in his socks but his smile can charm ducks off a pond. He is Tom's best friend and although she can do nothing about his disobedience or the holes in his socks she can feed him and she knows he will always be back for more.

"Yep." He looks at her with attentive brown eyes then glances sideways at the plates on the table. He had a habit of putting his chin in the air and watching everything that was going on without moving his head.

"It's ready. Please go and wash your hands. Both of you."

After they had gone she made a sandwich and sat at the kitchen table wondering when she would be the Captain's wife. When they married Jeff's promotion had been imminent but…here we are. He isn't Captain.

The birdsong clock above the fridge warbles half past one. A different bird sang a different song on the hour and on the half-hour. Half past one is a thrush. Three o'clock is her favourite.

A chaffinch. But she's sick of the bird clock. Not so much the birds but the tinny sound. The clock is old and should be thrown out but Tom insists that the clock stay where it is.

Today it's her turn to do a stint at Oxfam. Two o'clock to four o'clock. Sorting through bags of smelly jumble isn't her favourite pastime. A lot of it is only fit for the incinerator but she feels it's a good thing to do. And then she will do the shopping.

On Thursday it's her Course on Herbs and Herbalism. She doesn't want to miss that. Numbers are falling and it can't continue with less than ten people. The attractive woman who usually sits at the back of the room hasn't been recently. Probably on holiday. She's a bit aloof and keeps herself to herself but during a tea break they had got into conversation and discovered that she was a widow and the same age as Linda. So young to be a widow.

She's glad she joined the Course. It's no effort to sit and listen to the Lecturer giving all the amazing facts about plants growing in gardens and hedgerows and woods and fields providing cures long before drugs and pill popping became a hobby for so many people. And she is astonished to learn that the NASA Space Agency had tested the behaviour of house plants in sealed spaces. The researchers discovered that harmful toxins are removed from the air drawing them down to the roots where microbes absorb and destroy chemicals.

She puts the plate and mug in the sink, pauses at the big rubber plant in the hall, stroking it's smooth shiny leaves. She's very fond of this plant. She had learnt that it is an effective and natural air cleanser and she had also learnt that orchids are the only plant to give off oxygen through the night. She would never have known any of this had she not joined the Herb Course. She wanders upstairs to change from jeans into a sweater and skirt.

It will soon be Saturday and Michael will be here.

13

Linda steps out of the bathroom and is surprised to see Michael fastening the buttons on his shirt.

"Have to go."

"But...but...we're going to have dinner." She held her head with both hands. "It's all ready."

"Sorry, but I must go. Just had a call. One of the flock is very distressed. Can't ignore it."

Linda slumps on to the stool in front of the dressing table. She wants to stop him. Keep him here. Demand that he stays. But, yes he means it. He's going. Isn't that what he just said?

She stares at her reflection in the dressing table mirror, eyes blazing, her cheeks tinged as if an artist has smudged careless brush strokes across them. Then she pushes strands of silky hair behind each ear and picks up the hair brush, pointing it at her chin.

He had arrived punctually. Relaxed and confident. There was never any subterfuge about Michael. She gets the impression that he controls the world when he is wearing that sliver of white collar administering to old and young, visiting old peoples' homes, hospitals, officiating at weddings, baptisms, funerals.

Listening to confessions, allocating penance, making love to an absent husband's wife. Taking charge of a group of children. Giving special instruction to Tom and Jason. Playing football with them. Devising computer games for them. Drinking gin and tonic with his wealthy widows, who loved him. Taking tea with old ladies in their never-changing little rooms smelling of mothballs. They loved him, too.

Linda is not really surprised that priesthood appeals to him more than being Physical Training Instructor. Never having known his father, she can understand why he enjoys the family environment the priesthood offers.

Then they were upstairs, in her bedroom. She had decided to wear the lacy eau de nil, a model from Harrods. Jeff had bought it for her when the world was alight and bright and burning with lust and success and happiness.

She watched him unbutton his shirt slowly and arrange it on the back of the chair. Then he peeled off his jeans, folding them carefully and placing them on the tapestry stool. She decided that this extraordinary tidiness must be a result of his mother's training, and, of course, he would have had strict discipline at the Theological College.

He paused by the side of the bed in his dazzling white underpants, whisked them off and got into bed quickly. She has noticed this tendency to coyness. Perhaps it's because he's an only child. No rough and tumble with brothers. No rough and tumble with a father.

They were soon in the valley they know so well where all is peace and joy and calm. They had fallen asleep but she had woken to go to the bathroom and now, here he is, fully dressed and about to leave.

She turns to the mirror again. The tinge in her cheeks is fading and her mouth is hardening, ageing her face. It's Saturday night. And he's leaving. Damn him! She throws the hairbrush on to the dressing table and it slithers to the carpet.

He comes over and stands behind her stroking her shoulders with long, slim fingers. She springs to her feet and pushes him away.

"I'm sorry," Michael stands back. "Try and understand. After all, it is my job…"

"Yes, I know." She prowls around the bedroom, tapping the window sill, the back of the tapestry chair. "What time is it?"

"Half past seven."

"Tom won't be back until half past nine." She sits on the edge of the bed. "He and Jason have gone to the Bowling Alley. You

110

know, in the Amusement Arcade." She scoops up the hair brush and tosses it on to the dressing table. "Well, at least that's one worry less. You'll be gone before he gets back."

"But I've told you. That isn't a problem." He is at her side again, caressing her hand. "Tom knows I visit you. Don't worry."

Linda follows him downstairs and they stand facing each other in the hall. He reaches for his leather jacket draped over the banister without looking at it.

"Better luck next time," he kisses her on the cheek. "I'll give you a ring," and he was gone.

"Luck!" she yells after him but he doesn't hear. He's already at the bottom of the path. "What the hell has luck got to do with it?"

She slams the door and stares at the panels, surprised at her outburst. The footsteps die away and she wanders into the kitchen, takes a glass from the dishwasher and bangs it down on to the work top. She opens the fridge door, pulls out a bottle and fills the glass to the brim with white Caliterra wine. Flinty and dry. It suits her mood.

*****

It's Tuesday and, as promised, Michael is waiting for Tom and Jason in the crowded foyer of the Leisure Centre. It echoes with the piercing squeals of the children pushing and shoving each other with their bulging school bags wrenching shoulders out of sockets. He watches a boy with straggly brown hair getting a drink from the machine against the wall. Then he sees them galloping towards him."

"You're late," Michael puts a hand on Tom's blond hair and ruffles Jason's thick curls with the other.

"We got kept back," Jason kicks the leg of the chair.

"We were kept back," Michael corrects him. "Come along I've got the tickets."

He chooses a seat and scans the banks of empty bright blue seats marching down towards the edge of the swimming pool. There are few spectators this afternoon. At the far end several mothers clutching bags watch the pool anxiously.

Behind him three ladies bundled up in anoraks are unwrapping sweets. The air is damp, still and tiresome but he feels hot and slightly hung-over. A mixture of an over-spiced dinner and too much wine last night.

Soon the boys re-appear from the changing rooms hugging their school bags and trainers. Michael stuffs them under his seat.

"Off you go, But stay at this end."

The boys run towards the edge of the pool, their ivory skins gleaming, their buttocks smooth and taut in their swimming trunks. Tom's are black with the Nike tick of approval. Jason's are hand-me-downs from his older brother and they have been in the wash too many times. The emerald green has faded to a pale lemon.

The boys leap into the air together, holding their noses, yelling as they vanish in a cascade of water.

The pool is full of boys shouting and girls shrieking, paddling water at each other. Old men with shiny bald heads stroke the water with strong arms. Young men power across the pool like rockets.

A young mother is in the water encouraging her little boy to swim. He is scared stiff flapping his arms but going nowhere yet the mother persists, ignoring his yelping as he exhausts himself. Then she puts him on her back and swims to the ladder hauling herself out of the pool. She slides him to the wet, tiled floor, twitches the cups of her yellow bra, pulls down the edges of her yellow bikini pants then marches him off to the changing rooms without saying a word to the bewildered child.

Michael's eyes go back to the bobbing heads. Tom and Jason are in the middle of the pool with a group of boys.

Within twenty minutes they are back at his side, puffing and panting and dripping water.

"It's too crowded." Tom complains, wiping his face.

"Yes and him there," Jason points to a fat boy splashing water into the face of a girl. "He keeps grabbing me from underneath."

"Which boy?" Michael is on his feet gazing into the pool. "He mustn't do that."

"Doesn't matter," Jason embraces his wet chest. "I got him in the balls and came out before he could grab me again."

"Alright, go and get changed. Quickly, then we'll go and have something to eat."

Half an hour later they are sitting at a window table in Kentucky Fried Chicken in High Street.

"Would you like to come home with me?" Michael watches the boys devouring the food as if they hadn't been fed for a week. "I've got a new computer game. The latest."

"Oooh, yes," Tom snatches at the chicken leg.

"Have you got some Coke?" Jason swivels his eyes without moving his head, a sliver of meat hanging from the corner of his mouth.

"Of course," Michael sits back in his chair. "Plenty."

They walk up the short path dividing the tufty lawn from the narrow untidy garden. Michael unlocks the front door, steps into the hall and reaches for the phone.

"Go into the living room. I'm going to ring your mothers to let them know where you are."

Michael's house comes with his job. It's more than he could have dreamed of after student accommodation, sharing dormitories and bog standard bed-sitters. It has a square living room, an oblong dining room which is rarely used and a long narrow kitchen which is not used very much either. Upstairs there are two bedrooms, one of which he uses as a study. And there is a boxroom. A chatty cleaning lady, Mrs Anstey, comes for two hours once a week to gossip and restore order.

He'd given a great deal of thought to his future as a Physical Training Instructor and decided that teaching and promoting physical fitness tests, health counselling and organising sporting activities for muscular young men and women was not fulfilling enough for him.

So it was with much apprehension that he decided to tell his mother he didn't want to continue as a Physical Training Instructor. She had controlled and lived his life since he would walk. He was not going to be controlled by her any more. She must cut the umbilical cord, once and for all, so that he could be free. He wanted to join the priesthood. He was a believer and a scholar and needed the discipline to administer to a broader community, old and young.

And he was not going to ask her or to discuss it with her or even seek her opinion. His mind was made up. He was just going to tell her and wait for the storm to break.

He had timed it well. She was going to a ladies committee meeting at three o'clock and he decided to tell her after lunch instead of after dinner. His stomach was in turmoil as he went over the conversation. The statement of facts that he was about to deliver.

She was sitting, elegant as always, her frail body poised, bird-like as she listened, head on one side, manicured finger caressing a rope of jet beads, waiting for him to finish. Her response amazed him.

"The best thing you can possibly decide upon Michael. I'm so glad for you. I knew somehow that the sporty thing was not quite your calling." She got up, stepped towards him and embraced him. Immediately he caught the scent of her Floris perfume. It trailed after her loyally wherever she went. He always knew if she'd been into his room, even as a small boy.

"You do know, don't you," she stepped away, chin lowered as she blinked up at him with sad blue eyes, "I converted to Catholicism. As a young woman. Your grandmother never forgave me. Never got over it."

There was a pause and he didn't know what to say.

She went on, "Celibacy is a way of expressing love," and slowly lowered her slim frame into the chair.

He didn't know what to say to that either but it had all been easy. His mother was delighted and supported him all the way. The expected storm did not come and he had blended into the new life style effortlessly.

The theological studies had been a challenge and although he knew the promotion ladder was long and difficult he progressed steadily from the Seminary to the Vows of the Ordination and now he was Father Michael living in an unassuming red brick terraced house all to himself, not far from St Bernard's, a parish of young people, old people and middle-aged people. He took it all in his stride even the six thirty Mass on a Sunday morning, the ghost shift.

He doesn't have to concern himself too much about catering. Parishioners entertain him to lunch or dinner or drinks and family parties are a bonus. He accepts every invitation.

He likes confessions. They give him an inordinate power but he is surprised to realise that there seems to be no godliness in the Confessional. A broken relationship with God. Strange idea to tell your failings and lust to another human being, to voice the most furtive desires of your heart and body knowing that it is absolutely sacrosanct. And he had never heard anyone ask for forgiveness for being rude, or surly or unhelpful. The every day sins that so many of us commit. But whatever is confessed would never, ever be disclosed by the priest listening behind the gauze. Not even a murderer. He or she must give themselves up to the police not to the priest.

He just needs to be a good listener and he feels empowered listening to the churchgoers and their sins. Very few are anywhere near happily married. Most couples are together because everyone expects them to be. So away they go with a few words of encouragement, a simply penance of five Our Fathers, five Hail Marys and absolution. Go and get on with your life.

He replaces the phone and goes back into the living room.

Tom and Jason are sitting side by side on the carpet in front of the television ranging through the programmes.

"I've told your mothers where you are. Would you like some Coke? Crisps?"

"Yes, please."

Michael comes back. "What did you find on the television?"

"Nothing."

"Well, what about a Three Scrum?" Michael puts the remote control on top of the television.

"Ooh yea," Jason screws up the neck of a crisp bag, blows it up and explodes it with a loud bang.

Michael collects the squashed drink cans and crisp bags and puts them in the waste paper bin. "We have to move the settee to the wall. Like last time."

All three of them heave on the back of the settee. It is faded greeney-grey, bulky and shabby. Several small square cushions are just as tatty.

"Tom. Move the stool. Jason put the newspapers under the chair. That's it."

Now the centre of the room is clear apart from the flotsam and jetsam that has collected under the settee. Michael scoops up the Quality Street chocolate wrappers, a comb, a phone card, rosary beads and half a digestive biscuit. He puts the rosary beads inside a vase on the sideboard and tosses the rubbish into the waste paper bin.

"Barefoot please," and he kicks off his trainers and stands in the middle of the room, hands on hips. "Ready!"

Jason goes for Michael's legs and brings him down straight away. Tom piles in on top of Michael. There is puffing and panting and hissing and groaning and squealing, with arms and legs thrashing around in spindly confusion.

Suddenly Michael struggles free and throws himself on to the settee. Tom and Jason jump on top of him and bash him with the small square cushions. Michael's hands are groping freely in a wonderland of pubescent growth as blows from the cushions rain on him. Tom falls to the floor. Michael is now grappling with Jason's solid thighs but Jason brings up his knee and winds him.

"I want a drink." Tom is sitting on the carpet, knees hunched.

"Alright, cool it, boys." Michael struggles to his feet, smoothing his hair. "Getting too rough," he calls over his shoulder as he makes his way to the kitchen.

Tom leans over and whispers to Jason. "Shall we go?"

"Yea, but wait till we've had a drink."

Michael comes back with cans of Diet-pepsi. "Enough for today, eh boys? Better calm down with some television…"

The telephone rings. Michael puts down his can of drink and goes through to the hall.

"Come on," Tom is pushing his feet into his trainers. "Let's go."

Michael is still on the phone as they push past him and dash out of the front door clutching the cans of Diet-pepsi.

14

"My Mum says that's what makes the world go round," Tom picks up a stick and throws it into the canal.

"Well my Dad says it's fucking that makes the world go round." Jason digs his heels into the muddy path.

"My Mum won't let me use that word." Tom watches the stick float away. "Stops my pocket money. S'not fair. She calls it kopulating."

"What's that?" Jason has now scraped up a little pile of mud with his shoe heel.

"Don't know. Do elephants fuck or kopulate?" Tom pulls a fistful of grass from a clump and throws it into the water. "And what do fishes do? Saw a programme the other day. Couldn't see anything happening. Must have done it quick."

"They lay eggs. In the water." Jason rolls the ball of mud in the palms of his hands. "Then the man fish squirts all over the woman fish. That's how they do it. It's supposed to be the same as fucking. You end up with baby fishes."

Tom and Jason are squatting on the canal bank not half a mile from home, close to their little barn.

They decided not to go back to school this afternoon and cycled along the main road as far as the railway bridge then pushed their bikes along a muddy footpath, dipping their heads to avoid the dense, prickly branches from the overhanging hawthorn hedge. The motorway is high above them on the right, beyond the steep bank covered in bushes and shrubs festooned with plastic bags, beer cans, bottles, newspapers and old rags left by dossers. The high bank deadens the roar of the lorries pounding along to the industrial estate.

They crossed a narrow wooden bridge over the canal and followed the path into a field. There is a small barn in the corner. It is a ramshackle little building of crumbling grey stone and they have to push hard on the battered door to get inside with their bikes.

Along the length of this barn is a manger with a hay rack above it. One window with a broken pane looks out across the bare field and the earth floor is littered with straw. It's all derelict and dry and dreary and when the wind blows through the broken window it gets very cold.

They had found a log under the hedge, hauled it inside and on a wet day they sit here with cigarettes, crisps, sweets, biscuits, apples and anything else that might have come their way. They have never seen the farmer and they have told no one about their secret hideaway.

"Did you bring the cotton?" Tom yanks at a handful of grass and throws it into the canal. It spreads out like a green fan as it floats away.

"No, but I've got the hooks."

"We can't fish without the cotton."

"I know. So we can't fish. I'm hungry." Jason rolls another lump of mud into a ball and throws it into the water.

"So am I."

"We haven't got anything to eat." Jason looks sideways at Tom..

"Let's go…"

"Where are you going to say?" Jason asks.

"Father Michael's. He's always got something to eat." Tom stretches his legs and leans back on both hands. "But wait. He'll know we bunked off school."

"Yea. But he won't split on us. Didn't last time."

"And he'll want to scrum," Tom pushes out his bottom lip. "Hurt me last time."

"Yea. Hurt me too." Jason jumps to his feet. Gets too rough."

119

"If he does it again I'll thump him." Tom slips on the muddy bank.

"So will I. Come on let's go."

They race along the canal bank, scramble through the hole in the hedge and wheel their bikes out of the barn.

Michael is in the study working at his computer.

"You're early from school." He swings round on his swivel chair. "You have been to school, haven't you?"

"Got let out early." Jason stretched his thick little neck and looks away without moving his head.

Michael slaps the papers on his desk. "Now, the truth. What is it? Truanting? And look at your filthy hands and all that mud on your shoes. How many times have I told you. You must not play truant."

"Yea. But you can get us off." Jason kicks the shiny metal feet of the swivel chair.

"Last time I was able to convince the Headmaster that you were doing something for me. In a good cause. Remember all those leaflets you delivered. Well, there are only so many times I can help you. Come on now," He clicks on the mouse and the text on the screen expires with a tiny white spot. "Hungry?"

An hour later they had eaten hamburgers and drunk milk because there was no Coke left.

Michael glances at his watch. "School was out fifteen minutes ago."

Tom is playing with the computer. Jason pushes him out of the way to get at it.

"That's enough now. Please don't touch the keyboard. If you don't want to be found out you'd better be getting off home. There's a football match on Saturday. Southampton are playing Arsenal. Would you like to go?"

They turn to look at him. "Cor, brill."

The following Monday Tom and Jason are shuffling along the pavement, side by side. It's ten minutes past six, they have had their tea, told the truth about where they were going and are now making their way to West Park.

"Well, I'm not taking any more of it." Tom's hands are deep in the pockets of his jeans.

Jason is swinging one of his father's golf clubs. "What's up?"

"Nothing," Tom kicks an empty hamburger carton into the grass verge.

"Yes, there is," Jason skips in front of him, barring his way.

"He did something to me." Tom keeps his eyes on the pavement.

"When?" Jason steps aside and they continue on their way.

"Last Saturday. After the football match. You couldn't come 'cos you were helping your Dad."

Jason stretches the golf club above his head and brings it down across the back of his neck. "I've got something to tell you as well. Wait till we get to the Park."

"Yea, but you can't play golf in the Park."

"I'm not going to. Haven't got any golf balls."

"Well, then why did you bring the golf club?"

"Cos I wanted to. Come on, this way."

The Park is deserted except for an elderly man walking his Jack Russell terrier. It is yapping and straining at the leash, anxious to get at the mallards on the lake. The boys tumble on to the grass under the big willow tree.

"When did he do it to you?" Jason laid the golf club across his toes.

"I told you." Tom is watching the three ducks dreaming their way across the lake. "Last Saturday."

"Well, on the Thursday before," Jason jerks his left toe and the golf club rolls up his ankle. "I bumped into him outside Woolworth's and we went back to his house 'cos I was hungry and…"

There is a pause and the only noise comes from a police car roaring across the other side of the Park, blue lights flashing, klaxon blazing.

"What did he do to you? You tell first. You never said properly." Jason kicks the golf club away.

"D'you remember when I hurt my back. Last week. When we were climbing that tree at the canal? Well, when I saw him on Saturday I told him about my back and he said he would put some stuff on it."

"What happened?"

"He took me into his bedroom 'cos that's where this stuff was. For my back. He stretched me out across the bed and smoothed his hands on my back and legs and bum and then told me to turn over. Said he wanted to do the front of my legs. Then he…then he…he grabbed me. And… and…" Tom is staring across the lake. "He grabbed my hand and tried to make me touch him. You know where…" Tom gets to his feet and walks all around Jason. A fire engine honks as it chases another police car.

"I said, 'No, I'm going home' and started pulling on my jeans but he pushed me down…Saying all sorts of drivel…" Tom's voice is drowned by another police car braying its way along the road beyond the lake. "Made me feel bad. Scared me. Said I mustn't tell anybody."

"Promise," Jason holds the golf club across his knees. "That's what he tried to do to me. He pushed me down and jumped on top of me but I gave him such a belt in the belly it took his breath away. I scarpered straight away."

"What are we going to do?" Tom hugs his knees.

"I've been thinking about it." Jason smashes the golf club into the turf, wipes it clean and places at his side. "But we'll get him."

"How?"

"I'll tell you how," and he leans into Tom's face, whispering. "Do you think it will work?"

Tom stares into Jason's wide eyes. "Yea… yea… But it'll hurt him. That will hurt…"

"Serves him right. He hurt us. Should leave us alone." Jason caresses the gleaming shank of the golf club. "When shall we do it?"

"Next time we have a Three Scrum. But we'll have to get him drunk. And get the things together first." Tom stands up.

"He likes to drink. We'll need some wine." Jason picks up the golf club. "I know what we'll do. We'll get some Communion wine."

"Will it be strong enough to get him pissed?"

"Well, he's got a lot of bottles in that cupboard. Don't you remember? The night when those other boys were there? We can mix it to make it strong." Jason is staring at the three ducks. They are on the opposite side of the lake, squatting on the bank, fidgetting to make themselves comfortable. "But what if we get caught?"

"Won't get caught. People are always going to see him about something. Nobody will know we did it. Come on, let's go."

*****

The invitation came from Michael for the following Saturday afternoon. They were going to have a pizza and watch the Champions League.

Tom had nicked a bottle of Communion wine when they put away the vestments after Mass and stuffed it down the sleeve of his puff jacket. When he got home he hid it in his trainers at the bottom of the wardrobe.

Jason had swiped two white linen cloths and pushed them inside his anorak. When he got home he tore the white linen into strips, rolled them up and pushed them under his mattress.

Now Tom and Jason are standing side by side, ringing Michael's door bell.

"Come in, boys." Michael is wearing a red and white T-shirt and his black trousers.

The smell of pizza fills the kitchen.

"Smells good. We've brought a present." Tom pulls the bottle of wine from his puff jacket. He had decanted the Communion wine into an empty Côte de Rhone bottle and sealed it with a new cork he'd found at the back of the cutlery drawer, hammering it until it was flush with the neck of the bottle.

"My word, that's a fine bottle of wine," Michael studies the label.

"The best." Tom winks at Jason.

Two hours later, the pizza had been eaten, Tom and Jason have drunk a lot of Coca-Cola and Michael has drunk a lot of wine.

"Alright, boys. What about a Three Scrum. On the bed. Bring the rest of the drink."

Tom and Jason follow him upstairs clutching the cans and bottles. Michael takes the bottle of wine and puts it in the window sill.

"The cans of Coca-Cola can go here as well, and the gin. Then they won't get knocked over."

The dressing table is littered with plastic tumblers rolling between a hair brush, a comb, a pile of loose change and a wrist watch. A small television screen flickers on the rickety bamboo table in the corner.

Jason's eyes go to the rosary beads draped cross the corner of the mirror. Dark red shiny beads threaded together with a silver medallion and a silver cross dangling from the end.

He taps Tom on the shoulder and flicks his head towards the beads. Tom winks, peels off his puff jacket and throws it down. It lands near the bedroom door and looks like a black dog sleeping.

Half an hour later they are all sitting cross-legged on the bed. It has a wooden slatted headboard decorated with whirls and twirls meticulously carved a long time ago by Victorian craftsmen. The carvings are repeated on the slats at the foot of the bed.

They are all in their underpants. Tom's are yellow, red and blue patterned with the Bugs. Jason's are the faded green of the Ninja turtles. Michael's are mauve. All are wearing socks and all are slightly out of breath after the rough and tumble.

"Come on, let's have another Three Scrum." Jason winks at Tom.

"Alright," Michael drinks the gin as if it were water. "Just one more game. Can't play long. Have to go out tonight."

Once again the boys assault him with pillows and fists, heaving and pushing and avoiding his wild grabs. Michael's energy is fading and he is now lying flat on his back, panting for breath, quite drunk.

"Get dressed," Tom whispers to Jason.

They quickly pull on their track suits and push their feet into trainers.

"Be nice to me boys," Michael's eyes are closed and he is reaching out but finds nothing to touch. "Where are you?" Long white arms hover in the air above his head. He starts to sing in a low voice.

"Do you like this?" Tom runs his fingers in wriggly lines across Michael's chest.

"What are you doing?" he whispers.

"Just playing," Jason reaches for his anorak and pulls out the strips of linen hidden in the sleeves. He throws one length to Tom standing on the other side of the bed. "You like us to play with you."

"Of course, you know I do."

They tie a strip to each wrist, push his arms above his head and anchor them to the oak slats of the bedhead.

"Hey! What's going on?" Michael giggles, his eyes closed, head rolling from side to side.

"Taking off your pants." Together they tug at the mauve underpants and throw them into the corner near the bamboo table. "And now we're going to tie your legs. It won't hurt, honest. Like we did your arms. One either side, OK?"

"Alright," the voice is mellow. "That's nice."

Tom ties the linen strip to his left ankle and fastens it round one of the slats at the bottom of the bed. Jason is on his knees tying the strip to the right ankle. "Good."

Michael is now spread-eagled cross the bed, arms and legs firmly secured to each corner, still singing in a low voice.

Tom nods to Jason and together they smooth their cool hands over his lower abdomen and up across his chest.

"AAaah!" Michael whimpers. "Stop the room. It's spinning."

Now they are stroking the fat worm curled up in the black nest between Michael's legs, running their fingers up and down his thighs.

Michael moans and groans and gasps, tossing his head from side to side, the lank hair flopping across his forehead.

Jason reaches for the dark red rosary beads dangling from the corner of the dressing table mirror.

"Ready,?" Jason signals.

Tom nods and turns up the volume on the television. A crowd at a football match is roaring like ten thousand caged lions. The commentator is shouting above the din and the bedroom echoes with great rippling waves of cheers.

"Will they be strong enough?" Tom whispers.

"Don't be stupid, course they'll be strong enough." Jason hisses. "You know we tested them in the vestry."

"What are you doing now?" Michael is smiling at the ceiling.

The worm is now unrecognisable. Jason links the rosary beads round and round the shaft of inky brown tubular flesh then he gives the other end of the beads to Tom to thread through the loop.

"Ready now. Pull."

Michael screams. A long undulating high-pitched scream that carries beyond the bedroom, down the stairs and into the hall, filling the house with terror. He tries to put his hands to his crotch but he can't move.

"*Stop. Stop,*" the voice shrieks.

"Keep it tight." Jason grits is teeth.

Michael is bouncing up and down on the bed.

"AAaaah!." His voice has become a gurgle.

Tom grabs a small cushion from the bedside chair and stuffs it into Michael's mouth.

"Don't do that. You'll suffocate him." Jason throws the cushion to the floor. The blushed cheeks are turning grey. Tom reaches for the glass of gin and pours it over Michael's face. There is no reaction. He is quiet and still. No movement. No more words. His head is on one side, lips pulled back, mouth open, eyes closed.

"Let's go." Tom grabs the puff jacket and thunders down the stairs. Jason slides down the banisters.

The living room is a mess. The pizza box and some Coca-cola cans are scattered around the chairs. Dirty plates litter the settee. Peanuts and raisins look like rabbit droppings strewn across the carpet.

"Come on. Quick. Out..." Tom pushes on Jason's shoulders. The door slams and they streak down the garden path and run and run and run and don't stop until they get to the Co-op corner.

Tom leans on the shop window gasping for breath. "I've got the stitch. Do you think he'll be alright?"

"Bollocks. Teach him a lesson." Jason leans forward, his hands gripping his knees, sucking in air, staring at the pavement. Then he straightens up. "He'll get loose, sooner or later. Perhaps he'll leave us alone now." Jason wipes his forehead. "What shall we do? I've only got a pound."

"My Mum gave me some money. She was in a good mood. Painting her nails when I left. That means she's going out. And guess what? My Dad phoned last night. Soon be home. Said he'll take us camping."

"Same place as last time." Jason's head didn't move as his eyes swivelled to Tom. "By the river. So we can fish properly. That'll be cool."

"I reckon it's brill. Come on. We can go to the flicks," Tom starts to run again, "and we've got enough for an ice cream."

*****

Linda is sitting on the stool at her dressing table. It's half past seven and he's late. Unlike him. He is a pedantic time-keeper. She takes a sip of wine, staring at her reflection, pleased with her stylish hair cut, satisfied with her natural make-up. Waiting for her lover without a scruple of unease about her distant husband who is now on his way home. He had telephoned last night from some godforsaken port in South America.

"Linda, at last. I've got through…"

"Darling Jeff. Where are you?"

She didn't recognise his voice. It had been dismembered and recycled in short metallic spurts.

"Docked this morning. How are you? I've tried to get through so many times. I decided you must have been away. At your mother's or somewhere. How's Tom. Can I speak to him?"

"Yes, of course. Tom, come quickly" she called up the stairs.

"Hello Dad," the young clear voice rang with energy. "Where are you?"

"At Ocalaja. Look it upon your atlas. West coast of South America. I'm on the Bridge, Using a satellite phone." His eyes were fixed on the large map describing the different types of waves.

"When will you be home, Dad?"

"Soon and we'll go camping and fishing. How about that? Be good my son. Love you."

"Yea. Here's Mum again."

"Hello Linda." There was silence. He pressed his finger on the sticky tape on the corner of the map, waiting. "Linda, hello. Linda."

The line crackled and fizzled but there was no one there.

"The line's gone dead, Tom." She tried to redial without success.

"Where is he?" Tom asks.

"Get the Reader's Digest Atlas, Tom, you can find where it is." But they couldn't find the port Jeff had been phoning from and she

128

wasn't sure how it was spelt. "Dad will find it and explain."

"He'll be home soon, Mum," and Tom balances the atlas on his head as he returns it to the shelf. "Whippee."

Jeff home soon and here she is expecting Michael to arrive any minute.

She gets up from the dressing table and wanders to the window. The garden is unkempt. The daffodils should have been dead-headed. The wall flowers are crawling along the ground on dry stalks. Jeff loves the garden and spends hours pottering in it when he's on leave. She will definitely have to tidy it before he gets back and she really ought to keep it in better shape for him but the little herb garden in the far corner is thriving with rosemary, bay bush, the sage and parsley.

Her eyes skim the roofs of the parked cars, the neat lawns and gardens. There is not a soul nor a motorist in sight. No one. And not a sign of Michael.

She ambles down the stairs, clutching the empty wine glass. The wine is helping to numb the guilt, the sense of betrayal. But it's not the first betrayal in her life. When she was younger it had been different and she had not felt at all guilty, deceiving her parents because they never asked where she had been or what she had been doing so why should she feel guilty now. She had been sixteen and two weeks when she gave herself to that handsome Flying Officer at the Air Force Base in Cyprus and she wondered, even at that early age, who had invented guilt to plague mankind. She had not felt guilty, deceiving her parents. It had all been an adventure.

She goes into the lounge and pauses in front of the television cabinet but decides not to put it on. Saturday night. Football and lottery and women with big glossy mouths and men with rings in their ears and hairs in their noses and warts on their chins, all shouting and yelling at each other.

Something had delayed him. But why hasn't he phoned? She sinks on to the settee, tucking her feet under two little cushions. And yet, and yet, she knows she will forgive him. She needs him and he knows that but he never confesses to *his* need for her. His desires. Perhaps it's because he's not supposed to have them, these basic instincts, these desires born in all of us. It would be nice of him to admit that he wants her, even loves her. But he never admits to anything. It's almost as if she were being used.

She looks across the room to the telephone in the hall and remembers Jeff's call last night.

When they married she knew that Jeff, a Church of England Protestant would never convert. He firmly believed that the hierarchy was still doing battle with contraception while much of the Catholic developing world starved. He accepted that their children would enter the Roman Catholic faith but she hadn't realised just how much he detested the 'theatricals' as he calls it. To be fair he never discouraged Tom from attending Mass and doing all the things that a good Roman Catholic had to do.

She remembers they were sitting at the best table in The Orangerie of the Knightwood Hotel celebrating her birthday. Five year old Tom was at home in the suffocating care of her mother. She arrived from Crawley every time Jeff came on leave so that she could care for Tom insisting that she and Jeff should have quality time together.

But how could she say, 'please mother, don't come. We want to be alone. As a family.' And Jeff wanted quality time as well. He was very good about it and tolerated the punctual arrival of his mother-in-law.

Life and loving had been easier when Jeff had been on shorter voyages. Now his trips seemed endless. Long months of waiting and wishing and waiting. Doing her best with Tom. Doing her best to keep the house going. The garden, The bills. She needs someone to listen to her. Along comes Michael to help her with the garage doors.

The phone buzzes and she sweeps through to the hall, snatching it from its cradle.

"Hello."

"Lindaaa!. There you are." The voice is husky.

"Oh, oh," Linda's hand went to her throat. "Mother!"

"Yes, darling, s'me."

"What a surprise. How are you?"

"Fine." There is a pause and Linda detects the sound of a sip from a glass. "Just thought I'd have a little chat."

"Lovely," Linda chews on the broken nail on her little finger.

"How's Tom?" Her mother doesn't wait for a reply. "Been to the most maaarvellous party, darling. Just got home and I said to myself now why don't I give my little girl a call." She pauses. "President of the Rotary Club was there. You should have seen his wife. Always looks as if she's stepped from the front cover of Vogue. And that dreadful woman was there. You know, the one I told you about. Wears that awful costume jewellery. She's got nothing decent. That's why she wears that junk. Couldn't shake her off…"

"I'm…"

"Saw Isabel last week and we're going to the theatre on Thursday. And…guess what Linda?" There was a pause. "I've had a tint."

"A what?"

"A tint. I'm now champagne blonde. Can you imagine darling?"

"Mother I - er - " Linda stuttered. She must get her off the phone. She must keep the line clear for Michael's call.

"What is it darling?" There was another slurp. "And what are *you* doing? Have you heard from Jeff?"

"He phoned last night."

"Do let me know when he docks and I'll be there."

"He'll be home soon. Mother, must go. The kitchen, the stove…"

"Oh, what are you having for dinner darling? I'm not hungry. Ate too many canapés at the party. I'll just pour 'nother drink."

Linda grips a peg on the hat stand. She's feeling faint.

"Must go. Thank you for ringing." She slams down the receiver. "Damn, damn, damn you Mother." She spits at Tom's puff jacket hanging from the peg in front of her nose. If Michael had phoned the line would have been engaged. And as for Mother. Well, she never could say 'no' to the next gin and tonic. It was all those official functions when Daddy was in the Air Force.

"Damn." She marches into the kitchen. Her eyes go to the clock above the fridge, ticking it's maddening tick and she could hear the intermittent hum from the refrigerator. She is glad of the hum today. Reminds her of life. Things are happening if only inside a refrigerator.

Restless, she wanders back into the hall. Perhaps she's left the phone off the hook. No, it is in position. She can ring him. Parishioners are always phoning him, day and night. She picks up the pencil and taps it on the edge of the hall stand.

She hates this hall stand. It had come from her mother-in-law's home in Exeter. Jeff thought it was elegant. It's a disaster in her minimal scheme of things. Solid mahogany. Six feet tall. The elaborately spindled upper section frames an oval mirror with four solid brass hooks for Tom's baseball cap, his woolly hat, her navy blue beret and Jeff's Russian hat. Umbrellas languish on either side with their tips in a little metal tray underneath.

Grabbing the phone she stabs at the numbers. The phone is ringing but there's no answer. He's been called out on some emergency. Perhaps someone is dying. Or had an accident but wherever he is he could easily have given her quick call. There's no excuse. But perhaps he did try to ring her when her mother was on the phone. Number engaged. Damn her!

She goes back to the lounge and picks from the dishes of olives, the crisps, the nuts. Then she flops on to the settee nursing the dish of nuts. She puts it down, refills her glass and takes it upstairs, her mind a confusion of her mother with a champagne tint and Michael somewhere out there, but where? She reaches for her thick dressing gown and pulls it on. She is cold and she's getting light-headed.

15

Jeff watches from the wing of the Bridge as the pilot's launch splutters and coughs and disappears, swallowed by the river. Captain Ferrero is on his way to the next ship, and the next and then the next, all waiting patiently for their advisor to get them in to and out of the port. They cannot move without him.

He strides in to the Chartroom and stares at the last entry in the Log Book. There is it. In black and white. Chief Officer Jeffrey Bloxham assumed command of m.v. *Welland* at 03.35 hours Sunday, 16th March 1997. He smoothes his hands down his chest then glances at his wrist watch. He's been in command for just under one hour.

Time to check his ship. He hurries down to the weather deck and walks from fo'c'sle to stern. He's familiar with every inch of it but he's now legally responsible for it. Pausing amidships he peers into the darkness beyond the deck lights rippling across the shadowy river. Yes, Captain Ferrero is right. There's too much traffic for a pirate attack but he isn't taking any chances. He goes back to the Bridge.

The Third Officer is making coffee.

"Thank you," he takes the mug. "I want a patrol on the weather deck."

The Third Officer drops the spoon. "Yes, sir."

"Two men. Two hour shifts. Issue walkie-talkie radios and tell them to use the code word 'Mango' to call the Bridge in case of emergency. The walkie-talkies are in the signal locker in the Radio Room." He hands over a bunch of keys. "Be sure to insist on the code word. It's no good calling the Bridge and saying 'pirates on board.' Do you know why?"

The Third Officer jangles the keys in the palm of his hand.

"No sir."

"I'll tell you why." Jeff scans the neutral eyes in the hungry face with its woolly growth of beard. "The *Welland* had been ordered to anchorage off Buenaventura. It was eight o'clock at night when the Bo'sun saw a small vessel come alongside. There were eight hooded men in it. One man threw a grappling hook and they all scrambled up the side of the ship, bare-foot. The Bo'sun alerted the Bridge on his walkie-talkie and told them pirates on board. And do you know what? The Officer of the Watch thought he said 'Pilot on board.'"

The Third Officer meets Jeff's solid stare. "Did anyone get hurt?"

"The Second Officer had cuts on his legs. We hear these rumours going the rounds of the ships but when it really happens…"

"Bloody wars!" The Third Officer takes a gulp of his coffee.

"They had machetes and not guns, thank God. The ship's company fought them off. They were lucky. So I want a patrol on the weather deck. And the code word is 'Mango'. Understand?"

"Yes, sir," the Third Officer puts down his coffee mug and hurries into the Radio Room.

Jeff spurts down to his cabin, opens the door and slips off his shoes. He pads across to his night cabin and pushes the curtain aside. Undressing quickly he slips into bed. Fiona senses his nearness but does not abandon her cosy blanket of sleep.

Out there in the river all is quiet. There are no orange lights scorching the walls, no fork-lift trucks bleeping, no container lorries revving. Just the slap of water against the skin of the ship and the occasional vroom of a speed boat scurrying off to rendez-vous with heavens knows what assignment. The digital alarm clock winks at him. It's four forty five.

He's too hyped up to sleep. The events of the past new hours keep whirling around his head. Here they are, anchored in the river with the Captain ashore and he must prepare all documents for return alongside. He would need the spare keys to the Captain's accommodation to get at the paper work. The problem in the Radio Room will have to be fixed before sailing and they need an empty container. The facts march into the darkness of his mind and dissolve the tension in his body as he hovers on the edge of sleep then all is blackness until the bleep, bleep of his alarm clock tracks across the top of his head.

It is ten minutes to seven. Two hours of sleep have worked wonders. He decides not to have a shower. It might disturb Fiona so he washes and doesn't bother to shave. Then he bounds up the stairs, two at a time, pushing on the heavy door to the Chartroom.

"Any problems ?" He looks at the Third Officer staring out of the forward window, picking a spot on his neck.

"No, sir."

"Need the spare keys to the Captain's accommodation. They will be in the Radio Room. Come with me. And we'll need the Wireless Installation Inspection Certificate. It will be in his safe. The engineer's sure to ask for it."

The Radio Room is next to the Chartroom and is as gloomy and silent as a cave. Thick dark green curtains are drawn across the port windows and the dials on the banks of communication equipment are blind. The telex machine in the corner has spewed coils of paper across the deck creating a huge origami octopus.

Jeff selects a bunch of keys from the rack above the desk. The Third Officer is at his shoulder and they thunder down the stairs and swing left along the alleyway to the Captain's dayroom. Jeff pushes the key into the door and it swings open.

"B l o o d y w a r s..." Jeff moves to the settee.

"Fucking hell," the Third Officer whistles through his teeth.

Captain Pycroft is on the settee with a blanket draped across the lower half of his body. His chest is splattered with what looks like bird droppings. His hair is matted with the same muck and a dollop has landed on his left eyebrow. His head is at an angle towards the back of the settee, resting on a cushion. One arm dangles to the floor, the other flops across his stomach,

Jeff drops to his knees and reaches for the cold wrist. "There's a pulse. But it's weak."

He scans the dayroom then storms over to the fridge. There are three used glasses. "It would need more than three people to make this mess. What the hell's been going on?" He turns to face the Third Officer. "You were on watch. How did this lot get on board?"

"Don't know, sir. I didn't see anybody, sir."

"Somebody must have heard them. What about the Security Guard? Where was he?"

Jeff goes to the night cabin, yanks aside the curtain and peers inside. "Nobody's used the bed. Come on. We must get him in here. I'll take his head, you take his feet."

The inert body is slung like a hammock between them as they struggle through the curtain and heave him on to the bed. Jeff turns the body into the recovery position and brown spittle oozes from the Captain's mouth. The Third Officer fetches a towel from the bathroom and puts it on the pillow.

Jeff stands by the bed scrutinising the bare feet, the smooth legs, the waxy chest, the matted hair, the grey face. The breathing is heavy and laboured. He leans into the Captain's face.

"He's drunk." Jeff storms into the dayroom, goes to the desk and reaches for the phone, his eyes on the soil from the tubs that has been spilt across the carpet. A white cloth has been draped over the trellis.

"Ah, good morning Dowse. Chief Officer. Can you get up to the Captain's quarters. It's priority."

"Yes, sir, right away, sir."

He returns to the night cabin. "Make him as comfortable as you can. Clean that muck from his hair and face. We'll just have to wait until he's sobered up. With the load he's taken on board it may take some time before..." He was going to say before they got any sense out of this prat but instead he said, "before he can resume command. Check the Security Guards and report to me."

Jeff rattles down the stairs to his dayroom and pokes his head round the curtain. Fiona has gone. His world had been a different place a few hours ago and here he is with a legless Captain and this lot to sort out.

He shuffles through the cargo manifests, stowage plans, crew overtime lists and the oil consumption returns until he finds the telex from Head Office. The suspected cholera outbreak has not been confirmed and they can proceed to Callao as planned to discharge cargo and load fish meal.

The phone rings.

"Officer of the Watch, sir. I've spoken to the Chief of Security Guard. Nothing to report, sir. The watch changed at six o'clock this morning. No problems."

"Thank you," Jeff slams down the phone. "No problems, Huh!" Of course there are no problems. They probably get a cut on the takings. That's why nobody sees anything.

Heavy footsteps thump along the alleyway and Billy Lloyd turns sideways as he comes though the door. He always turns sideways as if allowing an invisible person to pass. It's his training. Not a lot of space down there in the Engine Room.

"Morning Billy. I was about to ring you." Jeff goes to the fridge and takes out two bottles of beer. "Need this. Or would you like something stronger?"

"No, a heart starter will do nicely." Billy's thick, solid body deflates as he sinks into the settee. "Well, what's the latest?"

"You may well ask. The Old Man didn't go ashore last night." Jeff takes a bottle of beer to his desk. "He was in his room. Getting pissed. The silly bugger's drunk himself legless. Don't know how many women he had last night but I've never seem such a pig's breakfast. I've checked the Security Guards. They know nothing and saw nothing." He slams his beer bottle on the desk. "We won't know what's been stolen until the Captain comes to his senses." He drains the bottle and goes to the fridge for another one.

"These women are as crafty as a cartload of monkeys. Have to be to survive." Billy crosses and uncrosses his ankles. "And why were we casting off at half past three for that bloody banana boat? Who do they think they are with their almighty dollars?"

"That bloody banana boat is bigger than we are and you know as well as I do that Drake Line aren't going to put their hands in their pockets if it's going to cost money to hold a berth and keep to our schedule." Jeff scratches his head as if the subject needs more consideration. "And then that dock strike. No labour. Didn't affect us after all because we had to pull anchor. By the way, the cholera scare is over. Telex from Head Office. Callao next port."

"And all that fish meal, eh!"

"'Fraid so. Six thousand tons of it. And if they decide to fumigate the holds we might have to go to anchor again. It's Sunday. Disinfecting holds will be the last thing on their minds. These Latin-Americans like to be at home with their families. Meals together, playing together, worshipping together. That's what keeps them all of a piece. The family."

Suddenly he is in the lounge at Coleridge Avenue with the sun shining across that oatmeal carpet. It shows every mark from Tom's trainers fresh from some rubbish dump he and Jason have been exploring. The family. That's where he should be, like these Latinos. Then there wouldn't be this worry trying to get a phone call through to Linda and Tom. Not here in this backwater with a wasted prat of a Captain and yet, and yet, he was here. The reason being his addiction to the sea, the challenge that lures him back again and again guiding a ship across these mysterious unfathomable oceans. Swallow the anchor? He shakes his head. These thoughts are for another time, not here and now. He must focus.

"Before anything can happen we need all our crew back on board. We'll have a muster when we get alongside."

"Talking about muster. I think we may have a stowaway or two."

"What do you mean?"

"We over-carried a couple of visitors. When he left the berth last night." Billy threw his head back and roared with laughter. "Just imagine. Sailing away in the night when all they wanted was a few dollars from a frustrated seaman!"

"You mean…"

"Yep." Billy prodded the arm of the settee with his thick finger.

"Saw these two luscious females on my way to the Engine Room this morning. Hiding in that empty cabin next to your office. Terrified they were. Told them to go down to the Galley and get some coffee."

"Where are they now?"

"God knows. On board somewhere."

"Oh, hell," Jeff pushes the manifests into the top drawer of his desk. "Let's hope the Blue Rinse twins don't see them"

"Aaah! They weren't born yesterday."

"Perhaps not but they will know International Maritime Law does not permit prostitution on the high seas."

"We're not on the high seas. We're anchored in this stinking river." Billy swigs his beer. "Besides, everybody knows the Police allow them through the dock gates. Relax."

"Relax!" Jeff goes to the port hole and gazes across the river but he doesn't see the canoes or the speedboats or the wild duck circling in the distance. "Seven of our crew ashore. They could be anywhere if they got into fisticuffs with the locals." He turns, slapping his thighs with his hands. "We've got two stowaways. We've got problems with the satellite. We've got three tons of coffee beans to load and we haven 't got a Captain."

"Oh, yes, we have." Billy puts the empty beer bottle to his lips and whistles. "Dry old do, this. I'll have the other wing if you don't mind. It's tough at the top Captain Bloxham."

*****

Bert Dowse is in the Galley, drops of moisture dampening his sparse fair hair. It looks like wet hay strewn across the top of his head. He's leaning on the work surface studying his cigarette, thin and spiky and hardly worth smoking but Dinty has made it for him. Fags are duty-free on board but Dinty likes to roll his own.

"My head hums," Bert sucks at the cigarette. "Lucky we got back from the Mission when we did." He straightens up with a grunt and gazes out of the port hole. "Ship's like a morgue. No end of 'em stranded ashore. They'll be spent up. And nowhere to go. It's

Sunday."

Dinty is sitting on his stool with a bucket of potatoes between his knees. He wipes his nose with the back of his hand. "Only church. And there's nowt to eat or drink there. Are the bloods on board?"

"Yea. Saw the Blue Rinse Twins when they got back yesterday afternoon. Met them on the stairs. Arguing as usual. Don't think Mrs Meredith went ashore. She's in her cabin. But I'll tell you something for nothing" Bert turns his bulky frame sideways to look at Dinty squatting on the stool. "Her bed weren't slept in last night."

"Perhaps she was at the Captain's party." Dinty chuckled. "Might do him good." He throws the last potato into the pan then he drains dirty water from the yellow plastic bucket and tips the potato peelings into the bin near the door.

"Wouldn't be her cup of tea. But then, you never know, do yer?" Bert blinks against the blue smoke curling into his eyes. "All I know is he were out for the count. They got him into his sack. Looks like his own grandfather this morning. Christ knows when he'll be on his feet again."

"Well, bugger me." Dinty pulls out his battered tin of tobacco and rolls another cigarette.. "But we're alright with this Chief. He knows what he's about."

"Thank God somebody does. Let's face it. That piss artist of a Captain hasn't a clue." Bert tosses his fag end out of the port hole. "How the bloody hell he got command is anybody's guess."

"Ah, hah!. A little bit here, a little bit there." Dinty slips his tobacco tin into his trouser pocket and dances around his stool, twiggy fingers scratching the palm of his hand, the skinny little cigarette wobbling between his lips. "We know how things happen. Never changes. Nothing like a bit of palm greasing."

Now he's in front of Bert staring from dark, bloodshot eyes, his lips pulled back into a straight line. "Spuds finished and now, since it's Sunday, we can pretend we're off duty. Let's celebrate." He shuffles across the Galley to the cupboard under the sink, reaches into a bucket and pulls out two bottles of beer. He gives them to Bert.

Bert places the neck of the bottle close to the edge of the work surface with his left hand and with the palm of his right hand smashes down on the cap of the bottle. It drops to the floor and rolls towards the waste bin. Then he does the same with the other bottle and passes it to Dinty.

"Cheers." Bert sank on to the stool.

"Well, what's up with the idiot?" Dinty's lips are pressed on the neck of the bottle as if he is playing a trumpet.

"Tanked up. I'm telling you Dinty. Never seen anything like it." Bert fidgets on the stool until he gets comfortable. "Some bloody shindig."

"Well, who were there?"

"Anybody's guess. He's a rum bugger." Bert straightens his back. It aches and his head aches after last night's binge at the Mission. "Sometimes there's half a dozen of 'em pelting those bloody buns. And dressing up for him. Do you remember when that woman threatened to sue?" Bert winces on his cigarette. "He took photos. Of her bare tits. Next time we docked she came back to get the pictures and he wouldn't give them to her. So she refused to leave the ship without 'em. Holding up the sailing she were. Pilot on board. Longshoremen waiting at the bollards All ready to cast off. A right bloody carry on it were. The Landing Agent sorted it out. As usual."

"Is he just hung-over then?"

"Looks half dead to me, Third Officer's keeping an eye on him." Bert gets up and the stool falls over. From the port hole he can see two fishermen sitting in a canoe about a hundred yards away, doing nothing. "I heard the Chief Officer and the Chief Engineer talking. They're worried stiff about him."

"Well, I don't see there's anything to worry about. He'll dry out. And anyway this Chief Officer runs the outfit. Time I got on with lunch." Dinty whacks the empty beer bottle into the bin and goes over to the shiny metal bath on the work bench. It is full of dismembered chickens. Legs, wings and breasts all jumbled together trying to find each other. "So, if they land him that means Chief Officer will be Master for the rest of the trip, eh?"

"That we should be so lucky." Bert belches and it echoes around the Galley.

*****

Joy is in her bra and panties, stretched out on the bed reading El Universo. She had bought the newspaper yesterday in Guayaquil.

"Listen to this. A Seminar has been held at Iquique proposing to link the Atlantic and Pacific coasts of South America by means of a high way across The Andes. Huh! I shall never live to see *that!*"

"See what?" Violet is sitting on the edge of the bed with her left foot on a stool, painting her toe nails.

"I've just told you. Please pay attention. I thought you wanted to know what was in the paper. This highway. An asphalt road. West to East across The Andes. From Peru, Bolivia and Chile to Paraguay, Brazil, Uruguay and Argentina. I can see it now. Transport cafes and container lorries and brothels. No more silent ravines and valleys and llamas with condors wheeling overhead."

"Take them years. All I can say to that is 'mañana'." Violet waggles her foot to dry the nail varnish.

Joy peers over the top of the newspaper. "It's time you got dressed."

"I'll get dressed when I'm ready."

"It's nearly time for lunch."

"It's Sunday so it's chicken and ice cream and I'm not hungry." Violet concentrates on the little toe. It's always difficult to get at. The years of wearing shoes that were too tight have squashed it into oblivion. "I'm fed up with waiting in the river. Going nowhere. Doing nothing." Violet screws the cap on the bottle of nail varnish.

Joy moves closer to peer at the freshly painted toe nails. "Fancy painting them that colour! You look as if you've got gangrene."

"It's Bilberry Frost. I like it." Violet pops the bottle of nail polish into her tartan makeup bag.

"Do you know what time it is?"

"No. And I don't care."

"It's twenty minutes to twelve."

"So what? Got a train to catch? And who are you to tell me when to get dressed."

"I'm not telling you. I just think that…"

"Yes, you are telling me. You just said 'it's time you got dressed'" Vi mimicked. "And I'll get dressed when I want to. Hardly swept a wink last night with all that hullabaloo."

"Nobody could sleep through that clatter."

Violet fishes the pink shell mirror from the makeup bag. "But why on earth were we sailing in the middle of the night?"

"Don't know. I've heard two versions. One from the Third Officer and the other from the Assistant Cook. You know, that little shrivelled up man, like a dried prune. But he's fun. Likes his bottle of beer."

"And what did they say?"

"The Third Officer, what's his name? Alec I think. He said the berth was needed by one of those big banana boats." Joy, hands on hips, watches her sister preening. "And the Assistant Cook said the dock workers went on strike at midnight. For more money. Take your choice. And does it matter? We shall get back alongside, sooner or later. They've got all those coffee beans to load."

Violet frowns at her reflection. "Well, I think we should know. We've every right to know. I've got a good mind to go and ask the Captain what's going on. Sitting out here in the middle of nowhere…"

"Cool it, Vi," Joy goes to the wardrobe. "That Captain and crew will have been on duty most of the night. What do you think all those bells were jangling for? That was the call to stations. For sailing. If they've got any sense they'll all be in bed now. So it's not a bit of good raising a rumpus with the Captain or anyone. Time for a drink." She pulls out the glasses. "You're too good at upsetting people. Leave it alone. We're not in port and there's no gangway. We can't go anywhere. Ice and lemon? And it's time we sorted out the gear." Joy pushes the bottle into the back of the wardrobe. "I think we should get it ready for going ashore in Southampton."

"But that's weeks away yet."

"Yes, I know. But once it's done we can forget about it." Joy wanders slowly round the cabin. "I think it's best if we do the same as last year."

"You mean…"

"Yes."

"But that's awfully fiddly."

"I know. But it works and it's safe. So the sooner we settle down to do it, the better. Perhaps after dinner tonight." Joy empties her glass.

"Alright. More tonic please. We've got everything we need. Let's do it."

16

Jeff is staring down at the inert body. The Third Officer is hovering at the foot of the bed. It is two hours since Captain Pycroft had been moved from the settee to his bedroom. His head is on one side, his eyes are closed, mouth slightly open, the only sound coming from the shallow breathing.

"Doesn't do anything, sir," The Third Officer is biting his lips. "Doesn't say anything."

"He's got a dreadful pallor. Should be coming to by now..." Jeff glances at the Third Officer. "We need a doctor. And it's Sunday. But we must get a doctor. Keep an eye on him."

Jeff marches along the alleyway and streaks up the stairs to the Bridge. He wrenches the phone from its bracket and punches in the numbers.

"Hello, Mr Modesto," Jeff can hear children's voices. High, shrill, excited voices. "This is Bloxham, Chief Officer, *Welland.* Sorry to disturb you. We have a problem. Need a Doctor immediately." Jeff stares across the river at the ships at anchor waiting to go alongside. "The Captain is ill."

"*Cojones. Hombre!* It's my daughter's party. Her First Communion today."

"I'm very sorry. But it's urgent." Jeff can hear the squeals and screams and music and can visualise the scene on a Sunday morning at Mr Modesto's home. His wife, the aunts, the uncles, the cousins, the grandmothers, the friends. All in their finery for a relaxed day, eating, drinking, celebrating that child's First Communion, celebrating being a family. Huh! Being a family. It touches a nerve again and his thoughts go to Coleridge Avenue. That's where he should be. At home with Linda and Tom. As a family. Not here dealing with a drunken Captain. These Latin-Americans know all about keeping the family together with their First Communions, anniversaries, birthdays, verbenas, fiestas. Yes, they know how to do it.

"I really am sorry but it's urgent."

"I call back," the angry voice barks and then the line went dead.

Within an hour Mr Modesto had contacted the duty doctor, booked a Cruz Roja launch to take them down the river to the *Welland*, deserted his family party and was now clambering up the gangway followed by a quick, lean man carrying a black bag.

Jeff is waiting for them at the Chief Officer's Office.

"This is Doctor Sanchez," Mr Modesto, grim-faced, stands aside as Jeff takes the cold hand. Doctor Sanchez is a tall, thin man wearing spectacles that seem too heavy for his long nose and his sallow face is pinched and anxious. He smiles but it doesn't reach his dark, deep-set eyes.

"This way please." Jeff leads the way up the stairs to the Captain's accommodation. The Third Officer pulls the curtain aside and they go into the night cabin.

Doctor Sanchez pushes his cumbersome spectacles up his nose and peers at Captain Pycroft. His head is still to one side, eyes still closed but he understands the questions and gives clear answers as Doctor Sanchez methodically checks and tests everything that needs checking and testing.

"You stay in bed. Understand?" Doctor Sanchez pulls the sheet across his chest in a maternal gesture. Then he glances at Jeff and nods.

Jeff swishes the curtain aside and leads the way up to the Bridge.

"It is serious," Doctor Sanchez puts his bag on the chart table, takes out a notebook and scribbles the details quickly. "He must be landed to hospital for tests. Blood, urine. Mr Modesto tells me you go alongside shortly."

146

"Yes, we have a berth waiting." Jeff goes to the Bridge window and takes in the long queue of vessels at anchor waiting to go alongside.

"I arrange priority clearance with Port Authority. An ambulance will meet you at the quayside." Doctor Sanchez takes his mobile phone from his pocket and steps on to the wing of the Bridge. Jeff can hear the rat-tat-tat of orders being given.

Half an hour later the Pilot arrives. Jeff has never met this one before. He is young. Thick eyebrows meet over his razor thin nose like a misplaced moustache and in spite of his breezy self-assurance there is a pensive sadness about him as he stands motionless on the Bridge.

The *Welland* slips along the river, past the ships at anchor, back to berth, turning slowly at the silver water tower and the gangway is made secure.

Two medics and two deck sailors are soon in the night cabin, swathing the Captain in a scarlet blanket. They transfer him from his bed to a stretcher and with great skill they manoeuvre it along alleyways, down stairways, and then they are at the gangway and the waiting ambulance.

Jeff watches from the wing of the Bridge as it speeds away then he goes back into the Chartroom and reaches for the Log Book. He enters the date and time of departure of Captain Peter Pycroft to Hospital Universitario, Calle Bolívar, Guayaquil.

Then he picks up the phone and speaks to Billy Lloyd. "Just landed the Captain. Nothing we can do until we get news from the hospital. So it's time for a beer."

"Or two," Billy laughs down the phone. "Your place or mine?"

"Better come here. Anything can happen and I must stand by."

Jeff keeps the phone in his hand and punches in Fiona's number and waits. No reply. She must be on deck. He'll explain later.

At half past nine the next morning Mr Modesto arrives at the Captain's dayroom just as Jeff gets back from Inspection, checking the mooring ropes, checking the gangway, checking the Security

Guards.

"Come in, what news?" He moves from his desk and sits by the side of Mr Modesto on the settee.

"Heart arrest. Dr Sanchez confirms that it will be at least a week before he gets results of all the tests."

A silence closes in on the dayroom outweighing the cacophony of sounds below on the quayside. Jeff gets up and paces to the window, smoothing his fingers over the scar on his cheek.

"Must talk to Southampton. Head Office will have to inform Mrs Pycroft."

"Yes, it's serious," Mr Modesto lights a cigarette.

"And it's up to them to decide. They could send a relief Master, or," he turns from the window, "They can put me in command. I'll use the satellite. Come with me."

Mr Modesto collects the papers strewn across the settee, stuffs them into his briefcase and follows Jeff to the Bridge. "Pilot booked for 1900 hours."

"Good. We're on our way. And we need a Captain." Jeff thumbs down the telephone list, presses the emergency Drake Line number and waits. This could be it. This could be the day he's been waiting for. Captain Jeffrey Bloxham. Master, m.v. *Welland*.

*****

"Fiona, please try and understand, " Jeff is at his desk in his dayroom. It's half past three and the dockside has died a siesta death. Nothing moves. And there isn't a dog in sight.

"I did try to ring you to explain what was going on. There was no reply."

"I went on deck until it got too hot."

"I'm sorry but I can't go ashore. Not with this uncertainty."

"Well, we managed it at Mahé. Last year…

"Yes, but that was different."

"Not really," Fiona is sitting on the settee, pouting her lips, swinging her leg. "*That* was a sick crew member." Her voice rises

148

to a trill.

"It is different. This is a sick Captain, Fiona. The Captain is responsible for the ship, the cargo, the crew, the passengers and at this moment he's in hospital. We do not have a Captain and I cannot leave the ship. It's out of the question. I'm waiting for Head Office to ring back."

"Of course," She eases herself out of the settee and wanders to this side. "Forgive me but you need a break. To get away. This has been such a strain on you, my darling." Her hands went to his cheeks.

"I'm sorry I'm so tense. But we're in a serious situation. I can do nothing until I hear from Southampton. Please try and understand." He gently pushes her cool hands away.

She picks up her sunglasses and makes for the door. "I'll go on deck for a while and leave you in peace."

He watches her walk slowly along the corridor, head down, his eyes on her long legs, her straight back. He's letting her down but there is nothing he can do about it. He's letting Linda down too, stuck out here on the west coast of South America and there is nothing he can do about it... Yes, there is. He could swallow the anchor. Go ashore. Finish with all this. No, this is not the day to go there. Not today, of all days.

He reaches for the cargo manifests but he can't concentrate on the disposition and discharge plans just now. He'll sort them out later. He wants to know if he'll be Master of his ship. But we're in mañana country and it's anybody's guess when the message will get through.

There is a clattering of footsteps down the stairs from the Bridge, then hurried paces along the corridor then John Bailey, Radio Officer stands in the doorway, smiling and waving a piece of paper.

"Just received, sir."

Jeff takes the telex. It is from Southampton.

"Confirm Jeffrey Bloxham in command m.v. *Welland* as from midnight 16th March 1997 for passage to Southampton. No crew replacement."

He stares at the dark green shiny leaves of the rubber plant. Then he reads the telex again. There it is, in black and white. He is Master. He is going to take his ship home. Captain Jeffrey Bloxham is going to sail into Southampton, Master of the *Welland* and Linda and Tom will be there waiting for him. He must ring her. And he must tell Tom. And Fiona must know.

17

Jeff is sitting at the desk behind the wall of exotic plants adorning the trellis in the Captain's dayroom. This is the third day of his promotion.

Since sailing from Guayaquil three and a half day's ago, the *Welland* has flirted with the seductive Pacific Ocean, engines gently vibrating to its capricious touch but last night as they approached Callao the *Welland* had been ordered to anchor in the bay. A chilly whisper swept through him, hardly discernible. There are cargo ships at anchor and the Peruvian Navy vessels are at their usual moorings. Lights twinkle from the shore half a mile away but he is taking no chances. Before turning in he had put a night patrol on duty again.

He can hear purposeful footsteps along the corridor and recognises them immediately.

"Morning sir. Bad news." The Bo'sun's weather-beaten face is haggard, the hair unkempt.

"Come in. Problems?"

"Yes, sir." The Bo'sun shakes his head.

"Sit down."

"That new mooring rope we ordered in Southampton. Well, we've lost half of it."

"What," Jeff springs to his feet, walks two paces and then comes back to his desk. "How?"

"Two deck sailors were on patrol. At four thirty this morning. They'd just got to the mooring deck when they saw a man hunched behind the bollards. They got a grip on his legs but they were greased. Couldn't hold him. Vaulted over the side into the drink. As agile as a monkey. Took the severed rope with him." The Bo'sun covers his knees with his powerful hands and stares at the carpet. "There was a small boat astern. Piled high with rope. The bugger were gone in a streak. Across the bay."

"But that rope is six inches thick. "Jeff fixes his eyes on the gaunt, bronzed face. "It would need a very sharp knife to cut it."

"He had a machete."

"Then we were lucky our men weren't attacked. But the rope will have to be replaced. Don't worry. You'll get your rope before we sail."

Jeff watches the Bo'sun disappear along the corridor. A good start to his command. More expense. Head Office will not be amused.

His eyes are on the calendar suspended by a rubber band. It depicts waterfalls of the world and has not been turned since sailing from Bilbao in February.

He sinks back in the swivel chair. It is more comfortable now that he has adjusted the height for his long back and long legs. The cleansing of Captain Pycroft's desk had taken some time. He'd sorted the papers and manifests and documents and there is now no danger of them toppling into the waste paper bin. Everything is in its place. On its clip. In its cupboard. He had given the porn magazines to Mr Modesto who had a market for everything. The contents of the Captain's safe had been checked, signed and witnessed and he had endorsed the ship's register.

The responsibilities energise him. He is familiar with every problem a cargo ship can throw at him and he takes them all in his stride. He taps the blotter with his pencil. He feels good. Now he's waiting for the Landing Agent.

He goes to the window. Down below men are humping black plastic bags of fish meal from a lorry parked at the ship's side and dumping them in a rope sling spread out on the quay. When a dozen bags have been piled up the rope sling is hooked on to the crane and hoisted into the hold. Barefoot and wearing scruffy shorts and shirts the men work quickly and quietly on eight hour shifts. They are agile, lean and quite young. Need to be. Fish meal weighs heavy.

He turns away pleased that the loading is going well. The Peruvian Port Authority run the docks efficiently and there is not a speck of rubbish anywhere. These docks are the cleanest he has seen in South America. It's the same at Paita and Pisco is so clean you could eat your dinner off the quay. And no women ever get through these dock gates. There are no bun fights on board the *Welland* in Peru.

As he watches the men his thoughts slip to Fiona. She's been a pillar of support over these last few days, passively observing all the twists and turns of visits from shore officials and telephone calls. Quietly carrying him away to the promised land at night.

She had insisted on going ashore, alone, out there in that chaos. But she's a seasoned traveller and knows exactly what she is about and she speaks the lingo. Of course, she had been disappointed and of course, he'd like to be ashore with her but today it is out of the question.

Then his thoughts slipped to the phone call. It had helped to settle his mind. Tom sounded bright and eager and excited but he was not sure about Linda. Once again there had been that lack of enthusiasm, the indifference. And once again he had felt a tremor of concern.

He hears a chink of pottery and he turns to see the Steward putting a tray of coffee on the low table.

"Thank you, Dowse. There'll be a cash issue tomorrow morning. After we've sailed,. Eleven o'clock. There'll be a notice on the board in the Crew Mess Room. Next port Buenaventura. Estimated Time of Arrival 1600 hours.

"Very good, sir," Bert hitches up his trousers with his elbows.

"Passengers all quiet?"

"Yes, sir," Bert sweeps his hand across his gleaming forehead. "Mrs Meredith ashore. Not back for lunch. The other ladies are in their cabin. Asked me not to disturb them. 'Spect they want to rest."

"That's good. If they're on board they can't get robbed. That

153

supermarket down the road is a mugger's paradise but the passengers will go there in spite of our warnings." Jeff pours himself a coffee.

"Shall I bring lunch topsides, sir?"

"No. I'll come down. I'm waiting for the Agent so lay for an extra please."

"Yes, sir." and Bert ambles off singing through his teeth.

Jeff takes his cup of coffee to the starboard window. The queue of lorries is endless, winding along the quayside and vanishing behind the warehouses. It will be hours before the loading is finished. Then he sees the Agent's black car speeding past the line of lorries. Tyres screech as it stops at the bottom of the gangway. Then a blue van rattles along and pulls up behind it, the words *'Proveeduria, Reparaciones y Servicios'* emblazoned on the side. Great. The ship's Chandler has arrived with the mooring rope.

*****

"Did you put the notice on the door?" Joy is covering the table with newspaper.

"Yes, I used that posh one. You know. From Las Brisas in Acapulco. And I've locked the door." Violet reaches in the cupboard above the wardrobe and pulls on the cord of a bulky orange lifejacket. It tumbles into her outstretched hands and she throws it on to the bed thrusting her long fingers into one of the pockets.

"There it is," she tosses the brown paper package on to the bed. "Damn. I've broken a nail."

"Don't open it yet. We must get everything ready first." Joy places the Sellotape, scissors, two teaspoons, a tumbler, a pile of tissues and small, transparent tubes of paper in an orderly row. Then she opens the brown paper parcel and slowly pours the white powder into the tumbler. "You sit there. Opposite. That's it." She leans back in her chair checking that everything is ready.

"I think they need to be about one inch long." Joy reaches for the scissors.

"Longer," Vi is fidgeting with the broken nail on her little finger.

"And we need two slivers of Sellotape. One for each end. Alright, that's your half." Joy pushes a small pile of tubes towards her. "This is mine. Be careful not to spill."

"That's why we've go the newspaper, isn't it?"

"I mean on the carpet." Joy is impatient. "The Steward will know what it is. So be careful."

"Don't suppose Bert will care a fig what we're up to. We'll do what we did last year. Remember that Philippino steward? Sharp as nine pence he was. We'll scatter talcum powder over the carpet when we've finished. Just in case." Violet puts spectacles on her long straight nose and studies the items on the table then she seals one end of the tube with a piece of Sellotape, picks up a teaspoon and fills the little tube with powder.

"Ready?" She holds the small capsule between her thumb and finger. Joy snips a sliver of Sellotape and seals the other end to form a small white sausage. "That's it. Easy-peasy."

They work quietly for an hour to the strains of Showtime favourites on the cassette recorder, helping each other to seal the little capsules. Then Violet gets up from the table with a groan.

"I'm getting stiff. Time for a break. It's nearly four o'clock. Where is everybody?" She supports her back with both hands. "The ship is very quiet. Not a footfall, and no noise from the docks as well."

"It's siesta time," Joy waits with a sliver of Sellotape on her finger.

"It's stuffy in here. Shall we open the port hole?" Vi fiddles with the port lugs.

"No, for heaven's sake. We can't do that. The Chief Engineer will go ballistic. I said, 'No' Vi." Joy pulls her sister away. "You got us into trouble last time. We can't open while we're in port and you know it."

"There's no need to be bossy." Vi shook herself free. "Let's go down to the Mess. I'm dying for a cup of tea."

"We've missed it." Joy smoothes some powder from the table

into her cupped hand.

"No we haven't. It's not quite four o'clock."

"Tea is three o'clock in port. Bert's probably gone ashore by now. And look at this lot. We can't go anywhere until we've finished."

Three quarters of an hour later the operating table has been completely dismantled.

Vi folds up the newspaper and the empty brown paper package from Pedro and stuffs it into her straw bag then she pushes it back in the bottom of the cupboard. "We must remember to get rid of that in a dustbin the next time we go shore."

"See, we did spill some," Joy peers down at the white dust frosting the carpet. "And we were so careful."

"No problem," Violet dives into the bathroom and comes back with a tin of Cussons' Imperial Leather talcum powder spraying it in a wide arc across the carpet.

"That's enough." Joy is standing near the door. "Stop, Vi. For heaven's sake. Enough."

"Want to be sure. Can't take any chances. "Violet falls to her knees and flicks her hand across the powder.

Joy is wiping the top of the table with a damp cloth. "Who would believe that it's such fiddly work. Why do we do it?"

"You know why we do it. And it's worth it." Vi sucks her broken finger nail.

Joy goes into the bathroom and throws the cloth into the bowl under the wash basin. Then she flops on to her bed. "Phew, I'm exhausted."

"So am I. We always get to this stage wondering if it is all worth it."

"Yes, and we always agree that it is."

"Ben will be pleased. And that's another trip paid for." Violet is preening in the pink shell mirror. "And I can get my teeth whitened. Let's celebrate."

"We're not home yet." Joy clasps her hands on top of her head.

156

"But we will be. Gin, or would you rather have a glass of wine."

18

Fiona left Jeff at four o'clock this morning when he was called to stations for docking, Now showered and dressed she is on deck to watch the *Welland* leave anchorage with the tugs nudging and coaxing her towards Berth No. 3.

Dawn is breaking and somewhere a sun is trying to penetrate a dirty yellow blanket of sulphuric fog hanging over Callao.

Shore passes are on the breakfast table and Fiona is leaving the Mess Room just as Joy and Vi arrive. They have never suggested a jaunt ashore together and Fiona is always ready with a good excuse, just in case.

She can take these ladies in small doses but the prospect of a day with all that bickering and carping makes her wince. So she is down the gangway just after nine o'clock gripping her navy blue Samsonite flight bag. A broad strap goes across her back and she keeps the bag in front of her. It contains a bottle of water, a banana, an apple and her medical kit in case of accident. A small zip compartment holds her shore pass, notebook and pencil. Dollar bills are stuffed in her Gossard Wonder-bra.

So it is with every confidence that she strides across the quayside passing men unloading white bags of soda ash on to pallets. Another group of men are clambering on and off lorries and others are lolling against the walls of the buildings, smoking cigarettes, watching her.

Fork-lift trucks scoop up steel rods and scurry away to dump them in a far corner of the warehouse creating a peal of church bells echoing to the metal girders of the roof.

At the end of the long, straight road there is a remarkable little island with lush green lawn and shrubs. Lorries approach at great speed with brakes squealing and tyres complaining but she waits for her chance, crosses safely and shows her pass to a policeman standing on the pavement near the metal turnstile.

"You alone?" The devastatingly handsome policeman fixes her with his burning black eyes. "Not safe to go alone."

"But…" Fiona smiles at him. "but I have friends. Peruvian friends. At the Inca Market. I'm going to visit them." It's a fib. She isn't going to see Bernardía and Maritsa today. She has decided to try and get to a place called Chosica in the foothills of the Andes, about thirty miles east of Callao. Her brochure says that it has a sunny climate above the fogs of Callao and that's all she knows about it.

She needs to distance herself from the ship. Jeff needs space around him with all the apparent disorder on board. She was sorry she had been so brittle with him but it would have been wonderful to come ashore together like they did in Mahé. She needs to get away from the sisters and she needs to talk to different people, see different things. Smell different scents. Stare at handsome faces, stare at work-weary faces. Admire the colourful clothes of the women. Everything is colour and music here in South America, so much colour and music that it almost obliterates the hardship and poverty all around.

She wants to come back fresh, energised by the challenge these people face everyday. Energised by their friendship, their smiles. Energised by Jeff, her raison d'être. Perhaps, but what is *his* purpose for existence? Is it this promotion to Captain? Is it his wife and son? The answer pops up quickly but she tosses it away knowing that there is no place, no future, no security for her with him. She smiles as she remembers a comment often made by Paul. 'Security is a coward's dream - there is no such thing' He was right, of course.

Her thoughts go back to last night's conversation.

"Why is it such a performance landing a Captain to hospital?" She was curled up on the settee. He was stalking the dayroom, pausing to look down on the docks then striding back to the settee.

"Well, everything has to be handed over to my control. The

159

official Log Book, the ship's register, the ship's articles. The Loadline Certificate. Manifests. Keys. And we had a problem." He pauses in front of her. "The Captain's keys were stolen in port so we had to get new ones cut. Then we had to make an inventory of all his personal belongings and clear them through Customs before they could be sent to the hospital. But it's all done and we've sailed. Thank goodness. He'll be flown home when he's fit to travel."

"And now. You're in charge, Captain Bloxham." She springs to her feet and flew into his arms.

"Yep. Confirmation from Head Office. Contract follows." He grasps her thick curls and holds her head back, searching the wide eyes. "You can never know how much this means to me, Fiona. I've waited so long, so long… But I would never have imagined in a thousand years that… that it would be like this! Taking command of a ship on the other side of the world." He releases her and steps away. "And I did not expect you to become such an integral part of my life. My double life of deceit."

"Well, I don't have a tinge of guilt so you can take me out of the equasion." She steps towards him and runs her finger over the scar on his cheek. "You know and I know that I am guilty of misconduct which means that my behaviour is not in accordance with accepted moral standards. So join the human race, Captain Bloxham"

"Yes, I am the Captain of my ship." His voice fades to a whisper clamping his arms around her waist. "Tonight we'll celebrate." And they did celebrate. With a lot of sparkling wine and music and laughter.

"Pass." The handsome policeman raises an arm and holds up a lorry for her to cross the road. "Be careful. Watch out for thieves."

Policemen always tell her to be careful and to watch out for thieves. Not bad, coming from a policeman but no one can guarantee safety, not even uniformed police. The rattling taxi twists its way through the rush hour traffic on the congested road from the Maritime port and soon they are bumper to bumper in the heart of Lima.

She asks the driver to wait while she calls at the Tourist Office in

Plaza de San Martín.

The young woman sitting at the desk looks up and smiles. "Buenas dias."

"Hello, is it possible for me to get to Chosica and back in a day? I'm on board the *Welland*. We docked this morning and I so much want to visit but I have limited time." She pauses. "I am alone because my husband is on duty all day and we sail this evening."

"You can easily get there and back in a day. Take a taxi to Parque Universitario and ask there for the bus. There is a regular service. When the bus is full it leaves then there will be another one."

"Thank you very much." and Fiona is rewarded with another radiant smile.

Next door to the Tourist Office is the Cambio so she changes some dollars onto soles and the taxi is on its way again.

"*Ya, estamos.*" The taxi driver leans his head back as if he had a stiff neck. "Parque Universitario."

She pays him and he zooms away into the chaos of the jam-packed streets.

Parque Universitario is a small park teeming with men and youths in colourful shirts. All have straight black hair and splendid profiles. They are hanging about under the trees, sitting on benches, squatting on the ground, their dark eyes riveted on the bag on her shoulders.

A throng of people scramble around street vendors with their tatty stalls, buying fruit, bread, bottles of water, cigarettes, newspapers, sweets, chocolates.

Buses are parked all around the Park but Fiona can't find one marked for Chosica so she goes to an old woman sitting at the side of a rickety little table. Her face is like crumpled leather but her eyes defy the years They are jet-black and young and happy and twinkling, holding centuries of secrets. Her layers of multi-coloured skirts also challenge the years. They would have whirled and swirled to the music of the zamponas in a frenzy of rhythm. Now they are spread around the old wooden box she is sitting on.

161

She is selling cigarettes and chewing gum and can't understand a word of Fiona's Castillian Spanish. Then it dawns on her that the woman is speaking Quechua, the language of the Inca that has survived for more than five hundred years.

Fiona looks around. A young girl is carrrying a plump baby wearing a hand-woven hat in magenta, scarlet and yellow.

"Dispénseme, por favor. I'm looking for the bus to Chosica…"

The girl points to a narrow street a few yards away. It is full of buses with drivers and conductors waving arms and yelling destinations at each other. Then she sees the mini-bus for Chosica. Crowds of people push and shove to get on with their babies and bundles and bags.

She pays the driver and settles herself in a window seat.

"Buenas dias," Fiona smiles at the elderly woman who sinks into the seat beside her. The mahogany face wreathes into a display of jagged, broken teeth. Her matted black hair is parted in the centre and scraped to the back of her head. Small bright eyes dance at the scene around her and Fiona realises that these worn out women somehow manage to retain their joy of living in their eyes. They are as bright as those of the old woman selling the cigarettes.

Soon the bus is edging its way through the outskirts of Lima passing pyramids of rubbish in the streets. Men, women, children and dogs are foraging amongst the filth. Small wonder they get cholera epidemics, Fiona thought, as she watches a woman shake out what appears to be a dead chicken and stuffs it into a colourful tapestry bag.

Beyond the rubbish she can see shacks clinging to the hill sides. They are constructed of old door frames, sheets of galvanised iron and cardboard cartons from the supermarkets. Washing hangs on clothes lines connecting the hovels to a neighbour like an umbilical cord, guaranteeing survival in the precarious existence of the shanty town.

As the bus shakes off the slums it continues to climb, bumping and shaking and rattling. Then the wheels are skimming over a good tarmac road slicing through the deep gorges with brooding grey mountains towering above. The windows are wide open and she could have reached out and touched that massive, solid wall.

Ahead she can see trees. Tall and strong. The bus continues along the gorge probing deeper into the heart of Chosica. Then the driver pulls up at the edge of a beautiful park. It is oval. She has never seen an oval park before. It is surrounded by a road and a pavement with very low iron railings, so low it would have been easy just to step over and into the park but that was prohibited. Little metal gates give access.

Palm trees with silver bark soar into the sky and she realises that they are unlikely to be palm trees with silver bark but that's what they look like. Beds of red and white and yellow flowers prosper between exotic shrubs. Dogs bounce around the old men and women sitting on the benches under the trees, dreaming of the past. Young mothers watch as toddlers play at their feet.

A breeze so light, so pure and clean, plays all around her as she wanders long the pavement circling the park. Makeshift stalls and trestles tables are laden with all manner of food and drink and services.

One man, smartly dressed in a light blue shirt, black trousers, white socks and beige shoes, is sitting on a stool at a card table in front of a typewriter. A pile of clean paper is anchored by a small stone. A dark-haired man of about forty is sitting next to him on a well-made bamboo chair. He is looking worried as he explains how he wants to reply to a letter he is holding. A younger man is standing at a diplomatic distance, clutching a file of papers, waiting for his turn.

She continues her circuit of the park following the pavement.

The women and children set the scene alive with their bright clothes. Such a burst of reds, blues, greens, they could have been dressed for a fiesta but this is not a holiday. This is an ordinary day in the life of these fascinating people. They stare at her, nod and go on their way. Clearly there are not many foreign visitors to their little town. Children follow, dancing around her, smiling, touching her skirt. No one asks for money and she hasn't seen a beggar. Fiona decides that she's just a curiosity with her pale skin, pale eyes, her pale hair. Here is someone different who has found their settled little world in the foothills of the Andes.

Beyond the park the road snakes around a huge rock overhang and she longs to keep on walking, right up to the mountains, into their world but she has no time. Turning back she is surprised to find an iron footbridge with red painted railings suspended over a fast flowing river. The water tumbles over rocks and boulders where three women are washing clothes. Children are splashing and squealing and spraying water over each other. A forceful wind sweeps down the valley and she raises her head and closes her eyes. It's like being on the deck of the *Welland.*

Crossing the bridge she goes down the concrete steps that lead to a narrow street buzzing with activity. There are fresh meat stalls with pigs' heads grinning at her, sheets of tripe look like unfinished knitting, chickens dead and alive next to a stall where fish, dead and alive, are expertly gutted by women with sharp eyes and even sharper knives.

She turns into another narrow street. Here there are potatoes, maize, beans and fruits she cannot identify. Barrels of olives, kiosks selling clothes, plastic kitchenware, cassette tapes.

An old, old man is bent over a last mending shoes.

Her eyes are on the lumpy woman with strong arms tossing the meat in the pan on top of the primitive stove. But all Fiona sees is an ultra-modern kitchen, fridges, freezers, micro-wave ovens The crowded commuter trains,. The rat race fermenting the worry about jobs, the mortgage repayments. The car repairs. The television and its moronic advertising. Those shopping malls.

Maritsa had told her that people grow their own food, cook it in the street and sell it in the street because most Peruvian houses do not have a kitchen. They do not have electricity and they do not have running water.

They weave blankets and sell them, they grow alfalfa and sell it. They have an inviolable appreciation of their spirituality and destiny. Going with the flow of the centuries of cultural heritage, not fighting it, not changing it, not destroying it. She envies them.

Pulling out her camera she approaches a woman, her skin weathered by years of wind and sun in the mountains. She is sitting under a bower of green fodder with sprigs of pretty mauve blooms. It is alfalfa for the animals. The old woman has placed a big bunch of fresh green leaves over her head to keep cool. At her feet is a bucket of coca leaves.

"*Con permiso?*" Fiona smiles and points at the camera.

The woman shakes her head from side to side. "No. Only foodstuffs. Not me."

The "foodstuffs" are herbs and plants and flowers that grow naturally and these people know what to do with them for health and medicinal purposes. Fiona respects her wishes and takes photos of the buckets of coca leaf, the chamomile with their daisy flowers and the thick green bunches of alfalfa suspended from the roof of her stall.

The other women at the meat stalls and fish stalls and fruit stalls do not want to be photographed either so she puts her camera away and wanders back to the café opposite the oval park.

She chooses a table under the trees and orders coffee. A young couple at the next table are in love, their fingers tracing each other's cheeks as if they were blind, touching each other's eyebrows, lingering over each other's lips.

She watches them kiss and again is aware of that yearning. Jeff. She wishes he could have come here. But it's no good wishing for anything. Wishing for Jeff to be free. Wishing for him to be with her to do things together. Life isn't like that. Jeff has a wife and son to support and she knows he will never leave them. But she wants him to see these things, this town and its remarkable people going about their daily lives with not a thought or a care for the world beyond that ridge of mountains over there, churned up all those millions of years ago.

There is a scrape of chair legs and the young lovers leave, hand in hand. She rummages deep in her bag to find her wrist watch. Nearly four o'clock. Time to go, time to leave this tranquil world and get back to the ship so she finishes her coffee and makes her way to the bus stop.

She hardly notices the return journey and is surprised that the mini-bus is now in the thick of traffic in Lima. She sees again the hovels clinging to the hillsides, the heaps of rubbish. People are still scavenging.

The bus crawls along with all the other buses and taxis and cars and donkey carts and mule carts and bicycles. Then they turn a corner and they are in Parque Universitario.

She jumps into a taxi next to the bus. The driver is young, handsome and talkative. A dangerous mixture. The Captain had warned her. It is not safe to travel alone in a taxi. She keeps her eyes on the road for familiar signs back to the ship. It would be easy to turn off into a back street, do the deed, rob her and dump her. No one would ever know her fate and her body would never be found.

"Turista, no?"

"No. My husband works on board. He's on duty all day."

"What do your husband? Capitano eh!"

"No. He's the Cook. He can never get ashore because he's always working. Everybody has to eat on board."

That satisfies the young driver and he has no more questions.

Fiona recognises the Cemetery. Not far now. It is on the right hand side set back from the road. Flower sellers are ranged on the wide pavement outside the wrought iron gates. Large, bulky women are surrounded by buckets of flowers vying with their brightly coloured skirts, offering relief to the joyless faces of the people filing through the gates to visit the graves.

At last the taxi zooms on to the roundabout in front of the checkpoint at the dock gates, she pays him and rummages in her bag for the shore pass. The policeman is on the phone. She stands and waits then he nods her through without a glance at her shore pass.

The doors of the grey blocks of warehouses are now all closed and the workmen have gone. Turning the corner she sees Berth 3 but there is nothing there. There is no ship. She must have come to the wrong place. Reaching into her bag she pulls out her shore pass again and then looks at the large number painted on the side of the huge shed. Yes, this is Berth No.3. But there is no *Welland.*

The gangway on the quayside looks like a sinister animal crouching, waiting to pounce. Broken pallets and strips of metal ribbon litter the deserted docks. There is not a soul in sight, only the seagulls wheeling overhead, screeching abuse. She is struggling for breath. Her vision is blurring. The quay beneath her feet tilts.

Behind her is a dirty white Portacabin with the words 'Cambio' painted above one of the windows. A metal rail separates it from the road and forces crew members into an orderly queue. There are no customers. She peeps through a window and sees two men sitting side by side at a long desk, counting money.

She knocks on the door but they ignore her so she goes back to the window. The biggest of the two men waves her away.

"Please. Please help me." She beats on the window with the palms of her hands "I don't want to change money. I need your help."

The two men look at each other than the biggest one gets up and comes to the window. He is solid and square with grey hairs curling round the buttons of the open neck of his white shirt.

"Closed." He glares at her. "Tomorrow."

"The *Welland*. The cargo ship. Docked this morning." She points. "It was over there at Berth 3. Where is it?"

"The *Belland?*" The man turns to his colleague. "What happened Paco?"

"It sailed." Paco comes to the window. He is tall and lean and holds a cigarette with great elegance. He draws in his hollow cheeks and then releases a ribbon of smoke. "Left this afternoon," and he ambles back to his desk.

Fiona steadies herself on the metal rail outside the Portacabin and stares at the empty slab of water in front of her. Gripping he rail she throws her head back, gasping for air.

How could the *Welland* sail without her? How could Jeff allow such a thing? After all, he is Captain now. She answers her question quickly. Cargo ships do not wait for anyone. There are repeated warnings. In the passenger ticket, in the literature. But she had checked the notice board on the gangway before leaving this morning. It had said shore leave ends at 1800. She reaches again for her wrist watch in the little pocket of her bag. It's twenty minutes past five.

The lights are still on in the Portacabin. She decides to ask if she can use their phone. Ring the Agent. She bangs on the door and waits. Then she goes to the window again. The office is empty. Their desks are tidy. The men have gone.

She gropes, hand over hand, along the metal rail. Her legs give way and she sinks on to an upturned red plastic beer crate at the side of the Portacabin. An icy wind sweeps through her freezing heart until she's sure it has stopped beating. She must do something. Go back to the dock gates and ask the police to phone the Agent.

She has about fifty dollars stuffed in her bra, she has no clothes other than what she is wearing. She has no passport, only her shore pass. She would need a hotel for the night and she would need more money to get to the *Welland* wherever it was.

And she's worried about being alone in a hotel overnight. She had had more than her fill of night intruders in hotels around the world. She had never forgotten the first scare in Hotel del Prado in Mexico City, before Paul shared her bed. Before... before... everything was 'before'.

It puzzled her as to how anyone could have a duplicate key to a bedroom in a prestigious hotel and had come to the conclusion that it must be a member of the hotel night staff on the prowl. They had access to the register and would know where the single women were accommodated.

Fiona was a light sleeper on spite of chronic jet lag but she had got her security in hotel bedrooms down to a fine art. There was always a piece of furniture, a coffee table or chair to haul across the room and wedge against the door handle. All that nightly furniture removal had ended when Paul came into her life. Paul... she sees him standing on front of her now, arms outstretched, smiling, on this deserted dock, so handsome, so sharp in uniform. Suddenly she is filled with the terror of loss.

"Oh, why did you leave me, Paul?" She covers her face with her hands, tears dampening her fingers, her shoulders shaking. A plane from the airport nearby roars up into the sky. Distant traffic noises hum on the edge of her consciousness. Everything around her looks alien. Everything is alien. She is stranded, thousands of miles from home, miles from her ship. Miles from Jeff.

She doesn't know how long she has been standing there but the thought of him anchors her to reality again. Paul and Jeff are synonymous. No, they aren't, she argued. Jeff is alive and Paul is dead. And Jeff is in command of the *Welland*. Perhaps he's contacted the Agent. She must find a telephone.

She tries to remember the itinerary as she plods along the endless dock road. Her legs ache, her feet are like dead weights and she's so tired, so hungry, so worried. She's fairly certain that after Callao it's back up the coast but she can't remember whether it 's Manta or Buenaventura in Colombia. Whichever it is she will have to fly there with documentation and money.

Now she is at the roundabout and then she's back at the dock gates. Ignoring the metal turnstile for pedestrians on the pavement she goes to the window of the little red brick office that straddles the roads in and out of the docks.

"Con permiso, Señor. Can you please help me?"

The policeman signals to her to pass through the side door into their hallowed domain. It's a stuffy, square office thick with cigarette smoke. There are two battered swivel chairs with torn upholstery on the armrests. A long desk is strewn with ledgers and papers and clip boards and a badly chipped white ash tray from Casa Loma Linda is overflowing with cigarette ends.

The walls are festooned with notices that have curled in on themselves. On the back of the door is a large poster of a beautiful brunette, eyeing the viewer with contempt. Fiona can almost hear the snarl. She is naked except for a mottled beige scarf swathed across her bosoms and between her legs. But it isn't a scarf, it's a snake.

Fiona sits on the edge of one of the swivel chairs. It is wonky so she holds one foot to the floor to keep it steady as she tells her story.

The handsome man towers over her. A younger policeman is diligently picking his teeth and appears not to be listening.

"I have the Landing Agent's telephone number here," she points to the page in her notebook.

169

"Your pass please."

Fiona hands it over.

"*Belland*." he turns the card over several times.

"As you see" she points, "shore leave doesn't end until 1800 hours but the ship has gone."

There is a rapid exchange of Spanish and then the young man reaches for a sheaf of papers on a clip below the window hatch.

"Wait a minute. Where's the Pilot's Rota," he fumbles through the papers, his slender brown fingers skimming down the list of ships and the Pilots allocated to them. "Ah, *Belland*. Here it is. Sails midnight."

"What! It's here?" Fiona jumps to her feet. "Well, where is it then?"

"Berth 9," the young policeman tosses the clip of papers on to the desk and straightens up.

"Oh, thank goodness. Thank goodness." She goes to the door. "Thank you very much. Where is Berth 9?"

"Straight along that road." He is pointing to the one she has already walked twice. "Turn right, past the Cambio on the left "

She can see a string of taxis parked on the short approach road to the dock gates. The drivers are standing around the food stall, eating.

"May I take a taxi?"

"Not permitted," the policeman puts his fingers into the pocket of his shirt and pulls out a packet of cigarettes. His colleague produces a lighter.

"Well - er - it's getting dark. And I'm nervous walking alone in the docks."

He put his head back and looks down his long, aquiline nose. "Sorry. No taxis permitted in the docks. You'll be safe. Nobody will harm you."

"But I'm not afraid of Peruvian men, It's the dogs that frighten me."

"Ah! No dogs." He turns to the papers on his desk.

"But there are," Fiona is pleading now. "They prowl around the stacks of containers. And they're wild... and diseased." She thought it better not to use the word 'rabid'. "Will someone walk with me. To Berth 9?"

"Not possible." The smoke from the cigarette in the corner of his mouth curls into his eyes and he squints. "No leave here. Sorry. You'll be OK."

Fiona sets off across the roundabout and on to the long deserted road past the warehouses. She must be thankful that she hasn't got to fly to the *Welland* in some far flung port along the west coast of South America. Her head aches and she feels quite sick but the *Welland* and Jeff are here, somewhere not far away.

She can hear a vehicle at the back of her and moves from the road to the safety of the pavement. It's a fork-lift truck.

"Where you goin?" The driver is a big, round jolly man with very white teeth and dark eyes set in little white saucers.

"The *Welland.*"

"Get up."

She hoists herself on to the seat. He slams into gear and they are on their way. It was like riding in a very tall dodgem car but she is surprised how slow it is. When watching them from the ship, as she often did, they seem to dart about the quayside at great speed.

"It's very kind of you. I thought I'd lost my ship. Thought it had sailed without me."

"Often have to move. Not enough berths. Berth 3 is longer than Berth 9."

It takes a few seconds for her weary brain to grasp what he means,. Of course, *Welland* is only quite small. But then, she wonders, why didn't they go to Berth 9 this morning. But her brain is too confused and she's too tired to make sense of anything.

The jolly man is whistling through his teeth and soon they are at Berth 9, a narrow quay with an overhang of shrubs and bushes and well away from the main thoroughfare of ships.

"I'm so very grateful to you. I've been to Chosica. It was lovely."

"Chosica! Ah! Very good." Those big eyes sway in their saucers. "We go there. For holidays. No fog."

The fork-lift zooms to the bottom of the gangway. Fiona slots a dollar bill into a crack in the rusty little dashboard. "Thank you very much. Goodbye."

"*Buena suerte*," he smiles his generous smile, pushes the dollar bill into his shirt pocket and buzzes away along the quayside.

She climbs the gangway slowly, with heavy legs, crosses the weather deck and steps inside. The Chief Officer's Office is deserted. She had hoped be would be there but, she reminds herself, Jeff isn't the Chief Officer now. He's the Captain.

She unlocks the cabin door, throws her bag on to the chair and kicks off her sandals. Then she unbuttons her blouse, steps out of her skirt and throws them across the cabin. She must shower but first she must let Jeff know that she is back on board but isn't sure which number to ring. Her hand hovers above the telephone but she turns away, all energy draining from her as the cabin begins to swirl. She reaches the bed and collapses in total exhaustion.

19

The unexpected departure of the *Welland* from Berth 3 is something Jeff could have done without but nobody argues with instructions from the Port Authority. Berth 3 was needed for a twenty eight thousand ton container ship. At eleven o'clock this morning the gangway had been dismantled and the *Welland* nosed her thirteen thousand tons around the corner to Berth 9. The Landing Agent instructed the foreman to re-route the fish meal lorries and loading resumed within half an hour.

Jeff is in his dayroom stretched out on the settee dragging himself from the anonymous world he'd been lured into after lunch. Cargo manifests have slipped from his fingers and are strewn across the carpet. With a bellowing yawn he reaches for them, slowly re-engaging with the world again. Loading of the fish meal is going well and the *Welland* is scheduled to sail at midnight. He glances at his wrist watch. It is 18.10.

Fiona. She hasn't phoned or sent a message to let him know that she's back on board.

He jumps to his feet in panic sending the manifests flying across the carpet again. He goes to his desk for no reason, stares at the papers, and moves back to the settee.

Out there, beyond the harbour, it's a free for all. Buses with drunken drivers crashing over ravines and buses crushed by rock falls and buses buried by landslides on those mountain roads.

Lorries, taxis and buses locking bumpers in the crowded streets and in downtown Lima the plazas are alive with thieves, urchins as crafty as monkeys and handsome lascivious men with a fondness for pale skins and blue eyes. Anything could happen.

He grabs his gloves from behind the door and rattles down the companionways to the weather deck. Dock workers are crawling over the hatches, clamping and checking. Metal clangs on metal as the containers on deck are made secure. Cranes whine, derricks groan. He finds the Bo'sun staring down into Hold No.2.

"How's it going?" He leans over the hatch cover and peers into the bowels of the ship.

"Need at least an hour and a half."

"OK." Jeff stares into the gaunt face. "Do you know if Ms Meredith is back on board?"

"Yes, sir."

"Good," he scrutinises the black bags piling up in the hold then goes aft to check the mooring lines, angry thoughts festering in his head as he marches along the quay. Of course, she's back. But why hadn't she phoned to tell him? Why did he have to ask his Bo'sun? And he is angry that he had fallen asleep and he is angry with Linda.

There is a Mobile Phone Man at every port. He appears from nowhere and stands by the ship's gangway all day and does a thriving business with crew members phoning home. He had followed the ship to Berth 9 and reclaimed his position at the bottom of the gangway. Jeff had tried to phone Linda after the *Welland* had been made secure. There had been no reply again.

Perhap's she's gone to visit her mother. Nana Clare commandeered Tom. In fact, she tries to take over the whole family. Almost a power game. Smothering Tom with sloppy kisses, expensive gifts and too many sweets, knowing full well he would always be back for more. Clare Jennings gave her only grandson everything he wanted. It isn't good for him but there is little Jeff can do. He is the absent father.

He mentally transports himself to Coleridge Avenue, to the telephone on the hall stand that Linda detests so much. He wants to tell her that he is now in command and after all these years of waiting he will be bringing the *Welland* into Southampton. And he wants to tell Tom his father is now Captain. Master of the *Welland*. But he can't get through and it's burning him up.

He dashes up to the passenger deck and taps on the cabin door. Fiona is standing in the middle of the cabin, looking dishevelled, a blue cotton robe hanging off one shoulder.

"Oh, Jeff, do come in." She turns quickly and trips over one of her sandals.

"I just wanted to be sure you were back on board. You didn't contact me." Her hair is dull with dust. Her skirt is in a crumpled heap on the settee. Her blouse is sliding off the back of the chair. The other sandal is near the bathroom door.

"Yes, I… No… er I…" She tugs on the belt of the robe.

"Fiona, you know you must always let me know that you're back. It's very important. For the operation of the ship, I mean." He glances again at the clothing strewn around the cabin. For one fleeting moment he suspects that she has had a visitor.

"I got a bit panicky. In fact, I was terrified. Thought you'd sailed without me." She went to the bed and shook the pillow. "Took me a while to find you - I mean the *Welland*."

"Had to move berth. But there was nothing I could do about it…"

"And then… when I got back… I was going to have a shower but…I crashed out. I was exhausted. Sorry about the mess. Look at me! I'm filthy. Kiss me."

He moved into her arms.

"Mmm, that's what I need. So you've had a busy day, Captain Bloxham. She hooks her arms around his neck and kisses him again. "How's the family?"

"Couldn't get through." He gently unclasps her arms and steps away. This reminder irritates. Why is it do difficult to get through? Never any answer. Where is Linda? What the hell is she doing? "We sail at midnight. Next port Buenaventura. Then the Canal then Cristóbal then Southampton. I'll give you a call when we've dropped the Pilot. It'll be late."

"And I promise to be clean."

"Must go."

He bounds up the stairs to the Master's suite with a smouldering hate burning in his head. He isn't sure where the hate has come from. Is it because Fiona had come back, expecting him to respond when she looks such a mess? Is it the frustration with Linda that is bringing him to bursting point? But she might be ill. Tom might be ill. Maybe her phone is out of order. The intense hostility is all mixed up and he hates himself for not knowing.

And the chances of a rendez-vous with Fiona tonight would be almost impossible and yet he has just given her hope. He could easily have explained that tonight would be difficult because midnight would mean one o'clock here in mañana country and he is exhausted. He hates the deceit. And there is more hate directed at Linda. He doesn't know what is going on at home and he hates himself for not knowing. And he's worried about her. He's worried about sailing, he's worried about Captain Pycroft which is a ridiculous concern to add to his list. Captain Pycroft can sink or swim. But if he sinks then Jeff would almost certainly remain Master.

He tosses his gloves on to the deck inside the door and marches across to the window. The queue of battered old lorries is wending its way around the quayside, the drivers smoking and joking and spitting and kicking against the wheels as they shunt up nearer to the *Welland* when an empty lorry speeds away. The Bo'sun had said and hour and a half.

"It's going to take longer," Jeff returns to his desk behind the jungle of plants. He must check that the satellite now works. The engineer arrived just as they moved to Berth 9 and he hadn't had a report from the Radio Officer yet. And he hadn't signed the invoice for the new mooring rope. And he must remember to collect the shore passes. They would not be allowed to sail until Immigration are satisfied that all crew and passengers are back on board.

*****

After four days slicing through the Pacific Ocean the *Welland* is now approaching Buenaventura, the most active commercial port in Colombia. The river is eighteen miles long and they have some distance to go yet.

Jeff is on the wing of the Bridge studying the Coastguard cutter zooming along on the starboard side, a hundred yards from the *Welland*. The cutter has guns mounted on tripods in the stern and bows with men in faded khaki fatigues moving about. And it's broad daylight. With that escort he is not going to waste energy worrying about pirates.

His eyes sweep the flat coastline with its mangrove swamps, its creeks and river mouths but all he sees is the telephone on the hall stand at Coleridge Avenue.

He storms back into the Chartroom. This river is dangerously shallow and *Welland* must hold her course. The Pilot is sitting in his chair, one foot on the foul weather rail, drinking coffee. Jeff has not met him before,. He's young and slim and good-looking but for Jeff's money he prefers a Pilot with a few grey hairs and a paunch to guide the *Welland* in this treacherous river.

At precisely two o'clock the vessel is secured alongside and succumbs to the relentless power of the sun scorching the decks, the holds, the crew, the dock workers. The dogs have crept away to sleep in the shade.

The Mobile Phone Man, tall and thin and dusty, is standing in the shade near a wooden shack. Jeff takes the little black slab from him and moves a short distance from the gangway. He marks the number and presses the phone to his left ear. He is hot and tired and hungry. He had been too busy for lunch because of a snarl-up in Hold No.1 when discharging began but this time he must be lucky. He must speak to Linda.

Close by is a solid, thick-set man wearing maroon trousers, a brown anorak and an orange baseball cap. Jeff can't think why the man is wearing so many clothes. It makes him sweat just to look at him. A cigarette droops from the corner of his mouth and one hand is in his pocket, the other holds a glinting chain. At the end of the chain is a Rottweiler dog, big and black and brooding, watching everything that moves.

Jeff keeps his eyes on the animal. The Landing Agent had said nothing about a Security Guard with a dog on the gangway but there it is, not missing a trick.

He scans the quayside as he waits for the phone to connect. Near the wire fence a man is fast asleep on an old wooden door. He wears no shoes and is naked to the waist. A few yards away three men are squatting on their haunches playing cards in the shade of a wooden hut. Then he sees the Galbraith sisters teetering down the gangway.

"Good afternoon, Captain," Violet waves.

"Good afternoon, Miss Galbraith." He watches as they stride across the quayside, giving the dog a wide berth and disappearing round the corner of a warehouse.

"Hello, Linda. Is that you? At last I've got you. Hello. Can you hear me? It's a very bad line."

"Yes, where are you? I can hear lots of noise." Her voice echoes along a tunnel.

"We're in Buenaventura. Sorry about the noise. I'm on the dock. How are you? Linda can you hear me? Is everything alright?"

"Hello Jeff, are you there? Miss you so much."

"Is Tom there?" Jeff watches the bright pink tongue that has slipped from the slavering jaws of the big, black dog a few yards away. He is surprised the tongue is so long and thin and delicate. "Let me speak to him."

"He's not here. He's with Jason. I'm worried about him. He's not eating. Not sleeping."

"Why?" He watches the Security Guard despatch the cigarette with a flick of his tongue. It lands in the water.

"Don't know. Won't tell me. Just says he wishes you were here. I've told him you'll be home soon. Do wish you were here, Jeff. I don't know…" There is a high-pitched squeal and then silence.

A fork-lift truck comes within a yard of his feet and reverses with its cheeky 'bleep-bleep'. He walks towards the stern of the ship and pauses between a pile of rope and a heap of rubbish.

"Hello, Linda. Are you there? There's good news. I'm now Master of the *Welland*. Captain at last. Tell you all about it when I get home. Hello, Linda?" He stares across the harbour. Ships are creeping in and out of berths with tugs fussing around the. "Linda, are you there?" There is an ear-splitting screech. "Linda?" He marks the number again. There is a continuous high-pitched grating sound then a long monotonous drone. The line is dead.

"Damn. She didn't hear me. She doesn't know and Tom doesn't know that I'm Captain. Damn and blast."

"Scuse me, sir. We've got a problem."

He turns to see the Bo'sun clattering down the gangway. "They've fucked up the stowage plans for Hold No.5. Can you come."

Jeff hands the phone to the man hovering at the back of him. "Lost the line. I'll try again before we sail."

He sprints up the gangway behind the Bo'sun and makes his way to Hold No.5 wondering what's wrong with Tom.

*****

The next morning Jeff is at his desk at a quarter to six. The *Welland* is sailing at seven thirty. Everything is on schedule in spite of the problem in Hold No. 5. Stevedores had read the wrong page of the manifest and loaded the wrong cargo into the wrong hold.

He had tried several times to get through to Linda again without success so he now has to sail not knowing what is bothering Tom. Worry gnaws at the edges of his mind as he checks and signs the invoices, the overtime sheets, the crew wage calculations. Tom is a healthy young boy. Why isn't he eating? Why isn't he sleeping?

The Landing Agent is perched on the edge of the settee, sipping quickly from a coffee cup cradled in his hands, his lean body bent like a willow towards the carpet. He looks as if he hadn't slept or weeks.

"There we are," Jeff shuffles the forms together.

"Shore passes? Need them." The sunken eyes look up at him. "Immigration and Customs will be here in half an hour."

Jeff pulls them from the clip on the calendar and hands them to the Landing Agent.

There is a heavy clumping of many feet on the stairs and the Second Officer is standing in the doorway.

"Sorry to interrupt, sir. Drugs Squad, sir." he steps aside and two men move into the dayroom, both are wearing khaki combat uniform and black boots.

"Good morning," Jeff took the hand and flinched at the vice-like grip. Two small grey eyes blink from a round hostile face. The silky brown hair has been shaved to within a centimetre of its existence. Jeff's eyes slip down to the revolver resting in a leather holster on the right hip.

"Armando Salguero." The man turns away.

The other man is just as big and strong with a mop of thick, black hair, shiny black eyes and a neat moustache. He, too, has a revolver at his right hip.

"Good morning, Manuel Campaláns."

"Please sit down," Jeff waves his arm in an arc around the room. They choose chairs near the low settee.

Mr Salguero strokes his large, square hands down his shirt then runs them across the top of his shaved head. "How many crew?"

"Twenty two," Jeff pulls out a copy of the manifest.

Mr Salguero glances at his colleague. "Get the rest of the men on board." He turns to Jeff. "Eight of them. Waiting in that white mini-bus," he nods towards the starboard window. "They search crew quarters and Storeroom,. Check sacks of flour in Potato Storeroom. I search officers and passengers. How many?"

"Eight officers," Jeff goes back to his desk and fishes out the passenger manifest. "And three passengers. But they'll be in bed."

"We search." Mr Salguero's vicious little eyes fragmented the room.

"Pilot will be here for sailing at seven o'clock," the Landing Agent interrupts. "In one hour."

"No problem," Mr Salguero clears his throat and turns to Mr Campaláns. *"Vamos."*

The Second Officer and Mr Campaláns march out and scuttle down the stairs.

"I start here."

Jeff's eyes are on Mr Salguero's broad back as he wrenches the cushions from the armchair and throws them to the floor.

*****

Voices in the alleyway disturb Joy from a shallow sleep. It is a quarter to six. Dawn is breaking and Mother Nature has washed the cabin with a sunrise from across the swamps, the mountains and forests blending it effortlessly in a roseate tinge. She would like her bedroom decorated in this colour.

Outside on the docks, she can hear the occasional thump of a container landing badly,. A lorry revving away. She raises her head and glances at the other bed. Violet's face is shrouded by a sheet.

Joy doesn't want to sleep again. If she does she'll wake up with a headache. Breakfast right now would go down well but it's too early to go to the Galley. She can hear a mumble of voices then footsteps stop near the door. There is a crisp knock. Just one. Sharp and loud. She sits up, head to one side. There it is again. Definitely someone at the door.

She scrambles out of bed and shakes Vi. "Wake up."

Vi grunts then a scrawny hand with painted talons finds its way out. "What's the matter?"

"There's somebody at the door."

Vi turns on to her back. "Go and open it. Bet there's nobody there."

Joy grabs the cotton housecoat, twitches her arms into the sleeves and throws open the door.

It is the Second Officer clutching his walkie-talkie. At his side is a giant of a man, wearing khaki shirt and trousers. A soldier. He has a gun on a belt around his waist.

"Sorry to disturb you, Miss Galbraith." The Second Officer shuffles from one foot to the other. "Drugs Squad would like to search your cabin."

"Now!" Joy gasps.

Violet is floundering out of bed in a flurry of sheets.

"Please come in," Joy steps back.

Violet is reaching for her housecoat.

The Drugs Officer steps inside. The Second Officer remains in the alleyway watching through the open door.

Joy and Violet face each other in their cotton nightdresses and cotton housecoats with hair unbrushed, bodies unwashed. Their eyes told each other to keep calm, breathe deeply and answer any questions truthfully. They look like carnival figures on stilts.

Violet has not a suggestion of makeup on her face. "Wish we'd known you were coming," she ties the belt of her housecoat and sits on the settee.

Joy frowns. Oh, please Vi, please don't start an argument. Not now. Not with this man. We could be in deep trouble. Just shut up and sit still.

The officer goes to the bathroom. He drops something in the washbasin Something metal. The cabinet door is opened and closed. There is a swish of the shower curtains. Then Joy can see him with his head halfway down the loo.

He comes out and opens the wardrobe. It has double doors. One side is for clothes and the other side has a series of narrow shelves. On one shelf are hair brushes, combs and mirrors. Below is the shelf for make-up and suntan oils. Below that are the medications. Oil of cloves for toothache, lavender oil, body lotion. And then... Joy's heart leaps to her throat. If he opens the box... She keeps her eyes riveted on his massive back. It fills the entire space of the open doors.

From the corner of her eye she sees Vi's hand go to her forehead. Keep calm, Vi. Don't do anything and most of all keep your mouth shut. This frightening man with a gun pokes and probes and peers at everything. Now he has the box of Boots suppositories in his hand. Joy and Vi had sealed both ends of the box with a bit of sellotape. He is turning the box over and over. Then he scrutinises the instructions.

"These," he turns to face them. "What for?"

"Well, they're for..." Joy falters. "Well, we bring them... In case we need them."

"What for?" The man shakes the box. It rattles.

Joy's legs are melting. "When you get to our age you've got to keep things working."

"You swallow them?"

He turns the box over and then measures its weight in the palm of his hand.

"No! Oh, no!" Joy strokes the lapel of her housecoat. "They're for the other end. Toilet. You know…"

Violet jumps to her feet, turns her back on him and bends down. "Here…" and she peers round her elbow, pointing to her bum. "You push them up here."

He frowns, screwing up the beady black eyes. His thick lips curl. Then he tosses the box back on to the shelf.

A whisper of air escapes from Joy's lungs. She watches him rummaging on the next shelf. This is where they keep their camera, spare films and batteries for the cassette player.

The bottom shelf is much deeper. They stow their deck bags and gin and wine and brandy here. He reaches for the bags, peers in and pushes them back. Then he moves to the fridge. There is only a slice of pineapple and some long-life milk. Above the fridge is another cupboard stuffed with a blanket. He pulls it out. Teaspoons, cups, teapot and sugar basin crash down spraying sugar across the top of the fridge.

"At night everything rattles so we cushion it all with the blanket," Vi explains.

He stares at Violet, then Joy. It is a chilling stare from a mask-like face. Then he pulls out the long drawers under the beds and finds newspapers and a copy of *The Lady* magazine.

Hands on hips he surveys the cabin then he goes to the door. The Second Officer is still there, standing like a sentry.

"Next," he barks and they were gone.

Joy shoots across the cabin and locks the door. "Oh, my goodness me, I feel faint." She flops on to the settee holding her head. "Need a drink."

Vi dives into the bottom of the wardrobe and pulls out the brandy bottle.

"What's the time?"

"Half past six," Violet is pacing around the cabin clutching the brandy bottle. "That was a close one. It's obscene. Waking people up at this hour. Ransacking our cabin. I shall complain to the Captain."

"Don't you dare. He can do nothing about it. Remember we're under the jurisdiction of the Port Authority when we're alongside and there's nothing he," Joy moves towards her sister and pokes a finger into her skinny left shoulder. "nor you nor I can do about it. We're guests in their country. So just shut up."

"But that's never happened before, has it?" Violet is running her hands through tangled curls. "Not on any of our trips."

"No. And I hope it doesn't happen again," Joy put the glasses on the table. "But you know as well as I do, the Americans are pouring over a billion dollars into Colombia for anti-drug operations. Bet that uniform he was wearing comes with the compliments of Uncle Sam."

"He looked like an American Marine, didn't he." Violet sinks on to the edge of the bed. "But they'll never stop it. Drug smuggling."

"No. It's market forces. Supply and demand." Now it's Joy's turn to be restless. She wanders across the cabin sipping her brandy. "Up there, in the mountains they're laughing all the way to the nearest Bank."

"Just like prostitution." Violet grimaces as she gulps the brandy. "No demand, no sale. And we get back to that idiotic European Union - whatever they call it now. With the Schengen Treaty they took away all the border control to the European countries and bingo, the drugs come in by the lorry load, by the bus load, in your belly, in your bra. Any which way. North, south east and west. The smugglers have never had it so good. And those poor little children abducted for the sex trade. It doesn't bear thinking about...."

"I know, I know. Vi..." Joy tries to stop the flow. "Vi, I'm sorry but I can't take any of your European diatribe this morning. Not after what we've just gone through." Joy is shouting. "So, please,

please drop it. We've had a lucky escape… and we're not home yet." She leans into Vi's face. "*And…* did you notice what he did with the box?"

Vi stares into her brandy glass.

"*Did you?"* Joy is shouting again.

"Yes," she whispered.

"He shook it!" Joy walks away. "*Shook it*! You see, I was absolutely right but you argued me blue in the face that we should pad the box so that it didn't rattle. You gave me a terrible row over that." She gulps some brandy. "If it had been solid he would have opened it. So, no more arguments in future."

She is standing over Vi again, a pitiful sight, hunched on the edge of the bed. Vi hates to be proved wrong and she hates to be seen without make-up. She looks so old and withered and Joy feels sorry for her.

"Would you like to shower first?"

20

Linda is in her dressing gown in the kitchen feeling grotty. Since her mother's telephone call just over an hour ago she has drunk quite a lot of wine to stifle the frustration of having to listen to her rattling on about her dyed hair and all the gossip that thrives in a cocktail party when all she wanted was to clear the line for Michael to ring. Damn her. Now she doesn't know whether he's been trying while the line was engaged. Damn her. And she'll be here at the drop of a hat when Jeff gets home to complicate matters. No. No she won't complicate matters because she doesn't know that the complication is and that's the way it will stay.

She decides to make some herbal tea and puts the kettle on. Her eyes go to the bird clock. It is ten minutes to ten. The back door slams and a waft of cool air slips into the kitchen.

"Hello Tom, was it good?" His cheeks are flushed, his shirt is hanging out of his track suit bottoms and his hair is ruffled.

"Yea," He stares back at her with a look she recognised. It's his guilty look. "Are you hungry?"

"Not very." He throws off his puff jacket and it slithers to the floor.

"What would you like? Some milk? Biscuits?"

"Milk, please." Tom sits at the table, fiddling with a fifty pence coin.

"What have you been up to, Tom? I know that look." she puts the glass of milk in front of him. "Come on, tell me. Have you quarrelled with Jason?"

"Course I haven't," Tom drinks his milk quickly and ignores the biscuits. "Going to bed. 'Night," and he comes to Linda's side, puts his long, loose arms around her neck and kisses her cheek.

"Night, Tom. Love you." She pats his bottom and he is gone, thumping up the stairs, slamming the bathroom door. There's definitely something wrong. Perhaps the film has upset him but he isn't going to talk about it tonight.

She sips her tea slowly, thinking about Michael and wondering why he hasn't phoned. She is bitterly disappointed. Huh! Who was it that said hope predominates in every mind until it has been suppressed by disappointment ? She can't remember but she's given up hope of hearing from him tonight.

Well, she is definitely not going to Mass tomorrow. She'll wait until he makes contact. Gives her an explanation. And an apology. Alright, she knows he's at the beck and call of all the parishioners but he could have phoned.

It was Tracey who brought the news when she came for coffee the next morning.

"He didn't take Mass today. It was that tall streak of a man, grey hair. Can't remember his name. And he still has halitosis. Really somebody should tell him." She is twisting the silky black fringe hair into little spikes. "And that woman. You know which one. She's always inviting Michael round for drinks. The rich widow. Well-dressed. Causes a lot of friction with the committee members. They resent her giving drinks parties for the priests."

"Oh, yes. I know who you mean. Always flying off to some exotic place for a holiday."

"Yes, and she's in her eighties you know." Tracey's sleepy hazel eyes blink slowly.

"I didn't know that. Doesn't look it. More coffee?"

"You don't when you've got money. Yes, please. Jim and I were on a bender last night. I could drink the well dry. Anyway she says he's had an accident."

"An accident?" Linda drops the spoon.

"Well, *she* of the drinks parties says he fell off a step ladder in the kitchen,. And Mr Granger - you know the Maths teacher - says he's gone on holiday."

"So who do we believe?" Linda puts both elbows on the table, cupping her chin.

"Don't know. There's something funny going on. More to this than meets the eye," Tracey finishes her coffee.

Linda's eyes are on Tracey's shiny black fringe of hair framing her round, good-natured face. If he was going on holiday why hadn't he mentioned it to her? And if he had had an accident he could still have found a moment to give her a quick ring. Just to put her mind at rest. Instead all of this, all this anxiety and worry. "Tell me, Tracey, is Jason alright?"

"Yes," Tracey caresses her bulbous stomach with both hands. "Why do you ask?"

"Well, Tom seemed very strange when he came in last night. Not at all himself. I wondered if the film had upset him. It was that gruesome thing with hairy apes dressed as men or men dressed as apes. I couldn't get anything out of him."

"Jason said they had a good time. Film was OK. No, I can't say he seemed any different. Must go."

"Let me know if you hear anything.. About Michael. And I'll do the same."

"We shall just have to wait and see. But it'll make a big difference to Jason and Tom." Tracey scoops up the keys. "If Michael doesn't turn up soon it'll put paid to their swimming. He usually takes them on a Tuesday. And he's always giving them treats. Swimming, football, camping, pizza parties. Don't know how we're going to break it to them, do you?"

"No," Linda twists the rings on her finger. "No, I don't."

"Play it by ear. Let's wait for them to ask. What do you think?"

Tracey is shaking the bunch of keys.

That's the one thing about Tracey. She never worries about anything. No point. Save your energy for better things, she says. Maybe it's because she has given birth three times, diminishing worry each time. Maybe it's because she has a clear conscience, playing it straight with Jim, no deception, no lies. Linda stares directly at Tracey across the kitchen table and envies her for playing it straight. How did she get herself into this maelstrom, this whirlpool of confusion? She knows the answer but can't face the reality of it today.

"Really must go. Thanks for the coffee."

*****

It is Sunday afternoon. Tom and Jason are on the canal bank shooting water into the air to see how high it will go.

"We'll need our sleeping bags and some food." Tom is kneeling at the edge of the canal filling his water pistol. "My Mum keeps asking but I'm not telling her anything. It's 'cos I wasn't hungry." He squirts a cascade of water over the canal. "She didn't go to Mass this morning. Don't know why 'cos she always goes. And if she'd gone she might have said something. About us going swimming with Michael, I mean. He usually takes us on a Tuesday. Then we would know."

"My Mum went. Said it was a different priest today." Jason is digging a hole in the turf with his penknife. "So we don't know what's happened to him. Do we?"

"Perhaps it's his day off." Tom suggested.

"He doesn't get days off. That's what he told us." Jason cleans the penknife on his jeans. "Do you think he's dead?"

"Course, he isn't." Tom glances at Jason for reassurance.

"Well, we don't know. He might be. But if we hide there nobody will find us. We've done it before. Gone missing, I mean."

"Yea, but we've never stayed all night."

"Well, I'll tell my Mum I'm coming to stay with you. And you can tell your Mum you're coming to stay with me. Then they won't know where we are." Jason slips the penknife into his pocket.

"What time shall be meet?"

"After tea." Jason snatches at a handful of cow parsley growing in a thick clump at the edge of the water.

189

"OK," Tom is shuffling from one foot to another, hands in his pockets, a bit uncertain about everything. "Where?"

"At the Park. Near the lake. Half past five. They know we often go there."

Jason tosses the long green stalks with the white flowers into the canal. "OK. Let's go."

*****

Linda was in the kitchen washing a lettuce.

"I'm going to take my sleeping bag 'cos me and Jason like to sleep downstairs. In the conservatory. It's like camping and we're not in anybody's way." Tom is at the fridge. "Can I take these?" He held up two cans of Diet Pepsi.

"Of course, you can darling," Linda dries her hands. "Better take some crisps as well. And there's some Mars bars. I'll make some sandwiches. Just in case you get hungry. Then you can both have a midnight feast, can't you?"

"Cool, Mum, that's cool." Tom watches his mother take the sunflower spread and ham from the fridge.

"There we are," She packs the neat little packages into the Reebok bag then she stuffs the cans of drink in the side pockets. "Now just behave. No fights. No water pistols. OK."

"No Mum," he grapples with the straps of the backpack, kisses her cheek and is out of the door, slamming it loudly.

The streets are quiet and he is soon in the Park. He isn't supposed to cycle in the Park but there's only an old lady with a little black dog that looks like a cat so he just peddles right over to the lake. He props his bike against the thick evergreen hedge surrounding the lake and sits down to wait for Jason.

Over at Britannia Way Jason's Mum is suspicious.

"Are you sure Tom's Mum can do with you? She didn't say anything about this when I saw her this morning." Tracey is up to her elbows in flour mixing a sponge cake for a raffle prize. Jason watches her dollop the mess into two round tins and put them in the oven.

"Yea." Jason's chin is in the air, his eyes moving sideways to look at his Mum. "She says we can sleep in the summer house. That's why I'm taking my sleeping bag."

"Alright then, since you've got holiday from school tomorrow you can go. You'd better take these," and she pulls two tins of Lilt orange drink from the fridge. Then she reaches for four packets of crisps from the Jacob 's cracker tin.

"Great, thanks Mum." Jason stuffs them into his Adidas bag.

"There's some Maltesers in the bowl over there. And just you behave. No football in the garden." She sinks into the kitchen chair, wiping her forehead with a tissue.

"No Mum," he grabs the backpack and swings it across his shoulders banging it on the door frame.

"Put it on properly, Jason, you'll pull your shoulders." Tracey calls from the door.

"OK." And he pushes his way out to the garden shed to get his bike. "M'off. Bye."

"Thought you was never coming." Tom jumps to his feet.

"Got lots of things to eat." Jason stays astride his bike. "And chocolate."

"So have I," Tom gets on to his bike and together they speed along the broad path and through the open wrought iron gates. Soon they are wheeling their bikes along the footpath and across the narrow bridge towards the little barn in the corner of the field.

Tom pushes on the rickety door hanging off its hinges and they squeeze through with their bikes and prop them against the end wall.

"Look! Here's the rope we brought last time," Jason pulls it out of the manger. "From Dad's garage. He doesn't know I took it but nobody's pinched it."

"Nobody comes here. We'll try and fix it in the tree." Tom throws his sleeping bag into the manger. "I've told Mum that we're sleeping in your conservatory tonight."

"My Mum thinks we're sleeping in your summer house." Jason goes to the dirty window with the broken pane of glass and looks out over the ploughed field. Threads of green in straight lines stretch over the field for as far as they eye can see.

"Yea, it's brill. And nobody knows where we are," Tom is shuffling through the straw littering the floor of the barn.

"But we haven't got any video and I didn't bring my computer game, did you?" Jason climbs into the manger and swings on the hay rack above. It cracks and two slats come away in his hand.

"No," Tom is on his hands and knees exploring a hole in the corner under the manger. "Do you think there'll be rats?"

"No. If there is we can kill them. So what shall we do now?"

"Let's go to the canal." Tom is examining the broken hay rack. "Bring the rope, And the fags."

The sycamore tree stands sentinel at the bend in the canal. It had started life as a sapling in the hedgerow years ago and now has a thick trunk and sturdy branches spreading in all directions forming a dark green canopy high above the canal.

"We'll tie the rope in that branch up there," Jason points, "and then we can swing right across and land under that hedge on the opposite bank. OK?"

"My Mum keeps asking if anything's the matter but I'm not telling her anything." Tom is tying a knot in the rope.

"Me neither. That's not strong enough. Give it to me." Jason's square jaw is set rigid as he struggles with the rope.

"But she's not fussing so much 'cos my Dad will be home soon." Tom snatches the rope back from Jason. "Needs a double knot. To take our weight."

"They don't know," Jason watches Tom's nimble fingers twisting the rope.

"There we are," Tom tests the rope. "Don't know what?"

"What we did to Father Michael." Jason swivels his eyes to Tom without moving his head.

"Nobody knows. And we're not telling anybody are we? Not ever." Tom grabs Jason's wrist and raises it above his head. "Serves him right."

"I reckon it must have hurt him quite a bit. It was cruel." Jason hurls the rope and it gets caught in the branches.

"No, it wasn't cruel. No more cruel than what he did to us. Do you think he'll ask us round again?"

"If he does I'm not going. That's what we agreed, isn't it. After the flicks?" Jason is at Tom's side gazing up at the rope tangled in the branches above.

"Yea. I'm not going either. But he won't ask us. Not after what we did to him. He'll be scared. And I'll tell you something else."

"What?"

"He won't tell anyone 'cos he knows what he did was wrong."

"Yea."

"I'm going up." Tom is now scaling the broad trunk of the tree, his trainers gripping the bark. Then he reaches a fork in the branches.

"What if he tells the police." Jason calls up to Tom.

"He won't." Tom is sitting astride the branch, working his way along. "Cos he's always told us not to tell anyone. And I'm not going to Mass again. Whatever my Mum says."

"Neither am I," Jason watches as Tom loops the rope around the branch.

"My Mum and your Mum go 'cos they like him. It's somebody to talk to while our Dads are away." He secures the rope and swings on it, gripping with both hands as he slithers down to the canal bank. "That's why he visits our house and your house. 'Cos he knows our Dads are away."

"But the trouble is…" Jason scratches his thick, curly hair.

"What?"

"We won't get any more football and swimming and camping

and pizza and Coca-cola. Will we?"

"No. But the grandmas will give us treats 'cos they've got nobody of their own. We'll be alright. You'll see." Tom is blowing on his sore hands to cool them.

"But if we don't go to Mass we won't see them."

"Yes, we will. They're always at school. Looking for somebody to treat. 'Cos now they're old they haven't got anyone like I just said. And when by Dad gets home he says he'll take us camping and swimming. And when my Nan comes she always gives me treats. Now who's going first?"

Tom and Jason are yelling and yodelling and swinging on the rope, climbing the tree in turns but they just can't swing strongly enough to get right across the canal. They rest for a while on the bank

"It's getting dark. We'll try again tomorrow, come on," and Tom springs along the canal path. "Race you to the barn."

In the failing light the barn looks sinister lurking under the thick hedge in the corner of the field. They close the door and together heave the log against it.

With hands stained with bark and grass and mud they set about the sandwiches and crisps and chocolate.

"Glad we got the rope fixed." Tom is munching a Mars bar. "Tomorrow we'll land on the other side of the canal."

"Yea. Bet you fifty pence I'll be the first to swing across," Jason blows up the crisp bag and smashes it between his fists.

"Bet you fifty pence I shall." Tom is wriggling into his sleeping bag.

"Are you scared?" Jason is looking up at the bits of straw caught in the broken tiles. "About being here?"

"No. Nothing to be scared of." Tom's voice is confident. "Night."

*****

The next morning Linda and Tracey are in the lounge discussing

194

the mystery of Father Michael over their coffee. Linda is in the easy chair near the window, head thrown back, staring at a little black dent in the shape of a question mark on the ceiling. She doesn't know how it got there.

It was made by Tom. One afternoon when she had gone to Oxfam, Jason brought one of his father's golf clubs and they decided to practice golf swings with no balls from the oatmeal carpet. He is taller than Jason and the club hit the ceiling leaving the small mysterious indentation.

Tracey is sitting on the floor, her back resting against the settee. "He's being moved."

"*What!* You mean…leaving?"

"Yes," Tracey cradles the coffee mug with both hands.

"How do you know?"

"Sue phoned. Last night. I decided it was too late to ring you. Her cleaning lady, you know, Mrs Anstey - she told her. She cleans for Michael as well."

"But…but…" Linda reaches for her mug of coffee. "What about the accident?"

"Gossip. They thrive on it. It's their oxygen. Can't live without it. He's gone on holiday, so Mrs Anstey says, and she should know. Doesn't know who's taking his place." Tracey struggles to heave thirteen stones on to her small, neat feet. "One thing's for sure. We'll never get anyone as dishy as Michael, will we? It's worth going to Mass just to see him. That's why he gets such good congregations. Pandering to all those frustrated women with his gorgeous eyes and gorgeous smile."

She yanks her yellow cotton T-shirt down over her unharnessed breasts. "Can't understand why a good-looking man like that would choose to be celibate, can you? I mean, it isn't natural, is it? Just imagine having it off with *him*?" She snaps a digestive biscuit in half and pops it into her mouth, "and he was so good with the boys. They'll miss him."

"Yes," Linda edges out of the armchair. "Tom hasn't mentioned Michael. Has Jason?"

"No, not a word," Tracey takes her mug through to the kitchen. "And yet the whole world used to revolve around him and the next swimming session or football match. Nothing we can do about it."

Linda follows Tracey and puts her coffee mug on the draining board. It's true. There is nothing she can do about it. Michael going away. Gone away. Without so much as a farewell, a goodbye. A phone call. Nothing. *Damn him.* Going on holiday and he didn't even mention it. He must have known about it, planned it.

She goes to the fridge and pulls out a bottle of Jacob's Creek Chardonnay. "Need this." She reaches for two glasses from the dish washer.

Tracey raises the glass to the light. "Cheers. Heard from Jeff lately?"

"Phoned Friday night. Lousy line. Said he was on a dockside somewhere but it sounded more like a jazz festival on the M3. I told him I was worried about Tom but I don't know whether he heard me. Then the line went dead. I've tried to get him back but they've sailed. Sometimes, Trace, I wonder if its all worth it?"

"What?"

"Being married to a man who works on the other side of the world."

"But you had your chance to join him. To sail with him on those fantastic voyages. I would've jumped at it."

"Yes, but, but... But Michael Nolan had turned up, unannounced, unexpected, fixing the garage doors. That's why she hadn't jumped at it. "I have to be here for Tom." She winces at the falsehood. She, Jeff and Tom could have been anywhere in the world, altogether as a family.

They are sitting opposite each other at the kitchen table. Linda narrows her eyes and watches Tracey over the top of her wine glass. Tracey has no idea of her affair with Michael and that's what makes it so difficult now. She longs to tell her, confess, to get her opinion and just to chat about it as Tracey would with her down to earth approach to life. Dear Tracey. Chock full of common sense. Never gets in a spin about anything. It's amazing how cheerful she

196

can be when the whole world seems to be falling apart. But, of course, Tracey's world isn't falling apart. Her husband isn't on the other side of the world.

"Frankly, Linda, I don't know how you can survive for three months without your man. I couldn't." Tracey pushes her glass across the table for a refill. "I don't know what Jim gets up to on his south coast business trips but he always seems glad to get back to me. And I never ask questions. Best not to know. Cheers."

"Well, I can't imagine Jeff having much of a time out there on that ship. They carry few passengers, less than twelve. And they are old and boring, so he says. Always asking questions. Always complaining, And when they dock the ship's company are loading and unloading cargo, often working all night, so I have no qualms about what Jeff does in his spare time. He'll be sleeping." Linda went to the fridge and put the cheese on the table. "Help yourself. Ritz biscuits in that tin."

"Thanks." Tracey nibbles on a biscuit then empties her glass quickly. "Must go. Thanks for the booze. And the coffee. I hope Jason behaved himself last night."

"What do you mean?"

"Jason. Said he was staying here last night."

"What!" Linda jumps to her feet, knocks the table and spills her wine. "But...but Tom told me he was staying over with Jason. They were going to sleep in your conservatory."

"He said what?" Tracey flops back in the kitchen chair. "Oh, my God."

"Have you seen them this morning?"

"No. Haven't seen Jason since he left last night. Said he was coming here." Tracey is on her feet.

"Tom left here to come to you!" Linda covers her mouth with both hands. "So they're both missing!"

The bird clock sang eleven thirty.

"Blast that bloody thing. It drives me crazy. Who needs it at a time like this?" She scowls at the clock. "We must tell the Police."

"Keep calm, Linda, keep calm. They've probably both gone to

mine. And there's no school today. They'll turn up." She picks another biscuit from the tin. "Must go. Keep in touch."

Linda leans back in the chair staring at the bottle of Jacob's Creek then she refills her glass, pacing around the kitchen, tapping the shiny work top, pushing on drawers with her hip, touching the Kenwood mixer. Tom. He's missing and Jason is missing. Where are they? And Jeff. She must get hold of Jeff. He should be here. It isn't fair that she has to deal with this on her own.

She wishes Tracey hadn't left. She wants to talk to her, steal some of her confidence. Ask her what to do about phoning Jeff. Be reassured. That was it. Reassurance. To put her mind at ease about Jeff and Tom and Jason. She wanders from the kitchen to the lounge, sipping wine quickly. And oh! If only she could tell Tracey about Michael.

After two more glasses of wine she goes to the telephone in the hall and reaches for the address book. She is in front of the hall stand staring into the mirror. It would have to go. She has said so many times. It may mean another argument with Jeff but it must go. Sentimental value. She hates this hall stand.

The face staring back at her looks tired. Her hair is untidy. The turbulent thoughts swirling around have made her look like a worried old woman. She studies the reflection for a moment then takes one of Tom's baseball caps and hangs it over the mirror then she thumbs through the index to find the number of Drake Line's offices and punches in the number.

21

It is two days since the *Welland* sailed from Buenaventura and she is now approaching the Panama Canal, enjoying her last flirtation with the Pacific.

Jeff is on the Bridge staring at the grey satin coiling gently to the horizon, his stomach in turmoil, his head on fire. The phone call had come through yesterday. By satellite.

"Tom's missing," and a volley of words followed by Linda sobbing uncontrollably into the phone.

"What do you mean? Missing?"

Her voice was too highly pitched for him to understand what she was trying to tell him. "Please Linda, speak slowly. It's a bad line. Take it easy. Didn't he go to school?"

"No, it's a holiday. For local elections. Tom and Jason. They're both missing."

"Well, he probably slept at Jason's."

"Yes. I mean 'no'. He was supposed to. But he's not at Jason's."

"Did they say where they were going?" Jeff's eyes are fixed on the radar screen, full of orange fireflies.

"Yes, they said they were coming here…"

"Linda, I'm not understanding the situation very well. Have you told the Police? Hello, Linda. Are you there?" The line went dead.

"To hell with these bloody phones. Where's Bailey?"

Within seconds Bailey was at the Chartroom door.

"Yes, sir."

"I've lost the line to Southampton. What's going on?"

"It's the congestion. In the Canal Zone, sir. Not a cat in hell's chance till we get clear of this traffic. But I'll keep trying."

Jeff steps on to the wing of the Bridge, exasperated. Bailey is right. Not a cat in hell's chance of getting through for hours. He stares across the vast ocean but cannot find an answer to the questions seething in his head. Linda must be worried to have got the satellite connection from Head Office and Head Office must have been equally alarmed to get her request. And now, grasping the boat rail until his knuckles are white, he has no answers to his questions. Tom is missing. Linda is hysterical.

There's only one thing he can do. He must get home. That is his place. She is his wife and Tom is his son. And he is missing. He must be there. The responsibility is his alone.

He turns from the wide expanse of indifferent sea and looks aft along the Boat Deck. He can see a deck bag and sandals near the boat rail. Fiona is in her deck chair under No. 2 boat. He bites the bit of dry skin on his thumb. He will have to tell her that he's leaving the ship at the next port.

She will never know how much it costs him. And Linda will never know how much it means to him either. After waiting all these years, all these long years, to take command he is now handing it back so that he can be at home with his wife and find his son.

He paces the deck trying to untangle the responsibilities reeling around his head, little bunches pulling this way and that. He is Master of the *Welland*, answerable for twenty two crew members, three passengers, hundreds of thousands of pounds worth of ship and cargo, and he was going to sail into Southampton standing on the Bridge as Master for the first time. He has a wife, a son, a lover and control of a ship. The responsibilities stand like an immoveable mountain range. The divided loyalties overwhelm him.

Decision made he goes to the Radio Room.

The telex has gone and he's now waiting for confirmation that

Head Office accepts his request to be repatriated on compassionate grounds. They can't really refuse but they will have to send a relief Captain to take over at Cristóbal.

He gazes across the grey satin sea. The *Welland* is alone but soon ships would be converging on Balbao from all directions, like bees round a honey pot.

He hears footsteps and John Bailey hurries towards him waving a piece of paper.

"Just arrived, sir," he smiles his perpetual smile.. "Lovely morning, sir."

"Thank you." Jeff scans the text. "Confirm Relief Captain Hugh Barraclough will take command *Welland* for passage to Southampton. Agente Naviero arranging your flight Cristóbal/London.

So there it is. The telex flutters in his hand as he leans on the rail staring at the sea, consulting its vast expanse, waiting for some response. But it just rolls on and on, unconcerned about telex messages and domestic problems. The sea is co-operating, making headway, gently pushing the *Welland*, at ease with itself.

The deed is done. And he has just given up his coveted crown. A hot, black ball of resentment churns around his stomach. He may never be offered promotion again. Then, perhaps Management might not hold it against him. Perhaps Drake Lines officials would understand. Presumably they had wives. And young sons.

But he cannot think beyond the immediate scene. The finalising of documents, accounts, Log Book, everything must be ship-shape to hand over to Captain Barraclough. He's heard the name but has never met him. When Dolphin Line merged with Drake he had been slotted into Drake Line's sea-going hierarchy.

The balmy breeze caresses his cheeks comforting him in a moment of sympathy. Sympathy for his brief reign as Captain. Sympathy for his problem at home. Sympathy for Fiona. She will be upset. But it's less than three weeks before Southampton and they would meet again soon. Laugh again, Love again.

His voyage leaves were occupied with Linda and Tom and the maintenance of the house and garden. He always came back to a jungle to hack through but he found it therapeutic and rewarding to reclaim some order and see the new growth. It was easy to meet Fiona. Sometimes the car needed a garage for servicing or repair and he needed newspapers on a Sunday and he had his Master Mariners' meetings.

He feels no guilt about having a wife and a lover and cannot discern the boundary between the two women. Three lives inextricably playing out their roles on different planets.

The magic of the early years of marriage had faded with Linda's negative attitude about his career plans. The overseas postings that would have offered so many possibilities for them all, especially Tom. He was an adventurer. Each time she had reneged and never for a convincing reason. Caring for her has taken the place of loving her. Now he is deceiving her.

Fiona. Grieving for a much-loved husband. She puts such a positive gloss on everything. He's never seen her weepy or depressed and she thrives on every challenge that comes her way. There must be moments of utter despair in her life yet he's never heard her whinge or complain about her loss. What was it she had said? They had been in his dayroom. 'Once you stop trying to make things what they are not, you can enjoy them for what they are.' And she never mentions the future. Plans, hopes, desires are deeply buried. She just lives her life, day by day because she says 'nothing matters'.

Being with her is fun. No, it's more than that. He is comfortable with her, depends on her but can't quite reach, can't quite identify that abstract thing that makes him depend on her. Perhaps it's all those years of smiling, listening, helping her passengers that makes it seem so natural that she smiles and listens and cares for him.

He folds the telex and pushes it into his shirt pocket. A group of deck sailors are working in the fo'c'sle. Amidships he can see the men rigging the pilot ladder. He grasps the boat rail and his eyes sweep the ocean clean again. Several ships have emerged from the Canal, sloughing it off like a chrysalis, free now to ply the Pacific ocean, heading south with their cargoes.

He marches into the Chartroom. Decision made. He must confirm to Head Office that he will leave the ship at Cristóbal. And he must tell Fiona.

*****

The next morning a hazy humidity clamps the *Welland* to the Pacific Ocean as she waits at anchor. She is now surrounded by container ships, tankers, break-bulk cargo ships, many of them from the other side of the world. Korea, Japan, China, all waiting for the visit of a motor launch bringing the Pilot to manoeuvre them through the Panama Canal.

Over to the starboard side a city of skyscrapers shimmer white in the heat. Posh hotels on the waterfront laze in their opulence and every once in a while a jet airliner soars into the clear, blue sky, gleaming as if it had come through a wash of silver before escaping from this earthly muddle.

The day wears on and the sun slips away and Panama City becomes a jeweller's display case of twinkling lights in a dark blue velvet sky.

As last the Pilot boards and the engines murmur as she noses through the breakwater and under the Bridge of the Americas. It is flood-lit with traffic like Dinky toys scooting across in both directions.

Jeff is in the Chartroom. It hums with quiet efficiency, punctuated by the clock above the echo-sounder as it clicks away each minute. There is a faint drone from the electrical equipment and the radar silently sweeps its screen.

The Second Officer stands by the main console. The young helmsman chews on his bottom lip as he concentrates on the steering. The atmosphere is tense.

"Two nine seven"

The inter-com from the ship to shore crackles and Jeff can hear a female voice on the VHF.

"Three zero four"

"Who's that woman?" Jeff is standing at the side of the Pilot, a bulky dark-haired man wearing spectacles.

"She's a Pilot," he keeps his eyes straight ahead. "Four two zero.

203

And we've got three female tug Captains. They're very good but they don't like the gentlemanly courtesies to be observed."

"What do you mean?" In the dim light Jeff can see the Pilot's strong profile traced against the orange lights overhead as they ease towards the Miraflores Lock.

"One point eight five. Well, I held the door for her to pass and said 'Ladies first', which is what most men would have said, and she replied that there are no men or women in the ship - only seamen! So there! Dead Slow Ahead."

"I suppose she's right." Jeff wanders to the wing of the Bridge and raises his chin to the night air. No wind. That's good news and will make life easier through the Canal. Below the mules are lining up on either side of the lock. The rattling pageant of locomotives is about to begin. Clanging and hooting and whistling as the *Welland* yields to the invasion of the Panamanian team. They are like an army of beetles in their smart brown overalls and yellow hard hats, scrambling around the bows and stern, manning the ropes to the mules that travel along the tram lines, hauling the *Welland* towards the locks.

He goes back into the Chartroom. The Pilot is drinking coffee and chanting his mantra to steer the *Welland* safely through this nerve-wracking ordeal.

"Hard to starboard."

Jeff's eyes are on the lock gates as they gradually open but his mind is elsewhere. The Agent had said Cristóbal nine o'clock in the morning. Before Cristóbal he must see Fiona. He must tell her he is relinquishing his command. Leaving to go home to take responsibility for his wife and son who is missing. It will not be easy for either of them.

*****

It is well past midnight when the *Welland* clears the Pedro Miguel locks and steams slowly towards the Gaillard Cut. The three passengers are on the Radar Deck above the Bridge and, as instructed, they are all standing clear of an area marked with broad white lines to avoid interference with the radar signal.

"I think this is the most interesting part of the Canal, don't you?" Fiona is leaning on the rail, a glass of wine swaying in her left hand. They are all in party mood and so is a group of off-duty crew men standing on the other side of the deck. The night is balmy, the sky is black velvet.

The lights nestling under the trees at the water's edge shine brilliant turquoise and a myriad of red and green lights are flashing intermittently on the hillsides giving a carnival atmosphere to the self-conscious operation of guiding a vessel safely through a narrow canal in the jungle to link two mighty oceans.

"Have some more," Fiona reaches for the bottle at her feet.

"It used to be called the Culebra Cut before Monsieur Gaillard came to the rescue." Joy is under the bright deck lights leafing through a brochure. "It says they named it after him. Nine miles long, so it says. Thousands of men died during the construction. Fever, snake bites, exhaustion. Makes me ill to think about it."

Vi isn't listening. She is twirling around in a flowing kaftan, waving her arms about, sloshing wine cross the deck. "We should have brought some music. I want to dance."

She glances at the men clutching cans of beer, huddled against the boat rail gazing into the thick, dark jungle. No one responds.

She is now dancing in the forbidden area of the Radar Deck swooping her skirt around. Suddenly she stops. "Listen!" She went to the boat rail. "I can hear somebody talking."

"It's the Pilot," Fiona steps on to the bottom rung of the boat rail and peers down,. "And the Captain. They're on the wing of the Bridge."

"Pity about our new Captain, isn't it?" Vi is off again, twirling around.

"Yes, just when we're getting used to him." Joy stuffs the brochure into the pocket of her skirt. "And he deserves to be Captain…"

"What's happened to him?" Fiona raises her glass to her lips very slowly.

"Didn't you know?" Vi calls from the other side of the deck.

"He's leaving us." She is now demonstrating a perilously dangerous step. Her long legs jack-knife towards the deck and she grabs the boat rail just in time.

"Leaving!" Fiona's voice cracks.

Vi gives up on her fandango and joins Fiona and Joy at the rail. "Phew! I got puffed. Well, that's what he heard. When we went down to the Galley for a snack. Bert told us."

"Told you what?"

"That he's leaving. Disembarking at the next port."

Fiona's heart thumps in her chest until it echoes in her ears. Since leaving anchorage at Balbao she had not visited him. He'd explained that he would be on the Bridge all night for the transit.

"But…but why?"

"Flying home. Bert didn't know for sure. Thought it was to do with his wife…"

Fiona's hand went to her lips and then slid to her throat. Something is blocking it and she is struggling for air. "Well that's a pity, isn't it?" Her voice fades.

Turning away she gazes beyond the boat rail. They are passing a small white commemorative plaque placed half-way up the rock wall of the Gaillard Cut. It is flood-lit and honours the memory of the thousands and thousands of men who had died here. But it slips past her without registering. She must speak to Jeff. But, he's there. On the Bridge. With the Pilot. And they would be there until daybreak. But why hasn't he told her? The rest of the ship know. And nosey-parker Vi knows.

Blood is boiling up to her neck, burning her ears. She needs to get away. To breathe. To absorb this item of news. To think through its meaning. To try to understand what's going on.

"Must go to the loo. Excuse me." And clutching the glass she storms across the deck and makes her way down the narrow stairways to her cabin.

She slams the door and leans on it. Jeff leaving the ship. And he hasn't told her. Why hasn't he told her? She hurls the wine glass across the cabin. It hits the handle of the bathroom door and scatters across the floor in sparkling shards.

She marches to the bed, slapping her hands on her thighs. Then she walks to the bathroom door stepping over the broken glass and moves to the wash basin, leaning into the mirror. She is shocked to see how old and tired she looks. She had looked old and tired before but Paul had always been there to comfort her, relax her. Take away the oldness and the fatigue. He understood.

But, she argues, Jeff understands. Yet he couldn't tell her his plans. Leaving the ship! She runs her fingers over her cheeks, massaging gently. There would be an explanation. She would know and when he does explain, when he does tell her just what is going on she will know exactly what to do. The gentle massaging restores her colour, relaxes her face. The storm in her head quietens. Yes, she know exactly what she will do.

22

"Why didn't you tell me?" Fiona hurls the question at him as she marches across the dayroom and pauses at the window. She folds her arms and glares at the scene below. It is the usual bleeping and revving and clouds of dust. The quayside at Cristóbal looks much the same as all other quaysides the ship has visited.

She looks quickly over her shoulder. Jeff is at his desk shuffling papers together. Then he gets up and walks slowly towards her. That loose, swaggering walk she knows so well. His head is tilted back, his eyes full of pain.

She opens her arms and hugs him, feeling the strength, the energy, the vibrancy of his body. "How could you?" she whispers.

"I have no choice, my darling, I must go." His voice is low. "I've spoken to my wife. She's quite distraught. In fact, she was hysterical. Tom's missing. She thought he was sleeping at his pal's but he's missing as well."

"Missing!"

"Yes, but I'm sure they'll turn up. He and Jason go off on these adventures." He holds her head with both hands. "I must get back. I must find out what's going on. It might be…"

"Of course, I'm sorry I was so angry but why did I have to hear it from that… that interfering old busybody. She'd been gossiping with the crew. Why couldn't you have told me?"

"I know…I know…but I've been rushed off my feet." He paces the dayroom eyes fixed on the carpet. "I was waiting for the right moment and it never came. I'm a coward. I couldn't find the right moment. And with the Panama Canal - well, we all need two heads for that transit." He returns to her side. "Forgive me. I knew it would upset you. It upsets me. But this is the dilemma I'm in. Can you begin to imagine how much this has cost me? Can anybody? Confirmed Master of the *Welland*. Something I've dreamed of all my life. To have command of my own ship. To sail her into Southampton. And now...!" He touches her cheek. "I've abandoned my control. I have no choice. I have to go." He buries his face in her hair. "And I have to leave you here."

"I'm sorry to be so selfish." She breaks away. "Of course you must go." She wanders back to his desk. "When do you leave?"

"We're waiting for the relief Captain. He's due this afternoon then I fly out tomorrow."

"Do you have your ticket?" Fiona stares at the sea of papers on the desk.

"Yes, the Agent brought it with the official papers when we docked."

"Show it to me. So that I can convince myself it's true."

He pulls open the second drawer of the desk and passes a wallet to her. "Here it is."

She flips through the wallet and reads the flight number and time of departure. "But you're flying from Panama City!"

"That's right. Have to take a domestic flight from here to Panama and get my connection there."

"But there isn't a reservation from here to Panama."

"No need. Just turn up at the airport. It's a domestic flight. A bit like a bus service."

"So, it's true," she flaps the wallet across her hand and gives it back to him. "You've convinced me."

"But you'll soon be in Southampton. Just the Atlantic."

"And The Azores."

"Rough weather never bothers you, my love. It won't be long and then I'll be ringing you." He put the wallet back in the drawer.

"Yes," her voice is distant as she slides her fingers along the edge of the easy chair, flicking imaginary dust from the top of the television screen, moving the ash tray to the centre of the low table. She is fidgeting. And she is thinking. Then she is back at his side. "You're going to be busy handing over this afternoon so perhaps I'll take a walk ashore."

"It's dodgy here."

"Everywhere is dodgy," she leans across the desk and kisses his scar.

"People get mugged within five minutes of going down the gangway."

"I'll be alright. Need to stretch my legs. And I have the Agent's name and phone number. I always take it with me when I go ashore. Just in case."

"Alright. Tomorrow morning will be very busy so I think we should say our goodbyes tonight. We'll make it very special."

"Yes please. I'm not good at farewells."

"It isn't farewell. It's *hasta pronto*. Shall we say eight o'clock. By then I will have vacated this penthouse. Back where I started this voyage. In the cabin next to yours. Captain Barraclough isn't likely to want a night on the town after a transatlantic flight."

"OK. So I'll go and see what Cristóbal looks like. Or should I say Colón. They join up don't they?

"Yes. Cristóbal is the port, part of the city of Colón. But do be careful."

She changes into her blue linen dress and stuffs the dollar bills into her bra, then she puts her passport and shore pass in the beige handbag, loops it across her back and shoulders and hurries down the stairways.

A taxi slithers to a halt at the bottom of the gangway and a man carrying a briefcase gets out. Fiona jumps in and the taxi is soon in the main street. It isn't far and she could have walked it but she's not in the mood to run the gauntlet of the street vendors and pickpockets today.

Soon she is outside the glass doors of a modern office block. It towers into the sky, glinting in the sun. She checks the address again and steps into a spacious lobby with its black leather sofas and black and white marble floors.

One glance at the Directory on the wall tells her she wants the second floor. She ignores the shiny elevator and goes up the broad stairs and finds herself in another airy lobby.

She sees a woman sitting at a very tidy reception desk.

"*Buenas tardes*," She is young with the air of a model about her. Glossy black hair cut exquisitely in a Mary Quant style, makeup so natural it is hardly noticeable but for the exceptionally long black eyelashes.

She is wearing a tailored linen suit in eau-de-nil with a distinctive butterfly brooch pinned to the lapel. The butterfly is beige and cream enamel and looks as if it has just alighted. Fiona did not expect to find such sophistication in Cristóbal.

"May I see Señor Alvarez please?" Fiona returns the smile. "I'm sorry I don't have an appointment."

*****

Captain Hugh Barraclough arrives at the m.v *Welland* at half past six. He heaves himself out of the Agent's car, glances around the docks, sniffs and then plods up the gangway. Jeff is waiting for him.

"Welcome aboard. Good flight?" Jeff holds out his hand.

"As good as any transatlantic flight can be I suppose." He takes the hand. "Panama City gets more like New York every day. And then I had to get that noisy crate to bring me here…"

Jeff inspects the rugged, mottled face, the hoary eyebrows, the watery eyes. Captain Barraclough is in his mid-fifties, slightly overweight, in need of a shave and he doesn't appear to be in a very good mood.

"Right. Our men will take care of your baggage. Let's go." And he led the way along the alleyway, up the stairways and throws open the door of the Captain's dayroom.

"Christ Almighty. It looks like a bloody jungle!" Captain Barraclough peels off his jacket.

"'Fraid so. Captain Pycroft created it. As you know he left us at Guayaquil."

"So I believe. And now you're deserting!" Captain Barraclough ambles across the room to the window.

"Domestic problem that won't wait." Jeff scans the broad back. He is definitely overweight and his ruddy complexion ages him. An untidy wedge of a man, a bit crusty, a drinker perhaps.

"Rotten luck, old boy." He turns away from the window and strides across the room, hands behind his back. He pauses, puts his head to one side and asks, "Any chance of a drink?"

"Of course. Beer, gin, Scotch."

"Scotch and water." He smiles to show slightly prominent teeth.

"I'd better put you in the picture." Jeff sinks into an easy chair. "After discharging of this cargo the next port is Southampton and I foresee no difficulties.

Captain Barraclough sprawls on the settee.

"Eight officers, fourteen ratings. All good men. No problems. Drugs search in Buenaventura. Clean ship. No alcoholics. No personality problems. I'm sorry to be leaving. The *Welland's* a happy ship." He keeps his eyes on the rugged face. And you will never know just how sorry I am to be leaving. All I've ever wanted and here I am handing my ship over to you at the stroke of a pen, just one signature and she's yours. My long awaited command gone. Phut! "We have three passengers. Manifests are on a clip on your desk."

"How pesty are they?" Captain Barraclough empties his glass and holds it out.

"No problems. Two sisters in their seventies but you'd never believe it. Like their gin. And a youngish widow. Keeps herself to herself."

"Oh does she, by jove! Captain Barraclough's hands went to loosen his tie. "Is she shacked up?"

Jeff freezes momentarily as he uncaps the bottle of Johnny Walker. "Not to my knowledge." He takes the glass to the Captain. "You must be hungry. Can I order something for you?"

"No thank you. I ate all that plastic muck on the 'plane. Wish I hadn't."

"Well then would you like to go through the legals before touring the ship?"

"Good idea," Captain Barraclough tosses back his Scotch.

"Were you thinking of going ashore tonight, sir?" Jeff holds the door open. "We can arrange a taxi for you."

"No. I shall turn in early. What about you?"

"No. I must do my packing when we've finished the handover." Jeff leads the way up the fourteen stairs and pushes open the door of the Chartroom.

"Here we are," he goes to the open Log Book on the chart table. "Ready for inspection and signature. And then perhaps you'd like to check the Master's safe."

*****

Fiona got a taxi back to the ship, had a quick shower and made it in time for dinner. The Mess was deserted except for Joy and Violet.

"Did you go ashore?" she asks.

"No," Joy helps herself to more salad. "We stayed on board watching the loading from the Bridge Deck."

"Until it got too hot, then we came in." Vi takes the last piece of bread. "Did you enjoy yourself? Can't think what on earth you could find to do here."

"Oh, I had some business to attend to," Fiona smiles, "and there are one or two interesting shops. It was a very successful jaunt for me."

Vi looks at her without raising her head. "It's our last port, isn't it? Now we have that dreary Atlantic Ocean. Bet it gets rough again."

"It's always rough near The Azores," Fiona cuts a piece of Stilton cheese. "But it won't worry me."

The meal continues in silence and then Violet leans back in her

213

chair, delicately dabbing the scarlet lips with her serviette.

"Tell me," her eyes are fixed on Fiona. "doesn't your husband like sea voyages?"

"What makes you think I have a husband?" Fiona has waited for such an opportunity and she is ready. She is going to sink this woman, once and for all.

"Well…you wear a wedding ring. So…" Vi feels the force of Joy's foot under the table.

"My husband is dead." Fiona watches Vi's face unravel and solidify into a mask. Silence stalks the Mess Room. Someone in the Galley drops a metal pan.

Fiona continued. "Tell me about your husband, Vi. Does he like sea voyages? Or perhaps you've never had a husband. Never had anyone to love."

Joy had told her about Tony Muncaster one afternoon when they were having tea alone. It was a bit below the belt but she was in the right mood to shoot down this bigot, this dogmatic, self-opinionated, gin-sloshing old bitch who had argued her way to South America and back. Silence hovers around the Mess Room, creeping into every corner and cupboard but finding no hiding place. Joy splutters into her coffee cup. Vi puts down her knife and sits back in the chair, staring at the calendar on the wall with its little square marker that is moved on by Bert every morning. One day less, one day nearer home.

"Of course, not everyone is lucky enough to fall in love. It's a painful process, being in love. It calls for a lot of giving without counting the cost." Fiona is in full flow as she stirs her coffee. "Many people abandon it after one painful experience. But there's no limit to the number of times you can be in love."

Vi sits like a statue, motionless.

"I think it's important to go on giving and not to count the cost." Fiona picks up her coffee cup. From the corner of her eye she can see a figure in the doorway of the Galley. It's Bert. He wipes his face with his white apron, hitches up his trousers with his elbows and disappears.

"It's a very humanising and humbling process and should never be discounted." Fiona finishes her coffee, gets up and leans on the back of the chair.

Violet is now staring down at the plate littered with bread crusts that she has discarded.

Fiona turns to Joy. "Excuse me. I must go."

*****

"Did you really say that?" Jeff hauls his travel bag off the bed, brings it into the dayroom and dumps it near the door.

"Yes, I did," Fiona is pleased with herself. More pleased than she could ever explain to Jeff. The outburst has left her with a calm satisfaction, an achievement but she is at a loss to analyse what she may have achieved.

"Very brave of you,." He goes back into the bedroom and checks the wardrobe again.

"Nothing brave about it. I've been longing to say it all trip. I don't know how Joy puts up with her."

"Well, remember you've got to put up with her for the rest of the trip."

"No problem." She jumps to her feet and swirls around until she stands in front of the music centre.

"By the way, the new Captain has arrived. Captain Barraclough."

"What did you make of him?"

"An experienced mariner." Jeff stands at her side as she sorts through the cassettes and that question echoes through his mind again. 'Is she shacked up'. He dismisses the nervousness immediately. Fiona will be able to deal with him. "Likes his Scotch. But you shouldn't have a problem."

"I want some music. Choose for me."

"Alright. What mood are you in?"

"Love. I'm in the mood for love." She sings, waltzing around the room, "simply because you're near me…"

"Here we go," he presses the buttons then takes Fiona's glass. "I'm so glad you're happy. It lifts me too."

215

"But we'll soon be together again. In my little bolt hole near the Park. It seems a long time since we were there."

"Yes, but remember I do have this problem to sort out. That's why I'm having to leave like this. The sooner I get home the sooner it will be solved. And the sooner I'll see you again." He moves to the drinks cabinet. "This isn't an easy parting. Especially after the fiasco of…"

"Stop," she points a finger at him. "We're not going back over anything. Let's drink to mañana."

*****

Bert Dowse is in the Crew Mess Room, checking. Someone has left the large basin of sugar uncovered and intoxicated flies are crawling around drowsily. Somebody has not put the coffee jar back in the cupboard and someone has left the bread on the bread board instead of replacing it in the bread bin.

Everything has to be stowed and locked in port and the key hidden behind the fire extinguisher at the entrance to the Mess Room. If not, the Mess Rooms would be stripped clean overnight. Everything gone, including the tables. Bert has rectified the failings of his fellow crew members and is now slumped at a table sitting opposite Dinty Lees.

"I'm telling you. She done my work for me." Bert tops up his tankard from the bottle of beer.

"What d'ya mean?" Dinty leans back in his chair tracing the pattern of the blue plastic tablecloth with a bony finger. Round and round the pale blue circles and then round and round the dark blue ones.

The Mess is deserted and so is the Crew Recreation Room. Most of the crew have gone ashore for their last fling.

"She and the Blue Rinses were still at the table when I was clearing up in the Galley after dinner. 'eard their voices. Could tell Mrs Meredith were having a go. Like you know what I mean. Her voice were higher than usual. She were laying the law down." Bert screws up his eyes against the smoke from his cigarette. "So I went to the door and by Christ she were letting Lipstick Lulu have it. All

216

about love and being married and caring." He smashes the cigarette end into the tin ash tray. "Lipstick Lulu didn't know what to do. You know what a mess she makes at table, pulling all the crusts from the bread. Allus leaves a bloody mess to clear up."

"Go on," Dinty is grinning.

"Well, I can tell you, I were proud of her. Been wanting to do it all trip. And she done it. Come on Dinty. Fill 'em up and let's drink to Mrs Meredith."

"Cheers," Dinty's thin little mouth scissors across his face. "And here's another toast for you. Bert. Here's to our Chief Mate."

"You mean, our Captain. Crying shame he's leaving tomorrow." Bert crashes his tankard against Dinty's. "Lousy rotten luck just when he'd got command. But when you come to think about it there isn't nothing else he could have done, is there? I mean, if there's trouble at home you've got to be there to sort it." He wasn't at home when Jean had been mowed down by a drunken driver. When he did get home it was all too late. Jean was never there again. And Keith, their only son. Keith with such promise. A whiz on the adding up and gadgets. Keith went off the rails and got locked up, left him in a bleak landscape. Empty, lonely. No, he should have been home. He'd been too late. "You need to be there."

"Yea. But like I said, he should've been Captain long ago." Dinty takes a deep swig. "There's no comparison with that piss artist we left behind in Guayaquil."

"No. But betya he'll be back."

"Not so sure," Dinty takes a cigarette from his little tin. "Drake Line medicals are strict. Don't reckon we'll see him again."

"With a bit of luck the Chief Mate'll be back. In command as Captain of the *Welland*. How about that, eh?"

"Yea, but you can't fart against thunder and them at the top stay at the top." Dinty jumps up and does a little dance around the table, hand outstretched, scratching his bony finger in the palm of his other hand "That's what it's all about, Bert."

"Don't care a fuck. Chief Mate'll be back. When it's all sorted." Bert drains his tankard, reaches down to the crate at his feet, pulls out two more bottles and places them on the table. "To the Captain of the *Welland*. He must feel gutted today."

"'ere we go, 'ere we go, 'ere we go." Dinty swings his tankard in the air sloshing beer across the plastic table cloth as he dances round the chairs. "And what about our new Captain?"

"Don't worry. As long as there's a bottle of Scotch he'll be alright."

"You sailed with him then?"

"No but one of me mates has. Jacko, the Carpenter, told me about him. No sweat. Good navigator. Good Skipper." Bert lurches across the table. "Now, Dinty, what we going to do?" Are we going to the Big Bamboo or are we going to the Mission or are we going to stay here."

"We're going to stay here," Dinty reaches for more beer from the crate, "and you're not going to get maudlin about a letter from Keith, like you allus do. We're staying here and we're getting tanked up. Then we'll do the same when we get to Southampton.

23

Linda puts the phone down, glowering at it, blaming it for what she has just done. She had phoned Jeff. In a panic. Perhaps she should've waited a little longer Tracey said so. But she was at her wit's end. Tom missing. Jason missing. Michael missing. Yes, she should have listened to Tracey who always made sense. Too late now.

The Personnel Manager at Drake Line had given her the satellite number of the *Welland* and she had got through quickly, pouring out her panic, her fears, in to a phone held by her husband thousands of miles away. She had told him that Tom was missing. She had told him that she was worried. She had told him that she wishes he were here. All of it true. But he's on the other side of the world and she should be able to cope with things while he's away.

If Michael had been here none of this would have happened. She wouldn't have needed to do anything, say any of these things to worry Jeff. Michael would have known what to do about Tom and Jason.

She wanders into the lounge. Her eyes go to the newspapers on the low octagonal table near the window then she glances at the carriage clock on the mantelpiece but nothing registers, not even the time. Everything in the lounge is strange. Nothing seems familiar. Terror strikes through her, scraping her nerves, gripping her stomach.

She edges round the back of the settee. Michael. It was all his fault. He's gone on holiday and hasn't had the courtesy to even mention it to her. He just doesn't care.

She circles the settee again but the lounge is not helping her. She is out of sync. With everything. She needs to talk to someone. Tracey. She'll give Tracey a ring.

"Thank goodness you're there, Trace. My head spins and I don't know which way to turn."

"What's the matter?"

"After you'd gone I rang the office. They gave me the number of the ship and I got through to Jeff. I've spoken to him."

"That's fantastic!" Tracey's voice is muffled. Linda can tell she is eating something.

"No, Trace, it's not fantastic. I should never have phoned him. They were about to transit the Panama Canal, of all places. He's told me that they all need two heads going through the Canal. I flipped. And he's going to be worried sick now and it's another couple of weeks before he's here. I shouldn't have told him Tom is missing.

"Don't worry."

"How can you say 'don't worry', Trace." Linda bites the nail on her little finger. "Where's Tom and where's Jason? Where are they?"

"Tell you what, Linda, why don't you come over here. We'll have some lunch together." Tracey is speaking slowly, carefully, "and we'll talk about it."

"OK. I'll leave a message on the kitchen table to say where I am. Just in case." Linda stares at Tom's baseball cap draped over the mirror. "I think we should tell the police."

"Stop worrying. If they're not back by late afternoon we'll have to."

Dear Trace. Takes everything in her stride. Worry is not a problem if you have a clear conscience. She chokes into a tissue and rushes to the bathroom.

*****

The barn is gloomy and cold in the dawn light. The two sleeping bags on the floor look like sacks of potatoes, then they move.

Tom is emerging like a chrysalis. "I heard something in the night, did you?"

"No. Why didn't you tell me?" Jason uncurls himself and sits up.

"Cos you were asleep."

"I got a bit cold. Round my head. What's time?"

"Don't know." Tom slews off his sleeping bag and peers out of the broken window at the open field rolling across to a hedge in the distance. "It's daytime. Smells funny in here."

"Well, it's cos nobody lives here. Properly. That's why it smells funny. It's just for cows and bulls. What shall we do today?"

"Let's go fishing. I've got the reel of black cotton and you brought the hooks, didn't you?"

"Yea," Jason jumps into the manger and swings on the hayrack. Another slat cracks off in his hands. "This wood's rotten. We haven 't got any worms. There's none in the canal bank 'cos I dug with my penknife."

"We'll use some bread. From the sandwiches." Tom is measuring out the cotton. "Let's have a drink and a Mars bar now and then we'll have a proper breakfast when we've caught the fish."

"Yea, we'll make a camp fire with that rotten wood. And the straw. And we can cook the fish for breakfast."

"Brill," Tom rummages into his bag and pulls out two cans of Lilt. "And after breakfast we'll go to our tree and swing over top the other side. Betya I'm first."

*****

Linda returned to Coleridge Avenue at four o'clock after a very liquid lunch. Tracey had convinced her that they should allow more time before contacting the police.

"Ring as soon as anything happens. OK." Tracey fills the doorway with her comfortable, lumpy body.

"Will do. Thanks for the TLC, Trace. Won't forget it."

When she opens the kitchen door she sees the scribbled message under the brown coffee mug on the table. It has not been touched.

"Tom. Jason. Are you here?" She calls as she goes from room to room. The silence mocks her. "Stupid, of course they're not here. Don't be such a fool." But in spite of Tracey's soothing presence, good lunch and bottle of Jacob's Creek Linda is still uptight, devouring the negatives. Tom. Anything could have happened to those boys. Terrible things happen. We see it on television news.

Back in the kitchen she pours herself a glass of wine and sits staring at it. What is she going to do about the quagmire she finds herself in? All of her own making. Michael, where is he? But Jeff will be here soon. It will be so good to see him.

The phone rings and she knocks over the glass spilling wine across the table as she dashes through to the hall. She snatches the phone from its cradle.

"Mrs Bloxham?" it is a man with a deep voice.

"Yes."

"Good afternoon. John Meekin. Personnel, Drake Line. We spoke the other day."

"Oh, yes."

"You needed the phone number to call your husband on the *Welland* remember? Well, we've had a telex message. The ship is at Cristóbal. Arrangements have been made for your husband to fly home and I just wanted to confirm that he will be arriving London Heathrow on Wednesday. Eleven thirty in the morning."

"That's the day after tomorrow." Linda holds her throat.

"He's on Flight No. AV 213."

Linda grabs the coat hook on the hall stand. "Oh…oh… Yes, yes, thank you. Say again please. Let me write it down."

"Flight No. AV 213 Wednesday 16th April arriving eleven thirty in the morning. Do you need any help to Heathrow?"

"Yes - er -no. Thank you very much Mr Meekin. That's fine."

Linda hears the phone cut and replaces the handset. Jeff leaving the ship! Flying home. The day after tomorrow. She must tell

Tracey. Straight away.

She picks up the phone again but before she can mark the number she hears the back door slam. She replaces the phone and goes to the kitchen. A bedraggled figure is standing near the door.

"TOM!"

"Hello Mum," he keeps his eyes on the floor, the Reebok bag dangling from his left hand.

"Tom, oh! Tom what happened?" She folds him into her arms and sobs into his filthy, slimy hair. "You're wet through. What on earth... Come here..."

She puts her arms around him again and the putrid smell of rotting vegetation gags in her throat. "Where have you been darling Tom? What happened?"

"Fell into the canal." Tom shifts from one wet trainer to the other, his eyes still glued to the floor.

"Jason. Where's Jason."

"Gone home. He fell into the canal as well."

24

The *Welland* left berth at Cristóbal at 1900 hours and was soon nosing past the flotilla of ships at anchor. There were large container ships, bulk carriers, tankers, glossy white refrigerated ships, all waiting to squeeze through the locks of the Panama Canal to the Pacific Ocean beyond.

Cristóbal is the last port before the long haul northwards. After sailing through the Mona Straits and leaving the Caribbean the escort of flying fish will abandon the *Welland* leaving her to the whims of the Atlantic Ocean getting moody and morose as she approaches The Azores.

Captain Barraclough is pounding the wheelhouse, pausing every now and again to take a quick look at the narrow exit to the breakwater and the fountain of water cascading over the rocks on either side. Those are dangerous rocks and that is a menacing sea out there to create such fury of spume and spray. The *Welland* must hold her course on low speed.

The Pilot is sitting in his chair, smoking a cheroot, seemingly without a care in the world. Of course, this Pilot can get a ship out of this breakwater blindfold. He's been doing it for years but Captain Barraclough can't relax until they are clear and the Pilot has gone.

Down below in the Mess Room Joy and Violet are having dinner.

"It's strange she didn't say she was disembarking." Violet prods the slice of beef.

"I'm not surprised at anything." Joy peels the cling film off the salad bowl and serves herself. "Not after your despicable behaviour…"

"Just what do you mean by that?" Vi puts down her knife and fork and clasps her hands in her lap.

"You know exactly what I mean, Vi, and if you don't I'll spell it out again. You had no business asking about her husband. And it serves you right that she dished it up to you in the way she did."

"Well, she's been a mystery from the start…"

"No she hasn't," Joy screws the cap on the salad dressing. "It's all quite clear to me. She's been widowed recently and sought the peace and calm of a cargo ship to help her get back on the rails again. Nothing mysterious about that."

"Well then, why has she left the ship? In this godforsaken port? What's she going to do, for heaven's sake? And why didn't she tell us? Didn't even say goodbye."

"Leave it alone," Joy takes a piece of bread. "She said yesterday that she had business to do. It could mean anything. Probably got friends or relatives here."

"Well, I get back to my original theory," Vi pushes her late away.

"Oh, and what was that?"

"That she's probably a prostitute…"

"Really, Vi, you're insufferable." Joy crumples up her serviette, tosses it on to the plate and gets up. "Excuse me, this is our last port. I'm going to watch the Pilot disembark."

The Pilot picks up his black bag and slings it over his shoulder then he shakes hands with Captain Barraclough and follows the Third Officer down the companion ways to the weather deck.

The launch is bobbing about like a cork in the strong cross currents so he waits for his chance before stepping off the ladder with expert timing. The launch coughs and splutters and zooms away into the dusky evening.

Captain Barraclough watches from the wing of the Bridge. Last

Pilot until Southampton. Now he can settle down to the Atlantic haul. Too early for weather forecasts around The Azores but they will come thick and fast.

He sinks into the Captain's chair, puts his foot on the rail and takes the mug of coffee offered by the Third Officer. He should get that pony tail cut off. Bloody ridiculous. An officer in the British Merchant Navy with a pony tail but he is powerless to order him to do so. Masters these days are master of very little in spite of the fact that they have to be Chief Stewards, Chief Pursers and Crew Pursers. Soon they wouldn't be needed at all. Ships will be sailing on remote control with not a human being to be found on the Bridge. He shivers involuntarily as he gazes at the horizon. To the west the sun is in its dying throes, reluctant to go, transforming the sky and tingeing the sea with molten gold.

Bloxham has buggered off to get back to is wife on some pretence or other. Those Galbraith sisters are a pain in the arse. Mrs. Meredith's visit at eight o'clock this morning had taken him by surprise and put him in very bad humour. Her timing had been faultless.

"Good morning Captain Barraclough."

There she stood in the doorway.

"I would like to leave the ship today." She smiled at him.

"Come in, sit down." He watched as she lowered herself into the chair at the side of his desk.

"But…but that's not possible. We're sailing today… and there are procedures. It all has to be arranged. Documented."

"Yes, I know. I visited the Agent's Office yesterday," she smiled at him again.

He leaned back in the chair studying the impudent face. "Why do you have to leave?"

"I have to go. I telephoned home and there are urgent matters that can't wait." She is fidgetting with the clasp on her handbag. Well, she knows they can wait. Like last year, after her trip on the *Witham*, she soon got back to her shore life, meeting and interacting with sociable and polite people and besides she didn't want to be here without Jeff, which is why she came. "The Agent has arranged my flight and I have my ticket."

"Oh, have you," he turned to the papers on his desk. "What about your baggage? And Customs and Immigration?"

"They cleared me last night." There was that smile again. "And the taxi will be here at ten thirty."

He half-turned, gripping the arm of his swivel chair trying to control his mounting anger at this flibbertigibbet sitting there telling him she was disembarking, now, today. "How can you get everything organised without my permission or knowledge? I am the Master."

"Well - er - yes, I know. I went to see Señor Alvarez, the Landing Agent, yesterday afternoon. He assured me that everything was in order. Then I came to see you last night to confirm but your door was closed and if the Captain's door is closed it means that he's not available and must not be disturbed, doesn't it?"

Of course, she's right. Clearly she knows the ship's routine. But it's a bloody nuisance. The manifest will have to be amended. All the records will have to be altered. The Log Book. But he cannot stop her. She's got it all buttoned up. "Does Captain Bloxham know you're disembarking?"

"No." Fiona sank back into the chair. "I didn't decide until after I'd made the phone calls ashore. Your door was closed and so was his, so I had to wait until now." She cleared her throat to swallow the deception. "There's just the matter of my safe deposit," her eyes went to his bedroom. Jeff's bedroom where they had spent so many hours. "I've paid the landing fees to Señor Alvarez."

"Good." Captain Barraclough heaves his body out of the chair and goes into his bedroom returning with the brown envelope.

"Would you like to check it?" He stood by her side.

She turned the package over. The signature and seal were intact. "I'm sure that won't be necessary." She met his eyes, smiled again and was gone.

He feels some disappointment. She would have relieved the boredom very nicely until Southampton. It's not often a cargo ship passenger is bedworthy.

He clutches his mug of coffee and watches the band of gold on the horizon sink into a small red button and then it, too disappears. Bloody shame. He puts his mug on the tray.

"I'll be in my dayroom," he speaks to no one in particular and clomps down the fourteen stairs.

Joy doesn't watch the Pilot disembark. She hurries to the cabin, cleans her teeth and reaches for her makeup bag. She doesn't want to dolly up too much, a fatal mistake at her age but she does want to look her best. A touch of rouge, just a blemish, a swish of grey eye shadow, everything looking natural.

She's so glad he's invited her. At last, after all those waves on deck when coming back from jaunts ashore. The cheery call from the bowels of the holds when supervising the loading of cargo. The mid-morning coffee during crew breaks.

"You didn't come for coffee." Violet sniffs, screws the top on the bottle of nail polish and tosses it into the drawer.

"The deck sailors invited me to their cabin and I had coffee with them. So interesting to hear their tales. They just live and die for the sea. I can understand it, in a way."

Joy has accepted several invitations to morning coffee and afternoon tea during crew breaks that Vi knows nothing about. But there had been no more inquisitions. She would never approve. Besides, it's none of her business.

Now it's nearly eight o'clock, the *Welland* and all its crew are homeward bound, there's an excitement about the ship and she is glamming up. Not for tea or coffee. It's an evening rendez-vous.

She steps away from the mirror, satisfied with what she sees, then she reaches in the bottom of the cupboard for a bottle of gin, stuffs it into her red straw bag and makes her way down the stairs, walking along the corridor, checking the names on the doors.

She passes the Laundry Room, the 2nd Engineer's cabin, the Engine Room Casing, the Chief Engineer's Dayroom, the cleaning Stores and then she stops in front of the next one and taps lightly.

The door opens and he steps back, smiles and signals for her to come in. The cabin seems bigger than she remembered but then it had been full of crew members. A spotless white cloth has been placed on the low table, set with dishes of nuts, olives, gherkins.

The long settee with its back to the bulkhead is draped in a colourful Peruvian blanket. Latin American music is playing softly from a music centre on the floor near the wardrobe. It is a haunting tango but she can't remember the title.

The atmosphere is relaxed, all lights have been suffused and give the cabin a mellow glow. He looks so sharp in his Levi jeans and a crisp pale blue shirt. He is wearing moccasins like the ones she bought in Manta. Hand-made in the softest leather. He seems taller tonight. Perhaps it's the smart clothes. And he is more handsome, his body flexible in its casual unhurried behaviour. Once again she notices the frisson of their first encounter when she saw him hauling ropes against a ferocious wind.

"Hello," she pulls the bottle of gin from the red straw bag and hands it to him. "You're off duty at last."

"And homeward bound," his gaunt, intense face seems younger in the soft lights. "Take a seat. What do you prefer? Gin or there's brandy, Scotch, wine…"

She sinks into the settee and looks around the cabin again. They could have been anywhere in the world but here they are, in a small cargo ship laden with coffee beans and fish meal, pushing its way through the Atlantic Ocean. Homeward bound.

"Gin please."

The Bo'sun reaches for two glasses.

25

The taxi speeds across the streets of Colón and is soon at the airport. An unpretentious huddle of buildings set in a vast expanse of wasteland. Jeff presents his passport and ticket to the young man wearing horn-rimmed spectacles. He flicks through the passport, raises his eyebrows and hands it back without looking up.

The small departure lounge is hot and crowded. Glancing around he decides the passengers for Panama are mainly business men, smoking, reading papers and drinking coffee. Two family groups sit on bright red chairs on the other side of the lounge. Children squeal and shout as they bounce off the bags and bundles, climbing on the back of chairs and swinging on the segregation ropes, pulling over the shiny chrome anchors.

A man in blue overalls is sweeping bits of paper, husks of nuts and chocolate wrappers into a dust pan on a long shaft. Two women are cleaning the huge windows. Jeff wanders to the far end of the row and sits down.

Outside he can see small aircraft resting on runways, like sleepy moths. Beyond the runway he can see the ocean. Already he is yearning for the sea. The clear, crystal air, the calm lazy days in the Pacific and its rolling grey satin, then the great white crests of water that rise and disappear until the Caribbean looks like dark blue satin. The ferocious gale force winds that come from nowhere to torment and tease the waves of confused swell pounding the noble little *Welland*. He closes his eyes and feels the wind and rain lashing his cheeks to ribbons.

Then he is on the wing of the Bridge gazing at the sea, that mysterious dead water that doesn't move, doesn't co-operate, refuses to accept a ship and leaves it impotent in a potent universe. He feels all these things as he sits, marooned, in this little departure lounge, missing the sea, missing the *Welland*, missing the power, the achievement of being Master, missing Fiona…concerned about Linda and Tom…

Holding the strap of his bag resting between his feet he gazes at the dull brown carpet. The image of Linda emerges. Well, soon he'd be home. Soon he'd know what was going on. He doesn't believe Tom is missing. Not in a sinister way. He and Jason would have gone off camping somewhere. He had done the same when he had been their age. But today is different. The world has moved on to unthinkable crimes and the horror strikes him. Perhaps Tom has been abducted. He pushes the idea to the back of his mind. The television and newspapers are full of such reports. He moves his thoughts quickly. To the handover yesterday.

The Chartroom. The open Log Book and he sees Captain Barraclough watching him sign away the promotion that he'd waited for so many long years. The cost of that signature in the Log Book is exorbitant but he knows he's done the right thing, giving up his command, flying home.

He looks around for reassurance. There is none. The parents sip their coffee while the children continue to bounce off the walls, the chairs and chase each other in circles. His eyes go to the stark, cream walls. There is not a poster nor a picture to trigger the imagination of a waiting passenger but the image of Fiona materialises. Last night, just hours go, in his night cabin she had been remarkably elated about the parting but then she never whinged or whined about anything. Took it all on the chin. Like losing Paul.

'Is she shacked up?' Captain Barraclough's question troubles him. He's decided that he was not a very agreeable person. Too cynical. Drank too much. But Fiona will know how to handle him, and she wouldn't have to tolerate this rather gauche man for long.

A female voice spurts an announcement in Spanish. It rattles like a machine gun along the walls of the lounge and people begin to round up the children and scramble for bags. They move across the lounge towards the boarding gate. He watches them. No point in joining the queue. He'd wait until they have all gone through.

"Hello," a voice rang out.

Turning he sees a tall woman in a cream linen suit and high-heeled shoes striding across the lounge towards him.

"*Fiona*"

She drops her Samsonite bag then he sees that she is clutching her passport and boarding pass.

"Yes, it's me. Flying home. With you."

He grabs his head with both hands. "But…but…what on earth?"

"But nothing, my love." She links her hand into his arm. "What's your seat number? Come on. They're boarding now."

Flight AV.213 from Panama City to London Heathrow is full to capacity, hot and noisy. Mothers placating restless children, business men browsing through briefcases and papers, younger men twitching their long legs nervously, confident young women touching up their lipstick, well-preserved older women with no such qualms, all settling to their long transatlantic flight.

Jeff and Fiona are in seats amidships close to two silent nuns. He had not been in the mood for conversation on the short flight from Colón and he has little to say to her now. In fact, he doesn't know what to say to her. This woman has become a stranger. His anger has subsided and he's too tired for an argument. A transatlantic flight is not the place to tell her that she really is out of order to follow him. But it's too late. Here she is, at his side fidgetting with her handbag.

How on earth did she engineer her disembarkation from the *Welland* with apparent ease and at such short notice? There would have been Immigration, Customs clearance, the Landing Agent, fees, the flight and payment for the ticket but then he reminds himself that she has been dealing with officials for years when flying. She would known exactly what to do.

A huge black cloud clamps him into his seat. A cloud of grudge, of disbelief, of resentment. His whole world has been turned upside down since that phone call. His son missing, his wife hysterical and he's signed away his promotion. And he's left the *Welland*. He needs to set things apart, arrange them with gaps in between so that he can get to grips with it all. Alone. Nothing she says or does can help him or Linda or Tom. This is *his* problem and has nothing to do with Fiona.

Doesn't she understand just what all this means to him? No, she doesn't understand. Linda doesn't understand. Nobody understands. Only he understands what it is to set your sights on an aim, a goal, an achievement and work towards it until you succeed. Most people just drift from one day to another, one week to another, year by year, untouched by ambition or desire or success, quite content with their lot. Always intending to do something. Members of the Going To Brigade.

His thoughts drift back to the *Witham* last year when she had approached him on the quayside at Mahé. That's where it all began. She had enticed him into her space and he had willingly become part of it and now here he is, lacking his own space, lacking his freedom to assert his identity. He is shocked that she is here when his one aim is to get back to his wife and find his son. He doesn't know how to deal with this inner conflict.

Dinner had been served, that plastic 'muck' as Captain Barraclough called it, and he had not been in the mood for in-flight movies or music. In fact, he was not in the mood for anything. He just wanted to sip his Scotch and soda, mellowing with the steady drone of the engines, the constant hum of muted conversations, the occasional squeal of a child, the bustling of the flight attendants and accept the unruffled release of the tension in Colón airport. Her arrival had frozen part of his being. Why hadn't he been pleased to see her? And what was he going to do at Heathrow?

Drake Line are very good on public relations and Linda would be there to meet him. He orders another Scotch and closes his eyes.

*****

Fiona would have preferred two seats on the skin of the plane instead of this row in the middle but there is nothing she can do about Avianca's seating plan. She has kicked off her shoes and slipped on cotton socks, looked through the brochures, read the

233

safety leaflet, the duty free booklet and she has declined the food.

She feels uncomfortable and isolated and sad, yes, sad. She wishes Jeff would say something to her, chat, talk, plan. Plan! How many times has she told herself that she can plan nothing. Neither can Jeff. After all, she's always expounding her theory that 'nothing matters' so why should Jeff be expected to make plans. They have never even discussed 'plans'. But she wants to connect with him, feel real again, human again. She needs him to pull her out of this isolation. To repair the rupture.

She glances sideways. His eyes are closed. Perhaps he's asleep. His hands are clasped across his lap, his long legs spread-eagled. Of course, he's tired, exhausted, worried. What a fool she is to have left the ship. She stares beyond at the carpet of clouds. Fluffy, weightless, useless. She should have stayed on board for the rest of the voyage instead of this irrational chase to the airport.

Why didn't she stop to think, understand that he needed to get home as soon as possible, alone and here she is just a passenger like everyone else on this hot and stuffy plane.

Her thoughts roam on, willy-nilly, tumbling and turning until she feels quite sick. Soon it will be Heathrow then she has to get to Southampton and when she gets home all she can do is resume that unpredictable sequence of events that she had set up after Paul, after…

When she went ashore in Cristóbal she tried to call Joanne but there was no reply so her sister doesn't know that she will be home sooner than expected. Fiona will walk into her flat, cold and empty, and there will be no provisions because Joanne doesn't know and there will be no fresh flowers because Joanne doesn't know. Oh! What a fool she was to have acted so impulsively. Too late now.

She must have dozed because the engine vibration has changed. They are descending to land. She looks at Jeff, his head back, yawning silently.

"Is someone meeting you?"

"No," she reaches for her handbag. "I couldn't get through to Joanne so she doesn't know that I am home sooner than expected."

There is a moment's silence.

Jeff ruffles his hair with both hands. "I'm sure Linda will be meeting me. So I could introduce you."

"Is that wise?"

"No. We are in uncharted territory Fiona, and I have no map."

"Well in that case, why don't we go our separate ways after collecting baggage."

"OK and I'll give you a ring when I have sorted my problem.

26

"Yes, Tom, I've already explained," Linda grips his hand. "Dad has left the ship."

"Why has he left the ship?" Tom trips over a sports bag.

"To come home. To be with us."

"Will he be Captain when he gets home?"

"Don't know. Come along."

They trail across the acres of polished floors in Heathrow Airport towards the Arrivals Hall.

"We have to wait here," Linda positions herself behind the first layer of people waiting at the thick rope barrier. He'll come through that opening there. Do you see where I mean?" She points.

"Near that policeman?" Tom peers round the side of a big man in a grey suit wearing a black turban.

"Yes. There'll be a lot of other people as well so you have to watch carefully."

The Arrivals Hall is ringing with announcements and quick squirts of music. Passengers, old and young, grey with fatigue, stream through the exit, struggling with holdalls slipping from their shoulders, trailing weary children, hugging sleepy babies as they push their luggage trolleys, scanning the sea of faces.

Sometimes they are six abreast coming through the opening, sometimes one weary, lonely person wanders past them, eyes down, clearly not expecting to be met. Jeff is tall and blond and he will be alone. She cannot possibly miss him. Looking around she is amazed that so many old people travel. Some go sailing by on a buggy, some are hobbling on sticks. How do they manage with their poor eyesight, their poor energy, their arthritic hips? But there they are, streaming out into the world again.

"Where's Dad?" Tom is stretching her fingers and pinching them.

"He'll come," Linda is getting anxious. He should have been out by now.

A flight from Bahrain has arrived and is spewing its bewildered passengers on to the concourse. Then she sees him striding along, a large bulky grip slung over one shoulder.

"*Dad, Dad...*" Tom dodges under the rope barrier and dashes across the open space.

Linda watches as Jeff drops his grip and sweeps Tom into his arms.

"TOM. There you are, my boy." and he buries his face in Tom's puff jacket stifling sobs that have come from nowhere. "My word, this is a surprise," Jeff stares into the eager, bright blue eyes as he fights to keep control. "Hello, my son."

"Dad, so glad you've come." Tom ruffles Jeff's thick, blond hair with his fingers. "Mum's over there. Come on."

"Linda," he takes her in his arms and catches a whiff of her perfume and remembers the honeymoon, The Seychelles, the good things, the happy memories. "Good to see you, Linda. My you look well," and he kisses her quickly on the lips.

"You've lost weight, Jeff. And you look tired."

"It's been a bit hectic. And it's a long flight." He looks at Tom again, energetic, restless. Then he takes his hand and squeezes it. Tom is not missing, he is right here at my side, fit and happy and Captain Barraclough is on the bridge of the *Welland*...where I should be...

"Come on. Let's go home."

*****

Captain Barraclough smoothes his brawny hands down his chest. Southampton Pilot on board and there it is, dear old Nab Tower.

The finest sight in the world. Home is the sailor, home from the sea.

Soon the tugs are nudging m.v. *Welland* alongside Berth 105 and she is made secure.

Joy and Violet are in their cabin with bags strewn across each bed.

"I'm going to wear mine," Joy pushes her arms into the green wool winter coat.

"It's a nuisance and I shall be too hot," Vi shakes out her tweed coat and folds it over her arm. "I'm going to carry mine. We always have this problem when we get back but there's no way we could have embarked in January without them and we always need them on deck until after The Azores. But winter coats are the least of our problems today."

"True. Who's going to carry. You or me?"

"I will."

"But you're carrying your coat and you have that bag and those stinking sea shells you insisted on bringing."

"I want them for the garden and I'm not going to discard them now. I'll carry. It's in my navy blue bag."

"Alright, if you insist. It doesn't matter really because we were cleared through Customs and Immigration at breakfast but you can't take anything for granted. They could 'do' us again."

"Unlikely."

"Just remember, stay calm, walk slowly. Let's go."

Laden with bags, coats and cameras they pick their way down the gangway and step on to dry land again.

Joy turns and gazes back at the *Welland*, such a good looking little ship, now crawling with crew and shore officials and dockers with cranes dangling, winches grinding, fork lifts fussing around the containers.

There is no sign of the Bo'sun but she has his telephone number tucked into the back of her address book. Adam Guthrie, 57 years old widower, still living alone in the matrimonial home at Hythe.

238

She hasn't told Vi about him. He said he would telephone. She is sure he will.

The Customs Hall is deserted. They pause, side by side, then stride slowly towards the 'Nothing to Declare' exit.

Violet's navy blue bag hangs loosely from her shoulder. It is stuffed with magazines, makeup, medication, sea shells and the unopened packet of Boots suppositories which will guarantee their next winter voyage.

There is not a Customs Officer in sight as a porter trails after them with their suitcases on a trolley. He loads them into the boot of the taxi.

They are soon back home, in their kitchen with the kettle on.

Joy reaches for the brown teapot. "Can never wait for this."

"Nobody can make tea properly beyond the Isle of Wight." Vi has collected the pile of mail from the hall table.

"Worth waiting for," Joy switches off the kettle. "And we've done it again. Put the Boots package on the table Vi. That's it."

Vi is sorting the mail making two piles. The telephone rings and they stare at each other.

"Who on earth can know that we are home?" Vi continues to filter the mail. "Ignore it."

"No," Joy goes into the hall and picks up the receiver. "Hello," she recognises the voice immediately. "Well, what a surprise. Are you home already?"

"Yes, doesn't take long for the old salts to get down the gangway and I knew you were through Customs and Immigration. I doubt if you have the kettle on yet but I just wanted to tell you that I have two tickets for next Saturday and was anxious to know that you were free."

"Well, yes. Thank you."

"Fine, it's a Latin American group touring the UK. I'll ring you again, after you've had your tea. And unpacked. Goodbye."

Joy replaces the phone, keeping her hand on it, staring at it, then she smiles and goes back into the kitchen.

"Who on earth was that?" Vi is clutching the tea cup with both hands.

"That was Adam Guthrie. You now, Bo'sun of the *Welland*."

"You mean that tall streak of a weather vane. Who has a knife in his leather belt? Not safe."

"Yes, the knife is for cutting rope that is jammed. He's invited me to a concert on Saturday. Apparently it's a Latin American group. Just imagine all those wonderful rhythms again…"

"Well…" Vi crashes her tea cup into the saucer, stands up, glares at Joy then she walks out of the kitchen, slamming the door.

*****

It is just a short walk from the Dock Gates to the Flying Angel Club in Southampton and seafarers find their way here as soon as they are off duty. It is one of the imposing red brick buildings in Queen's Terrace. Here they can eat, drink, read in the Reading Room, play indoor games, phone home, or sit quietly in the Chapel next to the secluded little garden.

Step through the door and inside is a mahogany bar that stretches the full length of a large oblong room full of tables and chairs. This afternoon it is smoky, dimly lit and disturbed only by a steady hum of voices and chink of glasses.

Several men are on high stools, leaning forward with elbows on the bar, chatting and occasionally bursting into raucous laughter. They are eager and excited, waiting to sail. Other men are sitting at tables. They are quieter, home from a tiring voyage, unwinding, relaxing, coming to terms with the world again.

Bert and Dinty are at their usual table at the far end of the room, in a corner near the door to the Games Room. Two empty glasses have been nudged across the table to make room for full ones. It is half past two and they are off duty until seven o'clock tomorrow morning.

"It were a crying shame," Dinty lights a thin cigarette.

"What's a crying shame?" Bert takes the cigarette offered.

"Chief Mate. But he'll be home now."

240

"His son were missing."

"You mean…that's why he left. That's what happened?"

"Yes. He had no choice did he, but to come home." Bert stares into his glass of beer. He didn't come home when Jean… and he should have done. And there's no word from Keith. He checked for mail before he left the *Welland*, this morning, just in case.

Dinty narrows his eyes. "A crying shame. But Chief Mate'll sort it out. You'll see."

Bert has a faraway look in his eyes. Dinty recognises it.

"Now don't get maudlin, Bert. We're home. Come on, drink up."

The door bursts open and a noisy group of men tumble in. Four of them, all wearing woolly hats, propping up a younger man in a bomber jacket and jeans. He is tall and thin and his knees have given way. His face is pale and gaunt and he is wearing a baseball cap back to front with a mop of brown hair curling around it.

Dinty edges through the tables to get to the bar, past the group who are guiding the young man in the baseball cap to a table. They sit him down but the young man jumps up immediately, waving his arms and singing 'Maggie, Maggie May…'"

"Not now, not now, Banger. Sit down. Have 'nother drink."

The fat man in the yellow woolly hat pushes him down into a chair again.

"Made an early start, didn't they?" Dinty is back with two more pints.

"Wonder what they're celebrating?" Bert takes a long swig.

"Easy, we'll find out."

The young man lolls back in his chair, legs sprawled under the table. "Said she was due today," he takes off his baseball cap then puts it back on again.

Bert's eyes are fixed on the young man slumped at the table with his friends.

"Dinty," Bert beckons for him to lean closer. "I know that voice. Listen."

The group are talking over each other then the baseball cap jerks to his feet again.

"Going for a leak." He pushes his way unsteadily past Bert and Dinty and goes along the corridor.

"I'll go with him. Don't want him absconding," and the little man in the green woolly hat laughs out loud.

"What you lot celebrating then?" Dinty calls across to the men at the table.

"It's Banger." Black woolly hat with the beard lights a cigarette. "Just left his University and says he's not going back. He's looking for someone."

"Do you know him then?" Bert lolls back in his chair.

"Yea. Met him in the Gangway Club. Insisted on coming here after a heart starter."

Bert gets up and knocks both glasses over as he squeezes out of the corner seat and goes to stand by the men at the table. Dinty follows.

The little man in the green woolly hat guides the young man back to join the group.

"We got company," the young man opens his arms wide. "Join party."

Bert looks into the soft brown eyes, now glassy with drink, the straight nose, the sunken cheeks, absorbing every detail of this face that he hadn't seen for such a long time. Keith is thinner, older but the voice. It's the voice that convinces him.

"I know you. What is your mother's name?"

"She's dead," he spat, "name was Jean."

"Your name is Keith isn't it? Keith Dowse?"

"Yea, but my friends call me Banger."

"Sit down, sit down," Black woolly hat shuffles the chairs to make room for Bert and Dinty and they are now all sitting together.

"I'm your father." Bert sinks into a chair.

Nobody speaks. The young man is leaning into Bert's face. "Office told me *Welland* was due yesterday but me and my mates decided to wait till today and we got kiboshed at the Gangway Club.

"Is that who you were looking for Banger?" Yellow woolly hat playfully pulls Keith's baseball cap. "You didn't tell us you were looking for yer Dad."

Bert reaches for Keith's hand. "You didn't write, my son." Bert's voice is low. "Not once."

Keith looks down at his feet, twizzling this baseball cap in his fingers. Then he looks into Bert's face sobering by the minute as reality takes over. "No point, Dad, you were away. All over the place… And there was nothing to say…in there." Keith picks up his glass and empties it quickly.

Bert pulls Keith to his feet and folds him in his arms, knocking over glasses of beer and ash trays until the table is awash.

Black woolly hat calls the barman over.

"Sorry about this mess. Now we've really got a party on our hands. We're celebrating. Drinks all round then more drinks.

27

Jeff is standing in the kitchen doorway with both arms flexed, supporting the door frame, one foot lazily in front of the other, watching Linda. He is just back from an appointment with the Marine Superintendent, Drake Line.

"How did it go?" She is shredding a lettuce with a new hairstyle which he likes, a new shade of lipstick which suits her and she is beautifully made up at half past eleven in the morning.

It's a week since he landed at Heathrow and as he watches her sweep the lettuce into a bowl he reflects on his ability to slip into domestic life so easily. But voyage leaves were always like this. Living in parallel worlds. Seafaring, an unpredictable world of problems and solutions. Domestic life rolling on, day by day. The gardening, the shopping, fixing her hair dryer, mending the twisted bracket on Tom's bike, taking him swimming last Tuesday, football match last Saturday. Just as if he had never been away.

"Well," she puts down the knife and stares at him, hands on hips. He moves into the kitchen and stands in front of her.

"Fine. I didn't know what to expect." He flicks his hand through her hair.

"Jeff, please, please tell me - how did it go?"

"Could have been dodgy but it went well, very, very well."

"Oh Jeff, I'm so glad. Come on then, tell me."

"Drake Line have given me three week's leave and then I resume command and sign on as Captain of the *Welland*"

Linda jumps into his arms. "Oh, Jeff, at last, at last! We've waited so long for this news and now..." She stands away.

244

"Captain Jeffrey Bloxham." She strokes the scar on his cheek and kisses it. "Did they say anything about Tom and…Tom not being missing after all?"

"No, the Marine Superintendent understood. He's a family man, too. They know I did the right thing in spite of the disruption it caused." He goes to the fridge and takes out a bottle of white wine. "This will do for now."

Linda takes two glasses from the cabinet. "Let's go into the lounge and make the most of the moment."

They flop on to the settee.

"Here's to Captain Bloxham," Linda chinks glasses.

"I must tell Tom. Where is he?"

"With Jason, somewhere. Yes, he will be so excited. I've been so concerned about him. Something upset him. And Jason. Wouldn't and still won't talk about it. Neither of them are saying what it is. But he does seem to be more settled. Especially now that you are back."

"Well, I've promised to take them camping before I go back so must get organised."

"They will love that. Do them good. It was all very fraught at the time and I panicked when they were missing. I shouldn't have phoned you. I'm sorry I lost it a bit. But you know, neither Tom nor Jason go to Mass anymore. Not since Father Michael left."

She had not heard a word from him, not a note or a phone call or message. Oh! What a tangled web she and Michael had woven. Now it's all over and it seems the most natural thing in the world to be sitting here by the side of the man she had deceived.

"Why did he leave?"

"Don't know. It was all so unexpected. I mean he got on well with everyone, spent a lot of time with the young boys, particularly with Tom and Jason."

"Surely there would be a reason. Somebody must now why he left."

"You'd think so. It's strange. There were all kinds of rumours at the time. That he had had an accident. That he went on holiday.

But who's to know what goes on. Anyway he's gone."

"Tom didn't say. I know Father Michael spent a lot of time with him and Jason. Perhaps that's what upset them both. But he did tell me about the night he and Jason went missing. Slept in some old barn.

"We've got a new priest. An older man."

"Well if Tom doesn't want to go to Mass, we won't make him." Jeff eases the glass from Linda's fingers and goes to the kitchen to refill them.

"Hey, I must get the lunch ready." Linda takes the glass.

"Lunch can wait. Come with me. Bring your glass."

Jeff takes Linda's hand and together they go upstairs.

*****

Jeff has phoned Fiona several times but has been foiled at every attempt. No reply. He never leaves a message so all he can do is to keep trying. It is two weeks since they parted at the baggage carousel in Heathrow and in ten day's time he will be sailing again. This time as Captain of the *m.v Welland*. The memory of the confusing and fragmented flight home has faded and he knows he did not handle it well but she should never have followed him to the airport. She should never have piled on more stress but that is now in the past. He is rested, his future is secure.

He's now at his Garage trying again to make contact with her as he had promised.

"Fiona, at last I've got you."

"Oh, hello. Yes, I've been a bit busy since I got back. You know how it is. Nice to hear from you."

He is now striding, two steps at a time, up the flight of stairs to 11 Merrick Court. The door opens immediately.

"Do come in," she smiles and steps back. "Such a long time," and she dissolves into his arms.

They separate and he steps back to look at her. She is wearing tailored black slacks and a cream silk blouse and nothing on her feet. There it is, the magic, luring him into her space again just when he had found his reliable, shock-proof space, his freedom to assert his identity at Coleridge Avenue. The enigma of this woman never ceases to haunt him. He studies the hazel eyes still with their hint of sadness, the chestnut curls, the freckles.

"Good to see you, Fiona."

"Come sit," she ushers him towards the settee.

He looks around the light and luminous room. Everything is just as he remembers. The cream carpet flecked with burnt orange. The pale beige settee, the cushions and the octagonal table.

"What would you like tea, coffee, glass of wine, Scotch?"

"Let's just talk awhile."

"OK." She sinks on to the settee beside him and reaches for his hand. "First - you. Tell me what happened. About Tom. I've been longing to know. It was all so chaotic at Heathrow when we parted. In fact, it was awful. The flight. The journey back to Southampton." She is tweaking his long fingers. "I should never have left the ship. And when you didn't phone..."

"But, I did phone. There was never an answer!"

"Well, sorry," She continues to stretch his fingers. "What about Tom?"

"Tom was not missing. He and his pal had had some kind of upset and decided to disappear for the night. No one seems to know what it was all about. They spent the night in an old barn near the canal and ended up falling in and arriving home wet through."

"So you needn't have left the *Welland*."

"No. But I wasn't to know that. Let's not go there, Fiona. It's past history. The good news is that I sail as Captain of the *Welland* next Tuesday."

"Whooppee," Fiona jumps to her feet and waltzes around. "You've been promoted! Now we are going to have a drink."

She bustles to the kitchen and he can hear the unmistakeable deep-throated pop as she opens the bottle of champagne.

"Terrific news. Here's to Captain Bloxham, Master of the *Welland*," and she passes him a glass.

"Thank you. It's a bit like seeing a film in slow motion, reflecting on the years of disappointments. It's been a long wait. But then, it is for most seafarers."

"Do you know what happened to Captain Pycroft. You know the man who had the heart attack in Guayaquil when you took over?"

"Yes. He made a good recovery but has been declared medically unfit for sea-going duties."

"Oh, my goodness. What will he do?"

"He is now Deputy General Manager at Drake Line's Head Office. Here in Southampton."

"Really! And that gruff man who took your place. What was his name?"

"Captain Barraclough. He's Master of the *Witham* for that long haul across the Indian Ocean. Remember?"

"How could I ever forget it!"

"Now tell me what have you been doing since I left you in Heathrow?"

"My usual. Nothing matters. So I have been doing my usual."

"And what is your usual Fiona?"

"I don't talk about it. And strangely enough, you have never asked. Not even when we first met on the *Witham*."

"Well, you just explained that you chose this apartment but found the same emptiness."

"Yes, and that's when I…"

The phone rings. Fiona stares at the occasional table, then at Jeff, then she puts down her glass and picks up the phone.

"Who?" She frowns and looks at Jeff. "Oh, yes, hello, nice to hear from you. How are you? What? When? Let me just see." She opens a drawer below the table and takes out a beige diary flicking through the pages. "Yes, that'll be fine. Let me know what time. Thank you. Goodbye."

She replaces the receiver, takes a pen out of the drawer and writes in the diary then she comes back to the settee and reaches for her glass, sipping quickly.

Jeff gets up and wanders to the large window and looks down at the manicured lawn, the well-behaved shrubs, the trees beyond. There is an awkward silence hovering around the room, prodding him with question marks. He turns to look at Fiona on the settee. She is smoothing her hands across her bare feet.

"Aren't you going to ask who that was?"

"Should I?" He turns to look at her. He has been caught off balance. Obviously it was a man and they are going to meet yet she had never hinted that there was any man in her life since Paul. He goes to her on the settee.

"Well," she pauses, "I think it would be better that you do. Let's freshen the glasses. I told you that I moved here to get a different view, a new perspective. But it was still so bleak, so empty and I longed for an opportunity to look good, feel good. To cut a long story short I decided to take a sort of unofficial part-time job." She keeps her eyes on her bare feet. "I escort lonely men. Men who have no one at their side for important or social engagements."

Jeff stiffens. "An escort!"

"Yes. It started quite by chance. One of Paul's colleagues with Meridian Airlines contacted me to ask if I would accompany his father-in-law to a business conference, cocktail party and dinner. And it seemed to grow from there. You know, Jeff, the world's full of lonely people, grieving people. And the ones I meet are successful, well-travelled - and need someone at their side for an important event. And I need someone to converse with, someone to listen to, someone to smile at. It comes quite naturally to me. Remember I was doing it for years in those Meridian airliners and I missed it so much after...

Jeff gets up and wanders to the window again, staring down at he lawn again but he doesn't see it.

"Do they pay you?"

"Oh no, no! Heaven forbid! I am just a sort of proxy, a substitute. You see I can understand their solitude, their isolation. That man who just phoned is a widower and needs someone at his side for an important conference dinner. Actually, Paul and I knew his brother who was a pilot. And I pine for intelligent conversation. It's almost non-existent today in the chattering class.

Jeff walks round the back of the settee. "And you book for a sea voyage each winter?"

"Well, yes. The first year I wanted to distance myself from my new perspective so decided on your cargo ship, then I came back to the *Welland*. You know why, surely." She leans over and kisses his scar. "Are you surprised?"

"Yes, it seems you have filled the emptiness well with your nothing matters. I'm glad, Fiona. It's good for you."

She goes to the tray and brings the bottle of champagne over to fill the glasses.

"No, no more thank you." He looks at his watch. "I have to go Fiona. I must collect the car from the garage. I'm taking Tom and his pal camping so there is much to do."

She stands frozen with the bottle in one hand.

"Oh, no. Then when will I see you?"

"I'll give you a ring before I sail. Must go."

THE END

Bibliography

David Beaty - *The Naked Pilot: The Human Factor in Aircraft Accidents*
   Published by Airlife Publishing Ltd. 1995.
   Previously published in hardback by Methuen 1991.

Oscar Lewis   *La Vida*
   First published in England by Martin Secker & Warburg Ltd 1967.

Act of Parliament of the United Kingdom of Great Britain and Ireland
   Offences against the Person Act 1861.

By the same author

Fiction
The Run of Time – Paperback (Amazon) & Kindle
The Triumph of Deceit – Paperback (Amazon) & Kindle

Non-fiction
Tiaras and T-shirts - Paperback (Amazon) & Kindle
Libya in Limbo - Kindle

Printed in Poland
by Amazon Fulfillment
Poland Sp. z o.o., Wrocław